Outside the Lines

by

Samantha Cayto

Red Cell Security Book 1

Outside the Lines

Cover Art by *Diana Carlile*

The Wild Rose Press, Inc.
PO Box 708
Adams Basin, NY 14410-0708
Visit us at www.thewilderroses.com

Publishing History
First Scarlet Rose Edition, 2016
Print ISBN 978-1-5092-1067-1
Digital ISBN 978-1-5092-1068-8

Published in the United States of America

Murder, stolen art, and sizzling passion...

"Is that your way of saying that you'd get hard for any man in your vicinity so I shouldn't take it personally?"

Dec worried the label of his bottle with this thumb, disbelieving that he was having this conversation at all. Felix would say it was because the time was right. As much as he valued the therapist's opinion, he couldn't quite believe that. He figured it was one more version of the kind of self-destructive behavior he thought was behind him.

"No, what I'm really saying is that you're the first guy to make me hard since the injuries that killed my career." There. If that revelation didn't send the man screaming out into the night, nothing would.

Instead, Jakes asked, "What injuries? I mean I know the PTSD, but what else?"

Dec shrugged. "Can't hear out of my right ear and my right knee is kind of shot."

Jakes slugged the rest of his beer back and stood. "Then I'll be sure to talk into your left ear and we'll be careful of your knee."

"Seriously?" Slamming his own bottle down on what served as his battered coffee table, Dec got vertical. "You think our fucking is a good idea?"

"Hell no. It's a spectacularly bad idea, but this"—he waved in the vicinity of his crotch—"isn't going anywhere that I can tell.

Chapter One

"John Boy, talk to me. Any hostiles in the vicinity?"

"Negative, sir. Nothing's moving except one goat."

Dec knew better than to take that news at face value. As good as his sniper was, the guy hailed from Omaha, not Krypton. He didn't rock x-ray vision like Superman, and his night vision goggles only did so much. The sleepy village nestled in the mountains of Kandahar had a certain squalid quaintness about it, all dark and quiet while his team approached. Still, he felt the itch between his shoulder blades, a sign he'd learned in the past not to ignore.

"Stay frosty, gentlemen, and lady." He cringed at his clumsiness, but he still hadn't gotten used to having a female attached to his team. No denying that having a woman on these night raids helped tremendously. Carter could interview the women and learn things he and his men couldn't. Still, he hadn't adjusted to the new reality, and even though his head told him Carter's gender didn't matter, he still worried about her being hurt just a tiny bit more than the others.

The quiet of the night shattered in a millisecond. That's all it took for an IED squirreled among the rocks strewn across the ground to turn his unease into a clusterfuck. The flash blinded him as dirt and dust flew into his face and the blast tore him off his feet. His world listed to one side as he went down. Bells rang in his ears, even while pain lanced his right one.

His hearing didn't wink out enough, though, for him to miss the screams of someone. Who? Someone to his left had triggered the explosion. Shit, Rios, young kid, a fucking tadpole. He had to get to him, but when he tried to roll to one side, agony engulfed his knee. He bit back his own scream, his body writhing on the ground. Carter's concerned face loomed over him. Her mouth moved, but no sound came out. None that he could hear anyway.

"What?" His one-word question echoed inside his head.

Carter's lips moved again, a silent plea.

"Status!" He tried to take command, figure out what had happened to his team. He was responsible for them. He had to get his shit together and lead them out of this fucking mess.

His body wouldn't obey. Nothing responded to his mental commands. The ringing in his ears, the pain shooting through his leg, and pressure on his chest kept him down and utterly useless. Why couldn't he move? Carter. It was Carter, climbing on top of him, squeezing the breath out of his lungs, holding him down with an implacable weight, and...licking his face? He had to get free. Oh, God, he couldn't breathe!

With a desperate cry, Dec wrenched out of his nightmare. His heart hammered a relentless tattoo, and his skin stretched tight over aching bones and muscle. When he opened his mouth to draw in some air, musky fur brushed over his lower lip. A velvety tongue lapped along his jaw line. The gentle touch and the knowledge it gave him of where he was eased his panic. Slowly, his muscles loosened and the tightness in his chest receded. His arms shook as he raised them to wrap them around the heavy body lying across his.

"Pax." He could barely hear the word, because he spoke so softly and his right ear was shot. He missed a lot since that day in Afghanistan. But the Belgium Malinois lying across him to stop his nightmare induced panic attack heard him well enough. She whined and lapped at him some more, not moving while he de-stressed by running his fingers through her thick coat.

When he felt steady enough, he patted her side a couple of times and gave her the command to get off. As soon as she leaped down to the side of the bed, he stretched his limbs in a wide X, shaking off the last of the tremors. His knee griped over the harsh treatment. He ignored it the same way he did just about every second of every day. A year's worth of physical therapy hadn't managed to rid him of the pain, so he pretended it didn't exist. He rolled over and reached toward his nightstand. Pax slid her muzzle between his hand and the piece of furniture.

Dec chuckled over the block and reassured her with a scratch under her chin. "It's okay, girl. I'm going for my phone, not my gun."

The dog cocked her head and gave him the fish eye before pulling back. He couldn't blame her suspicion. He did keep his forty in the dresser drawer, and there had been a couple of times in the past two years of his life when he'd been reaching for that very thing after one of his God-awful nightmares.

Those times were over, though. He'd made enough peace with the events of his last mission and had regained enough of an interest in life to reject any further thoughts of offing himself. He'd been a SEAL, for Christ's sake, and quitting wasn't the SEAL way.

With slower movements, he picked up his phone and saw that it was four forty-five. Shit, may as well get up. Trying to get back to sleep after a nightmare typically was its own nightmare. Kind of a relief really to be able to justify not even putting in the effort.

Stifling a groan, he shoved himself out of bed and stumbled on the way to the bathroom. Pax, bless her canine heart, shoved into him, giving him the leverage he needed to stay upright. Fucking knee. Okay, his therapist had allotted him one pity gripe over his physical limitations a day, and that had been it. He'd be all smiles for the next sixteen or so hours until he hit the sack again. Even if he fell flat on his fucking face in front of a crowd of people. And that thought did not count as a complaint. It was more in the family of a solemn vow.

Dec had to turn on the bathroom light in order to piss in the toilet and not around it, but he avoided looking at himself in the mirror. He didn't need to see his haggard face and unkempt hair. At Annapolis and while serving in the navy, he'd always kept it skull trimmed. Once he'd let it grow out a bit during rehab, he'd been reminded of how wavy and unruly it got. He really needed to get into the barber shop. He didn't know why he kept forgetting. It wasn't as if his days were chock-full of work.

After almost three months of being open for business, yet not having a single client, he'd almost reached a point where he had to think in terms of failure. God, how he hated that word, whether it applied to a mission or anything else in life. He'd always operated on the old adage of it not being an option. These days, with the deaths of two team members weighing on his conscience and a dwindling bank account reminding him that he was not made of money, he had to accept that failing was possible and even likely.

Not that it would happen today or even this week. Soon, though, he'd have to face the idea of laying off his two employees and maybe finding himself a real job. So far Red Cell Security operated as a very expensive hobby. Whatever had made him think he could return to his home town of Boston and set up a private security company when he had zero contacts in the area? Not that he'd ever had a large network of friends, and God knew his old man had never crawled out of a bottle long enough to develop business contacts.

And this was exactly how he ended up spiraling into obsessive thoughts. He needed to shut down his mind and get his body moving. After a quick wash and brush, he returned to his bedroom and pulled on a T-shirt, shorts, and running shoes. He tugged on his knee brace, knowing that, while it helped, it didn't stop his knee from hurting.

His physical therapist recommended he give up jogging in favor of something less stressful on his knee. Good advice that he'd promptly ignored. He loved running, had always found his escape in his feet hitting pavement. No way he'd let a little thing like his knee screaming in pain make him give it up. Yeah, not smart, but being insanely stubborn had helped him become a SEAL.

Pax padded up to him, her red service dog vest and

leash in her mouth. That was one of the things that made them so perfect for each other. She loved running as much as he did. He chuckled at the enthusiastic look she gave, ruffled the top of her head, and took the items out of her mouth. The vest wasn't technically legally necessary, but he liked using it anyway. His disabilities weren't exactly obvious, and he didn't like having to explain himself any time someone questioned Pax being allowed somewhere. He would have left the leash off, but that was required.

As an expertly trained bomb-sniffing and service dog, Pax responded to voice and hand commands perfectly. If he told her to stay, she stayed even if hell rained fire down around her. Unfortunately, Boston ordinances didn't recognize or trust that. Dec did, though. He trusted Pax with his life.

"Come on, girl. Let's go watch the sun come up."

Pax woofed very softly and eagerly headed for the door. They lived on the second floor of a six unit apartment building in the middle of the Brighton area of Boston. Lots of college students lived in their neighborhood, so the street was empty this early in a September morning. The kids would be up and about in several hours. Dec would be long gone, pretending to work in his office by that time. His warm up was brief, his nerves still jangling from the after effects of the nightmare. He needed to pound some pavement, work up a good sweat, to chase the remnants away.

He started slow, the only concession to his knee's fragility. Soon, though, he hit his stride, arms and legs pumping in fluid rhythm, his breathing steady. The twinge of pain from his knee was easy to ignore as his endorphins rose. The city noise around him was muted, a testament to the early hour and the fact that he heard it from one ear only. He always took a route that kept the street to his left and Pax kept pace at his right, acting as his substitute ear. He rarely needed her help with that or with balance when his knee went out.

No, her biggest function was to keep him calm while the mild chaos of everyday living swarmed around him, threatening his peace of mind. The bigger and noisier the crowd, the more likely Dec was to have a flashback. Suddenly, everyone looked like a hostile, and he went on high alert for snipers, IEDs, and suicide bombers. A panic attack would follow if not for the reassuring presence of Pax, threading him around people, acting as a barrier between him and others, and keeping him grounded emotionally. With Pax at his side, he felt calmer, safer, and not so alone.

By the time he made the loop back to his street, he'd gone five miles and was sopping wet. It might be September, but it was far from fall. The day promised to be a warm one. Pax gave a yip of delight when Dec slowed down and headed for their favorite coffee shop. It actually officially opened at six in the morning, catering to the early morning commuters as well as the student crowd later on. But so long as someone was there and the door unlocked, customers could go in. This early, no one was there except the young barista that always seemed to catch the first shift. Dec suspected the kid worked all night doing something else and picked up the coffee slinging job as a second source of income.

Dec opened the door and let Pax go first. She waited for him to enter, of course, but her tail wagged excitedly and she whined a bit when he didn't move fast enough to the counter. For a dog, she was a shameless flirt. The barista, Scott, lavished attention on her whenever they came in. He did so now, shooting Dec a brief smile before coming out from behind the counter with a bowl of water for Pax.

"Hey, girl." The pretty boy with the long, white-blond hair knelt down and petted her with genuine enthusiasm as she lapped up the water.

God, the kid couldn't be more than late teens, too skinny by half, the kind of twink that made older men drool. Not Dec's type, even though the kid had once come on to him, writing his number on Dec's coffee cup. The offer for no-strings sex had been obvious, but Dec wasn't ready for any kind of relationship, even one that amounted to a fuck buddy. Besides, that angel face had old eyes. He looked like a lot of young soldiers did once they'd seen battle. His innocence had been lost and in a way that couldn't be good. Given his own fucked-upedness, Dec was the last person who would be of any help.

Scott stood up and gave him a tired smile. "The usual?"

Dec rubbed his sweaty brow with the back of his hand. "Yeah, please, and may as well toss in an extra shot of espresso."

As he measured out the grounds, the boy glanced at Dec over his shoulder. "That kind of night, huh?"

"Yup." He stretched his neck, feeling the satisfying crack more than hearing it. He stretched his good leg by lifting his foot up to his ass. Without anyone else in the place, he felt relaxed.

"How's business?" Scott asked while he expertly created the large, two percent latte with the extra shot.

Dec made a face. "What business?" He shrugged. "No clients, no business."

"Dude, that sucks." The boy slid the coffee cup across the counter. "For what it's worth, I'm passing your card out to people I know."

"Thanks, man," Dec said, grabbing his drink. He'd been leaving cards with lots of the local businesses. Kind of a spaghetti against the wall approach that he didn't really expect to work. Nice of Scott to think of him, though. He handed over the money he owed for the overpriced, yet excellent coffee, then put a generous tip in the jar. He'd waited tables himself during college so he appreciated how much a low-wage earner like Scott needed dollars more than change.

The boy grinned, although the expression didn't quite reach his eyes. Yeah, he was a troubled kid for sure. "Thanks." He came around the counter to give Pax a final pat. "See you tomorrow, girl."

"We'll be here," Dec confirmed and, walking toward the door, he called for his dog. "Let's go, Pax."

He gulped down his caffeine fix on the relatively short walk back to his place, grabbed a shower, and dressed for his version of success—khaki pants, blue cotton buttoned-down, and casual loafers. He felt like a complete douche, but on the off chance he actually had a client wander in by accident looking for the dentist down the hall, he couldn't be hanging out in jeans, sneakers, and a snarky T-shirt. As he stepped out into the hallway, his neighbor and therapist stepped out, too.

"Oh, hey, Felix. Where're you headed this early?"

Felix Mathers, a middle-aged man with curly salt and pepper hair, and the only male on the planet that could pull off keeping his glasses hanging on a chain around his neck, gave him a sunny smile. "Declan, dearest boy," he said in a soft, slow cadence that betrayed his southern roots. "I have a doctor's appointment."

"Nothing serious, I hope." He started down the hall, and Felix fell into step on his left side because he knew about Dec's hearing deficit. Pax took her usual position on his right.

"Oh, nothing serious. Just some age-related girl trouble."

Dec inwardly rolled his eyes. As an old-time ex-drag queen, Felix had never lost his affectation of referring to himself often in female terms even though he wasn't transgender. Dec appreciated drag queens, like most gay men, and he also admired how a man of Felix's generation had been tremendously courageous to be out and proud even before Stonewall.

"Hmm, well if you need anything, be sure to let me know. It's not like my days and nights are chock-full."

Felix stopped on the front stoop and placed a hand with long, delicate fingers on Dec's arm. "I'm sorry to hear that. You need business and a hot man to keep you occupied."

Dec laughed off the observation. More than anyone, Felix understood at least why Dec chose to spend his nights alone. And, in his therapist persona, he'd been the one to urge Dec to take the chance of starting up his own security company. "I'll keep trying with one of those things, anyway. See you later."

With a wave and more jaunt to his step than he felt, Dec headed with Pax to the nearest T stop. The availability of public transportation had been one of the things to draw him to this part of Boston. Keeping a car in the city and finding and paying for parking was more effort and money than he wanted to tackle. Fortunately, the MBTA ran frequently and dumped him down into the Leather District, a section of the city not nearly as interesting and kinky as it sounded. It was a cheap place to maintain an office. If things took off, something less and less likely as the weeks passed, he'd hoped to move to the Financial District, where big business often located itself.

The one downside to riding the T, especially first thing in the morning, was the crowd of people joining him. After multiple tours in both Afghanistan and Iraq, Dec didn't do crowds very well. It didn't matter that his brain told him there were no suicide bombers lurking among the commuters. Every nerve ending vibrated, on high alert for sudden death.

He stood pressed against one end of the car as much as possible, glad to give up any chance at a seat to others, with Pax by his side. He knew she was on duty, sniffing for trouble the way she'd been taught to do as a bomb-detecting dog. He trusted her, if not his own instincts, to alert him to danger. He kept one hand on her at all times, just the feel of her fur a soothing reassurance.

He got looks, of course he did. People would eye Pax and her red vest, then glance up at him to see why he'd need a service dog. There was nothing for them to see except a face that couldn't quite erase the permanent scowl put there by years of being a SEAL no matter how hard he tried. Whatever strangers read in his expression, they quickly turned away.

Occasionally when college students rode with him, some of the girls were brave enough to coo over Pax and ask to pet her. He and Pax were always willing to oblige. He didn't want to be anti-social. The look some of those girls gave him, though, a sly appreciation for the very things that usually turned others off, made him uncomfortable. Even if he'd been into girls, he wouldn't have wanted to hook up with anyone simply because she found his dangerousness a turn-on.

The gazillion people getting on and off at each stop made progress slower than he liked. But although Boston was a pretty walkable city, he'd already tortured his knee enough for the day with his jog. He patiently waited for his stop and continued on for a few more blocks on foot. He didn't bother to hurry; nothing waiting for him to hurry for.

When he did arrive at his small office, his admin, Cindi, was already there watering the plants she'd bought and brought in herself. She said it made the place homier, and he couldn't disagree. So long as he didn't have to keep them alive, he had no objections.

The curvy blond with the short, corkscrew curls turned around and smiled. "Morning, Dec. Your nine o-clock is waiting in your office." Her heavily made-up eyes widened at him in unspoken warning. She tipped her head toward his inner office, the door for which stood open. Dec could just make out the back of a man sitting in his visitor chair.

Wait, what? He had a nine o-clock? Since when?

"Ah, thanks." He tried to ask her for more detail with his eyes, but she ignored him.

Putting her watering can down, she minced over to the make-shift coffee station on her impossibly high heels. Although Cindi had told him in her job interview that she'd only been living as a woman for a little more than a year, she'd gone full bore. He'd often seen her turn the heads of straight men. Not surprising given how pretty and ultra-feminine she was. She was also incredibly organized and reliable. He wished he had more for her to do. Worse, he hated the idea he might have to lay her off if business didn't pick up.

And, speaking of which, when she handed him coffee in his favorite mug, she made a point of saying. "I offered Mr. Johnson a cup, but he declined."

"Thanks." He meant it for more than the coffee, and Cindi's answering grin let him know she understood.

For the life of him, he couldn't remember anything about an appointment. No way he'd forgotten something like his first possible paying client coming, and Cindi certainly wouldn't have made a mistake about scheduling one, either.

He entered his office with Pax by his side and sized up the guy in the chair as he maneuvered around to put his drink on his desk. "Mr. Johnson?"

A tall, whip-thin man with a receding hairline of brown hair and skin that could charitably be called pasty stood up. He threw a jaundiced eye toward Pax before extending his hand past the cuff of his impeccable pinstriped suit. "Yes, Philip Johnson."

Dec took the offered hand for a dead fish kind of shake. Christ, even Cindi and Felix had harder grips. "I'm Declan Hunter, head of Red Cell Security. I'm sorry for the wait." He took his seat behind his Ikea desk and gestured for his guest to sit.

Not that the man had waited for permission. With a prissy sort of squat, he sat back down and crossed his legs. "Not at all, Mr. Hunter. I confess I fibbed a bit when I told your receptionist that I had an appointment." Johnson's voice held the kind of hot-potato Boston Brahmin accent that comics liked to make fun of. Having been born and raised in the Boston suburbs, Dec had a hard time believing it was genuine.

Dec tried to give a disarming smile but figured he failed. "No worries, Mr. Johnson. How can I help you?"

The man tugged at his coat cuff. "I'm the personal assistant to Mr. Stanford Place. Are you familiar with him?"

"Sorry, no."

Johnson sniffed in response. "Mr. Place is the scion of one of our older Boston families. A successful venture capitalist and a devoted patron and collector of the arts."

Because the man seemed to be waiting for some kind of a response, Dec tried to look impressed and nodded briefly, as if to say, of course, do go on dear fellow. It seemed to do the trick because Johnson got to the point.

"Mr. Place is in need of a security review and overhaul. He's been concerned—mildly—with a spate of oddly melodramatic threats made against him anonymously. He also has a very valuable art collection in his Beacon Hill home. He wants a new company to review his current home system, make suggestions as to how to increase its reliability, then implement them."

"I see." Dec bought a few seconds of time by taking a sip of coffee. He tried to hide his mounting excitement. This was exactly the type of work he'd been looking for. Personal security was his specialty. "What kind of threats are we talking about? Emails, letters, phone calls?"

Johnson wrinkled his nose. "Letters turning up in odd places at home, at work, even on his windshield. All made with cheap paper, the message spelled out with words cut from magazines, if you can believe that." He rolled his eyes. "Honestly, it's all so hokey, one has to believe that someone with a juvenile sense of humor and hopelessly stuck in a seventies TV drama is behind them."

Dec took another sip of his coffee and considered the information. It did seem ridiculous, except.... "Someone going to that much trouble is obviously obsessed with Mr. Place. That is not something to ignore. How many of these letters have there been and what did they say?"

Johnson uncrossed his legs and re-crossed with the other one. "There have been five, one a week on average, although never the same day of the week. The contents are brief and to the point. They all say that Mr. Place is an evil man who will get what's coming to him." Johnson shrugged. "Or words to that effect."

Putting down his mug, Dec leaned into his desk. "Do you have one of them with you?"

"Oh, no. Mr. Place burned every last one of them, the last two without even reading them."

"Seriously? Hasn't he even taken this to the police?"

"No. Mr. Place can be a bit, um, stiff-necked, shall we say. He's tough and not easily spooked. And he didn't get to be as successful as he is without being that way and without making tough decisions that not everyone has always liked. He hasn't taken the threats seriously, and honestly, I can't blame him. The delivery method is just too ridiculous for words."

"He still wants an overhaul of his security at home, though," Dec pointed out.

"Well, he's not *stupid*."

Dec thought it was plenty stupid to destroy evidence and not report repeated threats to the police. He didn't say that, of course. He wasn't going to blow his first opportunity for a client by being insulting. He changed tack instead.

"May I ask how you heard of my company?" As much as he didn't want to look a gift-horse in the mouth, he couldn't help but wonder how a guy like this ended up in his office.

"Your business card came across my path at some point or other," Johnson replied in a totally evasive way that got Dec's radar pinging. "Mr. Place values entrepreneurship, needless to say. He welcomes new blood providing fresh ideas to many aspects of his life. As his long-time assistant, I've had the opportunity to appreciate what he'd like. Based on my research of you, a former military man with a brand new business is just the sort of person Mr. Place would appreciate. Especially given his support for veterans in general and wounded ones in particular." He gave a pointed look at Pax, who sat placidly by Dec's chair. "When I mentioned you to him, he gave me the green light to pursue your engagement."

Okay, that made sense. He promoted his service as a SEAL to inspire confidence in potential customers. And he'd left his card all over the city, so the fact that even a rarified person like Johnson would have stumbled upon it was exactly what he'd intended all along. He wasn't sure how he felt about the veiled implication that hiring Dec was somehow an extension of Place's charity work. Then again, beggars couldn't be choosers. If Place liked the work that Dec's company did, he might recommend it to friends and business associates. It was just the kind of break Dec needed.

He gave Johnson his most ingratiating smile. "Thank you, sir. I appreciate your confidence in me. I'd be very interested in taking a look at Mr. Place's current home security. It's entirely possible, however, that it doesn't need any changes."

"Oh, no. Mr. Place wants a new system, regardless. He's the kind of man that always moves forward." Johnson reached inside his suit coat and pulled out a long, folded check. He had to stand up to hand it over to Dec. "I hope this is enough to fund a start for your time and equipment. Of course, I'll need an estimate of your total costs once you've seen the property."

Dec opened the check and almost choked on his spit. He swallowed hard before answering. "This is more than enough, thank you, sir." He glanced at the check again before looking at Johnson. "Don't you want me to work up an estimate before you pay me a retainer?"

Johnson waved away the question as if it were absurd. "Mr. Place and I have complete confidence that you'll do a wonderful job and for a fair price. Really, once he makes up his mind, Mr. Place is a full steam ahead sort of man. Decisive and demanding. You'll earn every penny of that check and more, I assure you."

With the check still glued to his finger and thumb, Dec stood up, too, ignoring the twinge in his knee. He signaled Pax to stay where she was as he escorted his new client out. Cindi sat at her desk, pretending to be busy with her computer, but of course she had nothing to do. She shot a disarming smile at Johnson when he passed her. Dec could swear the man stumbled a bit in reaction before regaining his almost prissy gate.

At the door, Johnson turned to speak with Dec. "I gave your admin my card. Please call me whenever you have a sense of when you'd be able to come and tour Mr. Place's residence. I'll set up the appointment."

"That sounds fine, and in the meantime, if Mr. Place receives any more threats, please keep it for me to look at. I'm not convinced it's harmless."

"Very well, if you insist. I'll pass that along to Mr. Place. I can't guarantee he'll comply, of course. Like I said, he's a bit stubborn," he added in a hushed, almost conspiratorial tone.

Dec held out his hand for another shake much as he didn't want to. "Thank you again, Mr. Johnson, for your trust in me and Red Cell Security. We won't disappoint."

Johnson gave a tepid smile to go with his limp shake. "I have no doubt of that, Mr. Hunter." He flicked a gaze at Cindi. "Ms. Keyes, it's been a pleasure."

"Likewise," Cindi rejoined with a dazzling smile that sent Johnson out the door on his once-again clumsy feet.

When he was sure Johnson was out of ear-shot, Dec turned to Cindi and chuckled. "Jesus, the Pentagon should weaponize your smile. If it were any more potent, I think Johnson would have fallen flat on his face."

Cindi shrugged and grinned impishly. "I have that effect on certain guys. The uptight ones like Johnson are the easiest to unsettle." Popping up, she hurried around her desk. "So, do we have a client?"

Her obvious glee infected Dec. He unfolded the check and held it up for her to see. "Why yes, Ms. Keyes, we do."

Cindi's mouth dropped open as she stared at the paper. "Holy shit! That's how much he's paying?"

"That's how much he's given as a *retainer*. The final amount is going to be much larger. Of course, most of that will be for equipment, but still." He couldn't help himself; he grabbed Cindi up in a hug and twirled her around once before setting her back down. "Sorry, if that was sexual harassment," he said with a laugh. "I just couldn't resist."

Cindi batted her lashes. "I'll just have to report you to HR, which is me." She cocked her head. "I find no merit in the complaint." She whooped and bounced up and down in her dangerous heels. "Oh my God, Dec, this is fantabulous."

"Yeah, it is." His grinned faded as the enormity of what had just happened hit his stomach. This was it. His first real break, the thing that could make his business or tank it. Oh man, a sense of dread settled over him. When he'd been a SEAL, he'd never worried about failure. Since that last mission and the epic failure it had become, he'd lost his bravado and much of his confidence. Felix had told him it was natural to have anxiety after such a cataclysmic event. Survivor's guilt, a feeling that he didn't deserve a future when others had lost theirs, was a common response as well. He just had to work through it. He and his company did deserve this chance. He could do a good job.

Shaking off the moment of doubt, he headed back to his office. "I'm going to call Malcom and see what his schedule is like this week to set up an appointment to study the property."

"He doesn't take or teach any classes on Wednesdays this semester."

Of course Cindi would know Mal's schedule. She and the MIT grad student that Dec had hired for the more technical computer-based security needs had become tight friends in the months since he'd employed them both.

"Okay, I'll just call and confirm he's not already tied up this Wednesday, then set up the appointment with Johnson." He stopped himself at the doorjamb. "Oh, and Cindi, let's order in some pizza for lunch."

"Yes, sir."

Once he was out of her sight, he allowed himself to close his eyes and take a deep breath. When he opened his eyes again, Pax sat staring at him with her head cocked to one side. He ruffled her head and sat heavily down in his chair. "This is it, girl. Our big break. We better not fuck it up."

With a whine, Pax laid her head on his thigh and looked up at him with her dewy brown eyes. Her message was clear. Dec barked out a laugh and rubbed her head again. "Yeah, I know. Stop worrying and start doing."

He picked up the phone and punched in the numbers.

Chapter Two

"I still can't believe how sick this place is." Malcolm made the observation with such a gleeful expression that Dec had to smile in response. "I mean, did you notice the drawing hanging in the master bathroom? That's a *Renoir*. Seriously, imagine having so much money that you can afford to hang a Renoir in the john."

Dec had indeed seen the drawing, and while he hadn't appreciated that it had been a Renoir, he did know expensive when he saw it, especially when it was encased in protective glass. The entire house, located in Louisburg Square, screamed expensive. Just owning so much real estate in this section of Boston confirmed his client, Mr. Place, was swimming in wealth. But once one had entered the building, even the most jaded of people could only stop and gape for a moment or two.

Everywhere he looked was all polished wood, deep carpeting, and plush furniture covered with rich fabrics in muted tones. Every room contained valuable accent pieces to catch one's attention and dazzle. No space went unattended, with paintings large and small hanging on the walls. Statues and vases, many overflowing with fresh-cut flowers, gracing corners and table tops depending on their size. Grace and beauty met one's eye with every turn of the head, and it all lived in a hushed world created by thick drapes that blocked the noise of the city outside.

Everything shined and glittered as well. Clearly an army of staff ruthlessly evicted every dust mote and vanquished all smudges, even though Dec hadn't encountered many people. Someone who had introduced himself as the majordomo, whatever the hell that meant, always let him in with a condescending air. Dec figured the man used a fancy word for butler, as if "butler" wasn't fancy enough on its own.

All Dec really cared about was the guy acted like someone had shoved a stick up his ass. He'd sniffed at the idea of Pax entering the immaculate space. Dec had stared the guy down and startled a couple of maids from time-to-time, who had given him a wide berth. Other than that, he'd mostly worked without encountering anyone, which suited him just fine. Being inside this home made him more uncomfortable than any hell hole he'd occupied during his career in the Navy.

He and Malcolm had taken two weeks to redo the security system, a task that both of them had relished, even though neither of them thought it necessary. Whoever put in the original system had used top-line stuff. Hard to believe Mr. Place had worried it wouldn't be protective enough of himself or his valuables. Yet, when Dec, his conscience not allowing him to do otherwise, broached the topic with Johnson, the secretary had insisted that Mr. Place wanted new and better. That insistence, plus the huge check that had cashed just fine, made Dec dismiss his doubts and get on with it. No more threats had been issued, either, or at least no one mentioned anything. Maybe some kook had been letting off steam after all, in which case, this expensive redo of security was doubly pointless. Still, who was he to question his client?

Malcolm was just finishing up the keypad for the door leading to the garage. On top of everything else, Place had an amazing three parking spots, a real luxury in the city. Dec estimated the value of all three of Place's vehicles put together was more than he might hope to earn in his lifetime. He'd allowed Mal a few minutes to drool over the machinery before getting on with the work. They'd stayed extra late to get the last of it done. No need to return the next day unless something went wrong. Dec was determined that the system would function perfectly from the get-go, and he trusted Mal to make sure of it.

Mal secured the plate and turned to Dec. "That's it, man. Our first job is finished." The handsome kid grinned like he'd been handed his favorite treat, and given how enamored the MIT grad student was about electronics, he kind of had.

Dec had slept a lot better in the last couple of weeks knowing that his business now had a chance. He knew Mal depended on the salary because his stipend for teaching was pitiful, yet his class schedule made fulltime employment impossible. He didn't come from a rich family, either.

During his interview for the job with Red Cell, Mal had told Dec how his whole village in India had pitched in to pay his way to come to MIT. He was determined to make money to give back to his community. Dec suspected the guy already sent some home. He also figured Mal wouldn't return to India if he could help it. Being gay was still hard in that country, especially for a rural boy. Having a job might help him get his green card once his studies were up.

Dec clapped the boy on his shoulder, a purely fraternal gesture. Mal's dark brown eyes and slender frame must turn a lot of heads in clubs, but like Scott, the younger man held no appeal. Dec liked more muscular men. Besides, although there was less than ten years difference between them, service had aged Dec to the point where he felt ancient next to the bright optimism of his employee.

"Good job. I couldn't have done this without you."

Mal grinned broadly, his teeth impossibly straight and bright white. "Ah, boss man, this wasn't a job as much as a party. I'm so stoked that this will lead to more work, too."

"Yeah, keep thinking those good thoughts. I figure a guy like Place must know a lot of people looking for security help. Word of mouth may be our ticket to success."

Mal picked up his satchel of extra parts and hoisted it onto his shoulder. "I'm counting on it. So, you need help going over the system with the client?"

Dec turned to lead the way up the steps to the first floor, Pax at his right side as usual. She'd been her typically patient self all through the long hours of work. "I actually went over the codes and how the keypads work earlier. He said he has a guest coming tonight and didn't want to be disturbed with *details*."

Dec was glad Mal walked behind him and didn't see the grimace he couldn't hold back. He didn't like his client all that much. The attitude of the majordomo wasn't so much different than the man they all worked for. Stanford Place wasn't very tall, certainly nowhere near Dec's own six-two, but he managed to look down his nose at Dec anyway.

Too bad, because he had the distinguished older man thing down pat. Not that Dec favored older men any more than younger ones. If he had, though, Place would have caught his eye. Underneath the tailored suits, there existed a fit body with sufficient masculine strength to tempt Dec. There supposedly was an ex-Mrs. Place, but Dec's gaydar pinged pretty strong the few times he'd been in Place's presence. He'd once caught the guy checking out Mal's ass in a fleeting encounter. While Mal did have a cute ass, something in the surreptitious leer bothered Dec.

They entered the entryway that led into an alley and stopped at the back door. "You better leave this way," Dec said. "If Place's guest arrives while you're using the front door, Place might have a fit."

Mal made a face. "Yeah, big shots the world over are the same. They don't like the help getting underfoot." Opening the door, he took one last look over his shoulder. "I sure am going to miss coming to this house, though. It's awesome."

Dec smiled. "Hopefully there'll be another awesome house soon."

With a final wave, he shut the door behind the boy and started up the back stairs. He intended to triple check every part of the house he could before leaving. Even though he and Mal had already double checked everything, his SEAL training wouldn't let him leave without one more walk through. He'd just have to avoid Place and his guest as best he could and slip out the back afterward.

His muffled footsteps on the deep pile of the runner unnerved him. With his hearing at fifty percent, he always felt at a disadvantage. Hard to hear the enemy sneaking up on you. Of course, that was Pax's job. She functioned as his right ear so that he didn't have to worry about something his head knew wouldn't happen anyway. Too bad the lizard part of his brain stubbornly remained mired in combat. It just couldn't accept that his life no longer involved sneak attacks.

Dec climbed all the way up to the top floor and began his methodical check. Every window had been wired, even the ones that would take someone trained by Cirque de Soleil to reach. The place was tight as a tick because Mr. Place's personal safety and tremendous amount of valuables needed that kind of reassurance.

Checking quickly and quietly, Dec was mindful of his client being somewhere below. There was also something faintly rude about traipsing through the guy's bedroom. He'd been there a few times, naturally, while installing the system. Now that night had fallen, however, he felt kind of like a stalker, drifting around the man's large, elegant poster bed to check the windows.

Ditto in the bathroom, all marble and mirrors. The spacious room was bigger than Dec's bedroom and had a decadent air about it, like some Roman bath used to seduce and sacrifice virgins or something. Thank God there were no windows in the walk-in closet, no need to hack his way through the jungle of clothing he'd spotted once through a half-open door.

As he made his way down to the second floor, where a sitting room existed, Dec could see a light on. Obviously, his client's guest had arrived and was being entertained by the master of the house. According to Johnson, none of the staff lived on site. Dec knew they'd left already. He resigned himself to not being able to double-check that one room. He used his SEAL-trained silence to pass the room unnoticed.

Pax, however, stopped and, turning her head toward the door, let out a soft whine. Weird. She never acted out. Using a hand signal, Dec silently commanded her to come to him. She did, but with obvious reluctance. Just as Dec turned to continue down the hall, a loud cry cut through even his reduced hearing.

Dec didn't hesitate. He had his concealed carry palmed before he'd taken one step toward the room. He rushed in without knocking and stared in stunned silence at what he saw.

Place stood in front of a fireplace, his handsome middle-aged profile with its swept-back graying hair highlighted by the flickering flames. He held a cut glass tumbler of amber liquid in one hand and a fistful of long, white-blond hair in the other. The boy kneeling by his side struggled to free himself. When Dec barged in, both men turned to stare at him.

Place's gaze shot daggers of annoyance, but Dec paid him little mind. It was Scott's silent plea shining through his beautiful blue eyes that held his attention.

Pax barked and moved forward.

"Pax, stay," Dec commanded. Although he didn't know exactly what was going on, he couldn't let his dog escalate matters in an effort to defend her friend. He quickly re-holstered his gun, too, because Jesus Christ, he wasn't about to shoot his own client.

"Mr. Hunter, what precisely do you think you're doing?" Place's cold, almost amused question sounded bizarre given the circumstances. He obviously wasn't happy about being interrupted.

Dec glanced from his client to the boy still hanging from the guy's brutal grip. Scott looked much different than he did in the coffee shop. Instead of worn jeans, his lower half was encased in black leather so tight it had the boy's cock and balls in a death grip. His midnight-blue silk shirt was open to the waist, exposing lots of smooth creamy skin.

Shit, Dec had always suspected the kid worked as a rent boy. That didn't lessen the shock of seeing him here at Place's house. And was that... Fuck, yeah, a red splotch marred Scott's pale cheek.

What a clusterfuck.

Dec had to dig deep for patience and answer the question in a civil tone instead of marching up to his client and punching him in the face. "I heard a cry of pain, Mr. Place."

The man smirked, took a sip of his drink, and shrugged. He still held Scott's hair in a death grip that the kid couldn't free himself from. Dec had known the man had strength, and here was the proof. "Joey and I are just playing. Nothing to be alarmed about and none of your business." The last bit was issued with an edge to it.

Joey? Who the fuck was Joey? Oh, right, Scott didn't use his real name with his tricks.

Dec took a deep breath and ran his hand across the back of his neck. What was he supposed to do now? He should have left with Mal, except that kind of thinking meant walking away from a problem, and he didn't do that. There was no choice here. None at all.

"It doesn't seem to me that Joey is enjoying this game the way you are. Sir." He tacked that on because it was ingrained when he really wanted to say "fucker" instead.

Place waggled Scott's head with his grip. "Nonsense. I assure you I've paid handsomely for just this kind of game."

"Fuck that," Scott spat out, his hands holding onto his head in an effort to counteract Place's grip. "I don't care what you say. The service made a mistake. I've already told you I don't do this kind of thing anymore. Let me go."

Dec had to hand it to the kid. He wasn't going down without a fight. His expression and tone told Dec that this wasn't some kind of twisted game where Scott only pretended not to like what his trick did to him. Scott really didn't like it, and the mounting desperation Dec saw in the boy's eyes made it impossible for Dec to convince himself otherwise. "You heard the boy, Mr. Place. Let him go."

Place nailed Dec with a hard look that undoubtedly usually got the man anything he wanted. "Must I remind you, Mr. Hunter, that you work for me?"

Dec sighed. "Yeah, I know, and I've installed your new security system just the way you wanted. That doesn't mean I'm going to walk away and let you brutalize this kid."

"You still have some money coming to you."

Jesus *fucking* Christ, what was that supposed to mean, that he wouldn't pay Dec the final amount due when the job was finished because he wouldn't let the guy beat the crap out of a rent boy? Dec stared into the man's eyes, and yup, that's exactly what he meant. Well, no way that was going to happen. Swallowing down his need to issue a threat in return, he forced his voice to go into the calm mode that people who knew him well meant he was about to blow.

"Let. Him. Go." He issued the order, then kept his gaze steady on the other man's.

A second ticked by. Two. Three. Finally, Place released Scott with a contemptuous flick of his hand and sauntered over to a wing chair by the fire. "Get out of my house. Both of you. Needless to say, I will do everything to ensure that neither of you gets work in this city ever again."

Yeah, that threat was the predictable no-shit icing on this how-the-hell-did-we-get-here cake. Dec didn't let his dismay show on his face. Instead, he stood silently while Scott scrambled to his feet, grabbed a black leather jacket from the nearby sofa, and bolted out the door. Dec signaled Pax to follow the boy, then brought up the rear, keeping his eyes on Place at all times. He needn't have bothered. The man sat sipping his drink and contemplating the flames as if no one else had ever been in the room.

Dec caught up with a stumbling Scott in the front entryway. He grabbed the kid by the elbow and brought him up short. After a brief, reflexive jerk, the boy stood still with his eyes downcast. Dec could see the bruise forming on the kid's cheek better, confirming it would turn ugly pretty fast. Man, Place must have walloped him a good one.

He kept his grip on Scott while leading him outside and down the stoop. It wasn't until they hit Beacon Street, that he let go. "Are you okay?"

"I'm fine," Scott said in a voice that sounded more weary than scared. He raised a palm to his injured face. "I've been hurt worse."

Dec winced inwardly at the observation. Sure, he'd

been hurt way worse, too, but that had been in battle, not in a well-appointed drawing room. "Have you, ah, dated Place before?"

Scott lowered his hand and snorted. "Yeah, about once every couple of months for a year now." He raised his gaze to Dec's. "He's one of the people I gave your card to."

Dec exhaled sharply. "Oh. I wondered how they'd found out about my company."

Scott looked away. "I'm sorry. I thought I could help, and instead, I've fucked everything up."

"That's bullshit." Even though a tiny part of Dec wanted to blame the kid as well, the better part of him stamped out that thought. A gay boy as young as Scott didn't become a sex worker for shits and giggles. It was a classic way for kids kicked out of their home or forced to run away to survive on the streets. Scott had obviously done well in the business given his clientele. That didn't give his tricks license to use him as a punching bag. "Has he hit you before?"

Scott just shrugged. Dec didn't think he'd answer until he finally said, "When I was younger, I had to take any tricks I could. Lots of guys like the twink look, you know? And some of them are into bondage and discipline." He shrugged again. "It pays better."

"Holy fuck," Dec muttered because he just couldn't hold back the response. When a guy as young as Scott referred to times when he was younger, that had to really mean the times when he was underage.

"I don't have to do that anymore, though," Scott added with conviction. "I'm not so desperate now. I tried to tell him, but he wouldn't listen. I didn't see the backhand coming. I'm usually better at avoiding a blow." A shudder ran through his slender frame.

Dec had the urge to wrap his arms around the boy for comfort. His anxiety over getting physically close to others, plus his worry that Scott would take it the wrong way, made him hesitate.

Pax, bless her, had no such trouble. With a woof, she brushed up against Scott's leg. He instinctively reached down to run his fingers through the fur on her head. His body visibly relaxed within seconds. Yeah, the dog had that effect on people, exactly why Dec had taken her in when her bomb detection handler had determined she was too burned out to be reliable anymore. Dec figured she was so good at handling his problems because she suffered her own doggie version of PTSD.

"Look," Dec said after a few seconds. "Let's both go home, put this crappy place behind us. If we cut across the Garden, we can get cabs in front of one of the hotels. My treat," he added because money had to be an even bigger issue for the kid.

With a final pat to Pax, Scott shook his head. "No need, thanks. I have an Uber account, or rather my service does. They're probably going to be mad about my walking out on Place, but fuck 'em." Pulling out his phone, he looked for an available car. "One is just a couple of minutes from here. I'm good," he added with an anemic smile.

Dec scanned the area around them. It wasn't much later than nine and there were plenty of people milling about. Scott was perfectly safe, except that the encounter with Place had left Dec on edge.

"I'll wait until you get picked up." He shrugged and gave the boy a wry smile. "I'm a worrier. What can

I say?"

Scott shot him a better, shier smile in return. "Thanks," he said in a soft voice. "For everything. If there's, ah, ever anything I can do for you in return…" His gaze was fixed on the ground as he made the offer.

Dec held up his hand. "Don't even go there. You don't have to offer me your body as payment. I did what needed to be done. End of story." His words came out a lot more harsh sounding than he intended.

Scott opened his mouth just as a car pulled up. His ride. Dec moved to open the door and usher him in. Before he pulled his second leg inside, Scott looked up at him from under his lashes.

"I didn't mean it like that. Or maybe I did. I don't know any other way, not anymore."

"I know," Dec replied in a hushed voice. His heart really ached for the kid. "Put some ice on your cheek when you get home."

Scott merely nodded in assent.

Dec shut the door and watched the car drive off. He took a deep breath and let it out slowly. "So, *that* happened," he said to no one in particular.

Pax woofed softly and rubbed against his leg much as she'd done with Scott. Dec gave her head an absentminded scratch.

Jamming his hands in his pockets, he bent back to stare up at the sky. The night was clear and a little cool with a hint of fall crispness. Fuck the idea of getting a cab; he'd walk home. His tiny apartment way over in Brighton was a far cry from the towering luxury of Beacon Hill and the Back Bay.

With his knee already protesting from repeated stair climbing, he set off toward the Garden. It would take him a while, but the walk would do his mental state some good. If he lucked out, he'd be too tired for nightmares. He wasn't going to worry about his business dying on the vine, either. Not tonight anyway. Plenty of time for that in the morning.

And, first thing he'd contact Johnson. Just because Place had his dick in a twist over losing his night of "fun" didn't mean Dec didn't deserve to get paid. He'd press the assistant about the check, then hope Place didn't have the clout to keep other clients away. It went without saying that no matter what, there'd be no testimonials coming from the man in the future.

****

Dec's knee uttered a steady scream by the time he limped his way up the front stoop of his building. The walk had certainly tired him out, although his mind still whirred, the scene in Place's house playing in an endless loop. He knew his obsessive thoughts weren't going to help in any way.

Felix had been working with him for months on this very issue. How Dec couldn't stop chewing over that last, fateful night when everything had gone to shit. The tricks Felix had taught him to break the cycle, like tapping his finger against his thigh or pressing his forefinger and thumb together or even just interacting with Pax, weren't working tonight. Nope, he kept seeing Scott's frightened eyes and Place's coldly disdainful ones and realizing over and over that nothing he could have done would have produced a different outcome.

Sweaty and achy, he decided to take a long, hot shower before trying for bed. He popped a couple of ibuprofen first for good measure. He'd been given lots of stronger narcotics during his recuperation yet hated the way they fuzzied up his thinking. Once the worst of the pain went away, he'd tossed the "good stuff" for over-the-counters instead. He'd worried about becoming an addict, too. His old man hadn't been the first person in his family to crawl into a bottle, so Dec knew addiction ran in the family. Things were bad, but they could always get worse if he let down his guard.

Because she was trained to stay with him no matter what, Pax padded after him into the tiny bathroom. He left the door open, knowing it would get uncomfortably steamy for her. He'd rather be a little cold getting out of the shower. Not the dog's fault Dec had once fallen deep enough into the well of self-pity that he'd actually toyed with suicide. Whether he would have gone through with it or not, his therapist at the time couldn't afford to play that game of is-he-serious and had added suicide prevention to Pax's training. In his more wry moments, Dec found it funny that his dog had to babysit him. He didn't want to upset her, either, by trying to override her training with a command to stay in the bedroom.

So he stripped down in front of his dog and stepped into the narrow shower stall. Fortunately, hot water wasn't a problem in the building. He turned the temperature up as much as he could stand and allowed the spray to boil his skin while he leaned against the wall with his eyes shut.

It didn't take long for the heat to loosen his muscles and the bands of tension to break up and drift away. It would help him get to sleep, but experience taught him to add an extra measure of help. He grabbed the bar of soap on the ledge near his head and lathered up his palms. Then he angled his hips away from the spray while he cupped his cock and balls.

The frosted glass of the shower door gave him some privacy while he stroked himself to hardness. Not that Pax would understand or even care what he was doing. Still, it eased his mind. There was something skeevy about beating off in front of his dog, regardless of gender.

Shortly after he'd woken at the hospital at Landstuhl, he'd experimented with his junk to make sure it still worked. Although he hadn't been hit in the groin, he'd still worried that there might have been some collateral damage. He'd freaked when nothing had happened, no hard-on, no real arousal at all. When he blurted out his horror to the psychiatrist who'd visited him days later, the guy had raised his eyebrows, shook his head, and essentially told Dec not to be such an ass. His body had suffered a major shock. Getting his rocks off was way down its priority list.

Give it time. He'd been advised, and damn if the guy hadn't been right.

The only problem was that while the hydraulics had come back online, it had devolved down to a physical release. There was no real joy in getting hard and coming. Sure, it set off endorphins or whatever, making him sleepy. That was all, though. The press of his fingers against his hardening flesh felt almost clinical to him, not much different than what he'd feel simply washing up. And his head certainly wasn't in the game.

From the onset of puberty, he'd always conjured up images of hot, naked men to goose his pleasure. From the earliest age, he could remember boys, not girls, caught his attention, peaked his interest, and eventually fueled his engine. Whether he pictured real boys he knew or men in magazines, movies, television, or the internet, his dick showed its appreciation by saluting the images and coming like a jackhammer in his fist.

Now? Nothing.

Every time he tried to imagine another man, not just the look but the feel of him given the years of sexual experience under his belt, his brain scattered. Try as he might, he couldn't hold any picture or tactile memory of what it felt like to be with another man. He'd lost the sense of what it was like to touch a man's skin, taste his cum, or bury himself inside the tight warmth of another man's hole. When he found the courage to broach the subject with Felix and ask him why, the therapist had, in typical fashion, thrown the question back at Dec. Why did *he* think his brain denied him the pleasure of such thoughts?

The therapeutic technique had pissed Dec off, but Felix had simply sat back, staring, patiently waiting for Dec to figure it out on his own. And he had, eventually. It hurt too much to think of men because Dec was pretty sure he wouldn't be able to connect with an actual real live man for a long time yet. Maybe never.

The psychological impact of his last mission not only made him anxious around people, it also gave him frequent nightmares. How could he possibly approach a guy when he could barely stand to be out in public? Even if by some miracle he did meet someone, how could he expose that someone to the mess inside Dec's head?

At most, he might manage a one-night stand, so long as one defined "night" as a couple of hours and not a whole night. The last thing anyone wanted, even with an anonymous fuck, was to be tossed out of bed from Dec's screaming. Worse—way, way worse—was, what if in the throes of a nightmare, Dec perceived his bed partner as the enemy and attacked him? Dec was trained to kill and do so quickly. The poor guy could be dead before Pax managed to intervene, which brought up the other problem of what kind of man wanted to fuck with a dog watching?

Nope. Not going to happen, so why give his brain or his dick false hope?

He clenched his fist more tightly around his cock and pumped with fast, even strokes. No point in trying to draw out the pleasure when there was little to be had. He tried, just for the hell of it, to picture the last guy he'd fucked. The man had been an Afghani soldier, and the fuck a quick and rough ride.

Christ, even with don't ask don't tell gone, Dec had remained discreet about his orientation. His teammates had always known because he felt he owed it to them to be completely open and honest. He still hadn't rubbed their noses in it, though. The Afghani risked even more, of course. Regardless of the local warlord openly keeping an adolescent boy as his personal sex slave with impunity, the law in that country could have caused the soldier his life if he'd been caught with another man. Dec had appreciated at the time, and still did, how lucky he was to live in a country where he didn't have to hide himself away.

His breath quickened with the pace of his hand, and his balls pulled up even tighter against his body. He squeezed them as he swiped his thumb through the slit of his cockhead. That little bite of pain, so unlike the pain in his knee or in his now-dead ear, drove him over the top. He came with a rush and a jerk of his body that almost, almost made him smile. It was more like a gritting of his teeth, a grim satisfaction of having completed a necessary task.

Leaning against the wall, he closed his eyes and let his breathing subside. Then he quickly washed the rest of his body and stepped out of the shower.

Pax lay on the floor, her muzzle on top of her paws. She lifted her head and stared back at him with her placid eyes, never demanding, always patiently waiting for him to make a move or give a command.

Christ, a wetness that had nothing to do with the shower pricked the back of his eyes. He was so lucky to have been given the chance to have her in his life. Maybe it was pathetic that he considered his best friend in the world to be his service dog. But, damn, he counted it a win in an otherwise shitty situation.

He grabbed a towel and started to dry his now-weary body off. "Come on, girl. Let's get some dinner and go to sleep. We'll worry about tomorrow, tomorrow."

Chapter Three

The victim's gaze remained fixed on the ceiling, unseeing of course given that the guy had been dead for hours. Sergeant Ryan Jakes followed the line of sight and had to admit that if the man hadn't died instantly when the bullets hit his heart, he at least had seen something beautiful in his final moments. The elaborate plaster work in the moldings around the ceiling's perimeter was nothing like the plain horse hair ceilings of his own two-family in Southie. Not that he'd expected anything different when he got the call while still at home. Beacon Hill held wealth that his half swamp Yankee, half Irish family would never see.

"Man, Jakie, just goes to show you."

He turned to look at his partner, Andres Diaz, who had just returned from walking through the house. "What's that?"

Andy shook his head. "All this money and you still end up dying before your time."

Ryan exhaled deeply. "Yeah, murder will do that. Find anything of interest?"

Andy got a glint in his eye that Ryan recognized as his partner's I-just-found-a-juicy-piece-of-evidence look. "Right this way."

He followed Andy out to the hallway and up the stairs to the third floor. Shit, a five story townhouse in Louisburg Square had to be worth at least ten mill. And that was just the real estate. The stuff inside, all the furniture and art, would have to fetch a whole fuck load more. That's why it made no sense that, so far, he'd seen nothing out of place. At the moment, robbery seemed an unlikely motive. He followed Andy into the vic's bedroom—had to be given its size and décor—and right into a walk-in closet about the size of Ryan's living room.

Andy led him to the very end and pointed dramatically past a bunch of suits shoved to one side of the hanging rod. A narrow doorway stood open. "After you."

Ryan stepped past his partner and into a small, windowless treasure room. There was no other word for it. He stopped at the entryway and stared, much as he'd done with the ceiling in the sitting room. All along the walls and in a neat row down the middle of the room stood glass cases filled with various art objects, from coins to ornamental knifes to… Was that? Yup, looked like one of those Faberge eggs that even a poor Southie boy had heard off. Paintings hung on the walls, too, and over in the far corner was a high-back chair and a small round table with a decanter of amber liquid.

"Is this fucking freaky, or what?" Andy's breath tickled Ryan's neck.

Ryan moved farther into the room to get a better look at the walls next to the doorway, and that's when he spotted the empty space. In the middle of the wall to the left, in perfect alignment with the chair on the other side of the room was a whole lot of nothing. A really big empty space. Well, the hooks that had been used for a picture were still stuck into the plaster, but whatever had hung on them was missing.

He stepped back to scrutinize the entire wall, and there was no doubt in his mind that something had been taken. The placement of the hooks indicated only one thing. It would make no sense to have space between two other paintings when there was additional unused space on the other side of the last piece.

"Now we know what the motivation for the murder was," Andy said, joining him.

Ryan slapped his hands on his hips. "Yeah, I guess we do, except…"

He craned his neck around to get a better look at the rest of the stuff on display. Yup, definitely one of those adorable, jewel-encrusted Faberge eggs. This one looked like a gold hen carrying a deep blue egg in its beak.

Leaving Andy, he sauntered down the line of cases, ogling up close what they contained—jewelry, carved ivory tusks, a shrunken head? Ick. And right next to it, a mummified hand with tattered wrapping. Lovely. He shuddered and moved on.

One case contained a bunch of dishware with swastikas on them. Nazi collectibles, how nice. Although he had no way of knowing, because of his limited education in art, he suspected that much, if not all, of what he saw was illegal or illegally gained. Why else would it be hidden away in a house crammed full of other expensive stuff? Or maybe some of it, like the Nazi dishes, was just too damn immoral to display where anyone could see it.

In the far corner to the left of the chair, he spied for the first time a marble figure of a boy with half his arms and all his dick broken off. The statue stood within stroking distance of the seat. Had the victim, Place, really sat in that chair, fondling the smooth, cold ass of the Roman or Greek boy or whatever the hell ancient culture it had come from?

Ryan winced and proceeded to the chair. He sat down and settled back, perusing the contents of the room. Yeah, this spot gave one the perfect view of all the goodies on display, especially the art hanging on the walls, and in particular the now-empty spot. He could easily imagine Place sitting there like some Bond villain, sipping whisky and maybe jacking off to the thrilling sight of his ill-gotten gain, if not the feel of the marble boy. Of course, he had just leaped to certain conclusions, but the whole set up made no sense otherwise.

"How did you find this place anyway?" he asked his partner.

Andy had been peering at some black and white drawing of a girl sitting and knitting. "I think this is a Van Gogh."

Andy sounded kind of awe struck, but Ryan wasn't so impressed. The whole damn house was littered with expensive artwork. His interest was in why this room in particular existed and why the hell someone would commit murder and take only what appeared to be one thing.

"How did you discover this room, Sherlock?" he repeated with a note of exasperation. While his partner was a morning person, Ryan hadn't had enough coffee yet to make him good company.

Andy straightened and turned to look at him. "I thought there might be a safe in the back of the closet. It's a pretty classic hiding place for one. The door was easy to spot once I moved the clothes around because it was open." He shrugged. "I guess the murderer knew the security code. You saw the number pad next to the knob, right?"

Yeah, Ryan had seen it. A standard looking one with nine digits and a zero button at the bottom. The question was whether the killer knew the code or got it out of Place before killing him. "I wonder who knew about this room and if anyone other than Place had the code?"

"Good question. The guy with the stick up his ass, the one who called the murder in, said the vic's personal assistant was on his way. If anyone has it, it's probably one of them." He grinned. "You look comfy. Do you think Place has a fluffy white cat?"

Ryan grinned back because, of course, he'd been thinking the same thing. He hefted himself out of the chair and walked toward the door. "Let's go see what we can find out from the help. Bet the ME is here now, too."

As they hit the second floor, they saw that lots of people had joined the party. He poked his head back into the murder site only long enough to consult with the ME. The slender back and curvy hips of the person leaning over the vic confirmed that his favorite medical examiner, Dr. Barnes, was on the case.

Not that he was into women, but if he were, she would do it for him. Except, word was that she had already set up house with two detectives on the force. Two. No room for a third guy even if he were interested.

He entered the room and stepping over the legs of the deceased, he squatted down across from her. "What's the verdict, doc?"

Barnes gave him her trademark ironic grin. "He's dead and has been since shortly after midnight, I'd say." She waved her hand over the blood-soaked chest. "Two bullets to the chest, and one at least must have struck him in the heart if not both. I'll know better once I open him up."

"Any signs of a struggle or torture?"

Pressing her lips into a thin line, she gave a short shake of her head. "Not that I can see. No ligature marks on his wrists, no bruising on the knuckles or scrapes under his nails. I'd say he was either surprised by his killer or was kept at a distance because of the weapon."

With a nod, Ryan stood back up. "Thanks, doc. I'll leave you to it."

He found his partner in what looked like the formal living room, braced against dark walnut wainscoting with his arms folded in front of him. He watched the butler guy hover over an anemic-looking man who sat in a big winged back chair with his boney hand covering his lips.

"This just isn't possible. He was fine when I left him yesterday evening." A shudder ran through the almost delicate frame.

Ryan joined Andy at the wall. He resisted the urge to run his fingers down the fine wood. This aspect of the Place home more than anything impressed him because he made furniture as a hobby. Oh, man, the things he could create with this quality material. A thrill raced through his blood, probably the same feeling Place had experienced every time he occupied his treasure room. Maybe he and the victim had more in common than he would have imagined, except that none of the wood Ryan worked with was covered in proverbial human blood.

"This the personal assistant?" he murmured to his partner. When Andy nodded, Ryan said, "You take Mr. Belvedere down to the kitchen and get a more formal statement out of him and the rest of the staff. I'll see what this guy knows. Sounds like he might have been the last person to be with the vic. Other than the killer, of course," he added with a raised eyebrow.

Pushing off to an upright position, Andy herded the butler out of the room. Ryan waited until they'd left before approaching the assistant. "I'm Sergeant Ryan Jakes, the lead detective on this homicide, Mr..."

The man sat up straighter and removed his hand from his bloodless lips. "I'm Philip Johnson."

Ryan took out his pocket notebook and pen. "You were Mr. Place's secretary?"

Johnson's back stiffened. "His personal assistant."

Ryan clicked his pen. "I'm sorry. I don't get the distinction."

Johnson managed to look down at Ryan even from his lower ground position. "As Mr. Place's personal assistant, I aided him in all aspects of his business and personal life."

"Uh huh." Ryan wrote *personal assistant = up your own hole* on his pad.

Johnson took a deep, stuttering breath. "I will never forgive myself for his murder."

That got Ryan's attention. "Wait, what? Are you saying you killed Mr. Place?"

"Don't be absurd!" Johnson glared up at Ryan before blinking and looking away. "I simply meant that I should have tried harder to convince Mr. Place to take the threats against him more seriously, to take them to the police instead of hiring a new security company."

Ryan held up his hand. "Whoa, wait, *again*. What threats and what new security company?" Seconds ticked by in silence. He was on the verge of asking his questions once more *with feeling* when, with a sniff of disdain or grief—hard to say which—Johnson returned his gaze to Ryan.

"Mr. Place had received random notes with vague threats of how he'd pay for his blood-sucking ways or words to that effect. Unfortunately, Mr. Place didn't take them seriously. He only allowed me, grudgingly, to have his security redone here at home."

Ryan gripped his pen a little tighter, the only outward appearance he'd allow of his mounting frustration. How could someone as obviously educated and successful as Place not realize the importance of going to the police with something like criminal threats? Looking to private security as the solution only made Ryan's job harder, and of course, it hadn't worked after all anyway. "I don't suppose you or he kept any of the notes?"

Johnson shook his head, a look of remorse crossing his face. "No. Mr. Place burned or shredded every one of them."

"Of course he did." With a sigh he didn't bother to hide, Ryan propped his ass on the arm of the companion chair to Johnson's left. "What security team did he use and who would have had the codes to get into the house?"

Johnson reached into his breast pocket and pulled out a white card. He held it out to Ryan, his arm stretched, yet his body unyielding. Ryan was the one who had to move to make their fingers meet. The small show of power irked Ryan, but he had a feeling that was going to be his default feeling for the remainder of this case. Damn, rich people and the people who worked for them bugged the shit out of him.

He looked at the card and frowned at the name of the company and its president. "Red Cell Security? Never heard of them." He found that fact, in and of itself, strange. An upscale security firm working the carriage trade should be one he recognized given his years of service in the district assigned to Beacon Hill.

Johnson sniffed again, this time clearly with disdain. "A new company. The founder is a former navy SEAL. Mr. Place always valued service to one's country, and naturally one assumed that a SEAL would be knowledgeable and competent."

"How did you learn of the company? Did one of Mr. Place's friends or business associates recommend them?" A robbery and murder right on the heels of a security change rang lots of bells for Ryan. None of them good.

Johnson's gaze skittered away. "Something like that. I really couldn't say who."

Yeah, you could, but you won't. Interesting. He decided not to press the point for the moment, merely pocketed the card. Red Cell Security's modest address in the Leather District would be his next stop. He tried a different tack instead. "What kind of work did this company do for Mr. Place?"

"They redid all of the security for the house, here," Johnson replied with a delicate shrug of one shoulder. "They were supposed to finish last night."

Ryan lifted his head sharply from his pad. "They

were here last night? Until when?"

Another shrug. "I really couldn't say." That seemed to be the guy's default verbal expression. "Certainly, they were still here past six when I left for a dinner engagement."

"With whom?"

"Oh, dear." Johnson rolled his eyes. "I suppose I'm a suspect, like in some hideously crass murder mystery. God, Mr. Place would be so embarrassed by all of this tawdry digging into his affairs. He was a very private man, you know."

"I bet, but he's dead, so I'm thinking embarrassment is the least of his concerns. I have to explore all avenues."

"Yes, of course." Johnson waved his hand in dismissal. "I enjoyed the company of a woman I've been dating for a few weeks. I left her apartment after five o'clock this morning in order to return to my home and get properly dressed for the day. I suppose you need her name and contact information?"

"Yes, please." He watched Johnson dig another card, this one out of his wallet, and took it when he passed it over. He caught the name of the law firm in raised black letters before he saw her name. It didn't mean anything to him, except the snarkier side of him wondered what this woman, or anyone for that matter, would see in the effete personal assistant. Still, the information would have to be followed up on. Procedure in a murder investigation was ninety percent tedium.

He tucked the card into his jacket pocket. "So, Mr. Johnson, did the new security system include the hidden room in the back of Mr. Place's bedroom closet?" He asked the question as if it were merely the next routine question among dozens.

Johnson blinked back at him, seemingly nonplussed. "I have no idea what you're talking about."

"Really? I thought you handled all of Mr. Place's affairs. My partner found an open, yet secured, room containing a variety of art works. It appears that something is missing. We were hoping you could clue us in on what that item might be."

Johnson sat up away from the back of the chair, his demeanor turning fierce. "I repeat. I have no idea what you are talking about. Mr. Place's art collection is well known in this city, but there is no secret room."

"I'm sorry to disagree with you, sir. I just came from there. Does Mr. Place own a Faberge egg?"

The abrupt question left Johnson speechless for a second. "No, he doesn't. It's one of the things he'd always hoped to acquire. Regrettably, someone has always out bid him on the rare occasions when the opportunity arose."

Ryan tapped his notebook against his thigh and frowned. "Hmm, there's this golden chicken figurine with a blue egg in its mouth, standing by a gold basket." He shrugged. "Looked like one of those Faberge egg things to me. Of course, I'm just a cop and have only posters hanging on my walls."

Johnson licked his lower lip, the first sign of true nervousness. "That sounds like Hen with Sapphire Pendant. It's one of the lost eggs."

"Not anymore it's not. Lost, I mean. Because I just saw it upstairs."

With a new-found bound of energy, Johnson popped out of his chair. "I need to see that room."

Ryan moved more slowly, standing up straight, shaking his head. "Sorry, sir. That's not possible. Unless you have knowledge of what that room contained and consequently what might be missing, I can't let you in there. It's part of the crime scene."

Johnson clearly didn't like that answer. Probably not used to being told no on anything. "Very well. I suppose I'll have to accustom myself to being in the dark and on the sidelines with regard to Mr. Place's affairs now that he's gone."

"Yeah, about that. Who is Mr. Place's heir? Do you know? The butler said there is no Mrs. Place. Not anymore anyway, and no children. Is that right?"

"Yes," came the icy reply.

"And he wasn't dating anyone?"

"Mr. Place squired a number of women to functions around town, but had no special lady that I know of."

Ryan kept his eyes from rolling at the arcane way in which the stuck-up assistant described Place's dating life. "So, no one important enough to leave his stuff to."

"I wouldn't think so. I expect Mr. Place's brother, a man he hasn't seen in some time, might be the heir, as well as certain charities he's been involved with over the years. Mr. Place's estate planning lawyer would be able to tell you."

"What's his name?"

"You have *her* card already."

Ryan's coffee-deprived brain took a few seconds for him to catch up. He gave the man a wry grin. "Right."

Johnson's pale, smooth cheek pinked up just a bit, the only indication that he found being his boss's lawyer's lover embarrassing. "And just for your edification, Sergeant. Bentley is a majordomo, not a butler."

Ryan raised his eyebrows. "The difference being?"

Now Johnson's face cracked into a look that some might describe as a smile. "The same as that of a personal assistant to a secretary."

"Of course." Ryan allowed the sigh to stay inside of him. This case already sucked in too many ways to count. A high profile victim meant the higher ups would be breathing down his ass by noon to find the perps. Add in possibly stolen artwork, and you had an open invitation for the feds to come stick their nose in. That was always a party to be missed.

There was nothing he could do to change any of it, however, so he needed to stop whining and start slogging away. The best place to begin after the household interviews were done was this security company. At a minimum, these guys had failed in their goal to protect their client. At worse, they'd somehow been a plant all along and facilitated the murder.

Either way, he was looking forward to having a little chat with one Mr. Declan Hunter.

****

Dec toyed with the last of his coffee, his gaze fixed on the less than awesome view of the city that his office window afforded. After a typically miserable night's sleep, he'd gone for his usual run. He tried not to worry about how Scott wasn't there when he'd gone in for his morning coffee, told himself that the kid probably had called in sick so that he didn't have to explain his bruised face.

Still, it bothered him. He hoped it didn't mean that

the boy had been fired or forced to leave Boston. The idea of Place having that kind of clout that quickly really was the stuff of bad suspense movies.

Since coming to the office, he'd found one thing after another to take up his time and delay the inevitable call he had to make to Johnson. No matter how pissed off Place was about his night being ruined by Dec's intervention, the job had been completed and the final payment was owed.

Of course, Dec knew that if Johnson put up a fuss about paying due to his boss's assholery, there would be little to be done about it. Dec wasn't going to blow what little profit he'd already received on a long, drawn out court battle. Place had the deeper pockets and would have his high-priced lawyers drag the whole thing out until Dec's own funds ran dry. His only hope was that Johnson had more integrity than Dec's gut told him he did.

He gulped down the last of his coffee and swirled his chair around to face his desk. Time to stop being such a chicken-shit about the whole thing and call the guy. Just as he picked up the phone, however, his door opened.

Cindi stuck her face inside. "Um, Dec? Sorry to disturb you but there are some people here who need to speak with you." The serious look on her face and her tone, coupled with the fact that she had elected to open the door and not just call him through the intercom, raised the hairs on the back of his neck.

"What's going on?" He stood up as he asked the question, and his change in demeanor caused Pax to get up as well. She trained her gaze on the receptionist, on high alert.

Cindi opened the door more fully and stepped to one side. "Detective Sergeant Ryan Jakes and Detective Andres Diaz of the Boston Police Department to see you, sir." Her formality, so different from her usual perky self, sent him right to Defcon One.

Two men inched past her to enter his office. The first one through was average height, sleek more than slender, with olive-toned skin and short, straight dark brown hair. He was classically handsome and well-dressed in a navy blue suit, white shirt, and red tie. Everything pressed and spit-polished to a shine that would have satisfied any senior chief doing an inspection of his crew. He figured this must be Diaz, and swarthy men had always done it for him. Perhaps because it made a nice contrast to his own pale skin and dirty-blond hair. But as appealing a sight as the man made, it was the guy who swaggered on his partner's heels that really caught, and held, Dec's attention.

This must be Jakes, the senior man if rank meant anything, and it did on the police force like in the military. This guy had pale skin similar to Dec's, yet darker hair that held a hint of red in it. Cut short almost to a buzz, it covered a head with a square-jawed face. Green eyes stared right at Dec, piercing, judging. They reminded him of his grandmother's fierce, almost feral, cat that had never missed an opportunity to scratch him if he got too close.

In contrast to his partner's turned-out appearance, Jakes looked rumpled with his barely tied tie and his ill-fitting suit. He really needed to wear a larger size, in Dec's estimation. The fabric stretched over bulging muscles so tightly, it looked like the seams might break apart at any moment. Not that he would complain if they did.

Whoa. Where had that stray thought come from?

He registered his alarming interest in the man in the millisecond it took him to scrutinize and catalogue his visitors. Putting it aside to maybe analyze later, he nodded. "Gentlemen."

He knew how to hide his feelings, to play it cool when inside, he was anything but. Having cops show up at his door couldn't be good news. Christ, he hoped it didn't have anything to do with Scott not being at the coffee house that morning. Had something happened to the kid, and if so, had Place sicced the cops on Dec in retaliation? Was there even any chance that a trail would lead to someone as careful and high-placed as Place even if the rent boy had been hurt or killed or even offed himself? Didn't seem likely, and man, he was getting way ahead of the game. Before he could question why they were at his office, the men flipped open their I.D.s for him to see.

Only Jakes did the talking. "Mr. Hunter, as your receptionist stated, we're Jakes and Diaz from Boston P.D. We need to speak with you, please."

Oh, and how awkward that last word tumbled off the guy's tongue. Jakes was clearly a typical Alpha male type and social niceties didn't come naturally. Dec could relate. He was the same way or used to be when serving in the Teams. As the senior man on any op, it had always fallen to him to sit with village elders, sipping tea, making small talk through his team linguist. The very definition of awkward to his way of thinking.

The cops stood eying him as much as he did them, waiting for a response. "Sure, although I can't imagine why." He nodded at Cindi. "Thanks, Cindi."

"My pleasure, boss." She paused before shutting the door. "May I get you gentlemen any coffee?" Dec could hear the reluctance in her offer, way too formal and so not her usual bubbly self.

Diaz flashed her a bright smile. "No, thank you, ma'am."

Surprisingly, Jakes also smiled at her and holy fuck, just for a brief and frightening moment, Dec would have given his left nut to have the guy turn that heart-stopping, toe-curling, blood-boiling look his way. "I'd love a cup, black, if it's no trouble."

Even Cindi, the one used to making guys' dicks hard, not the other way around, made a gushing sound. "No, trouble at all. I'll be right back." She almost walked into the door instead of away from it.

Jakes' smile dropped the moment he set his gaze back on Dec. The cop became all business. "Mind if we sit down, Mr. Hunter?"

Dec gestured toward his visitor chairs. "Please." He sat down himself without waiting for them.

Diaz plopped into his chair immediately, but Jakes took a second to step closer to the desk and extend his hand toward Pax's nose. He gave her a few seconds to sniff his fingers before patting her head, then sitting down. "Beautiful dog," he said while he took a small flip pad and pen out of his pocket.

Dec wasn't sure what made the man more appealing, that dazzling smile that transformed his face into movie star quality sex appeal or his obvious comfort around and appreciation of Pax. "Thanks, she's my service dog."

"Right," Jakes replied perusing his notebook. "Former Navy SEAL, honorably discharged on a medical about two years ago."

Okay, so they'd researched him, no big surprise. Whatever was up, digging into people's lives was what cops did. Before he could demand they get to the point of this little visit, Cindi returned with a cup of coffee. She'd used one of the six visitor cups with a saucer underneath. The almost delicate china looked ludicrous when she placed it in front of the jacked guy.

Once again, the cop dazzled her with his smile. "Thank you, ma'am."

"My pleasure. If there's anything else I can do, please let me know." Cindi had recovered enough from the shock of Jakes' charm to return to her usual flirty self.

Jakes gave her a firm, short nod of acknowledgment before focusing back on Dec. Apparently, the guy was immune to Cindi's feminine appeal, which meant either he was gay or knew Cindi was transgender and not as open-minded about it as his "ma'am" would have indicated. And why the fuck did Dec even care, let alone wish that it was the former and not the latter?

The cop picked up the small cup with his large hand, cradling it in his palm, and took a long, healthy swallow. Left handed, no ring. And double fuck that Dec would even notice such a thing.

"What's this all about?" He barked out the question, his limited patience, with himself most of all, at an end.

Jakes looked at him over the rim of the cup as he took another gulp. His thick neck worked the liquid down before he dropped his bomb. "Stanford Place is dead, murdered to be exact."

Dec stared back at the man, a gaping fish look no doubt, while he absorbed the shocking information. "You're shitting me?" Whatever polish he'd strived to deliver as a business man vanished. "How the hell did that happen?"

The cop's gaze remained steady on Dec, obviously measuring his reaction, weighing how to respond to his question. Asshole acted like Dec was a suspect, which of course, he fucking well was. *Shit.*

"I don't have an alibi, fyi, if it happened sometime last night." God, he sounded defensive to his own ears.

Jakes coolly stared back at him, almost unblinking, still drinking his coffee. He drained the cup and placed it carefully back on its saucer. "It did, around midnight." He flipped over a new piece of paper in his notebook. "I understand from Place's *personal assistant* that you were recently hired to redo the home security system after Place received anonymous threats."

Dec had to look away. Guilt ate at his gut. Jesus, a man was murdered on his watch. He should have pressed Place to go to the police, and he shouldn't have left that house until he was sure Place would activate the system. Hell, he should have set the alarm himself. He'd been too focused on making sure Scott got out and home okay.

Ah, fuck, again. *Scott.* Had the boy returned to Place's house to exact revenge?

Dec got ahold of himself and pretended he was being debriefed after a mission. Keep it simple. "Approximately two weeks ago—Cindi can confirm the date—Johnson came in and hired me to redo Place's security. He did say at the time that Place had received written threats from an unsub and also had a valuable art collection that he worried about protecting. Despite having a good system already, he wanted a new one. I obliged. My tech guy and I left shortly before nine p.m. last night."

Jakes flipped a page. "Malcolm Srinivasan. An Indian national and MIT grad student."

"Right. You've done your homework." Of course he had. Dec already knew that. It rankled him more, though, knowing that a cop had rifled through Mal's life. He didn't care about himself so much. His people meant everything to him, and he wanted to protect them as much as possible.

Jakes quirked the left side of his mouth up, a half smile that tugged at Dec's cock despite his growing apprehension and irritation. That stupid appendage, which had spent the last two years phoning it in, shouted out a "hey there" in his jeans. Really? Now? Now was when his long dormant libido decided to wake the fuck back up?

Christ, he really was a basket case. In the back of his mind, he could see Felix smiling at the good news, but Dec couldn't muster any enthusiasm. The last guy, the very last guy on the planet, Dec should be attracted to was the lead cop in the murder investigation of Dec's very first client.

"Mal left before I did and never formally met the client. Only I did. Mal didn't even talk to Johnson." Determined to protect his team, Dec wanted Mal in the clear immediately. "Cindi met Johnson the one time he came here, and she never went to the client's house." *There. Just focus those cat eyes on me, not my people. Damn it.*

The tip of Jakes' tongue poked past his surprisingly

full lips. "Cindi, with two i's, Keyes, formerly known as Keith Keyes."

Dec's grip tightened on his armrests, his hackles raised. Leaning forward just a bit, he bore his gaze into the cop's. He'd practically made tadpoles shit their pants with that gaze before, and those were SEALs, afraid of nothing and no one. He wanted this man to understand the shaky ground on which he tread. It didn't matter that both Jakes and Diaz had called Cindi ma'am. He intended to make damn sure they knew they needed to treat his admin with respect.

"That's right," he bit out. "And I'm telling you *she* didn't know Place."

"We appreciate your trying to do our job for us, Mr. Hunter, but you know we have to follow a certain procedure, earn our paychecks." He gave Dec a "so sorry" kind of smirk that made Dec want to smack it off the guy's face. Or maybe kiss it off.

No. Nope, not going there.

Jakes continued. "We'll need to ask Ms. Keyes ourselves before we leave, and we'll be getting in touch with Mr. Srinivasan." His expression softened. "We're not interested in making innocent people miserable. We won't be digging into stuff that's not pertinent to the case, either."

Somewhat mollified that his team wasn't going to be harassed, Dec eased back into his chair. Because the sudden spike in his adrenaline fed his overall anxiety, he reached over to stroke Pax's head. Bless her little doggie heart, she was right there within reach.

Jakes tracked the movement. His cop brain probably doing the quick math about what kind of service Pax might be providing. Shame rose inside Dec before he could squelch it, then he heard Felix's voice reminding him that there was nothing unmanly about PTSD. Yeah, like he ever really bought *that* story. He wouldn't let Jakes see how he felt, however.

"I appreciate that," he allowed, happy his voice was steady. "I want to help, of course I do. I set up the man's new security. Was he murdered in his home? Was the alarm by-passed?"

Instead of answering his question, the cop responded with one of his own. "How long after your associate did you leave?"

Dec held in the sigh of frustration. "Less than half an hour. I did a final walk-through of the house as much as I could to triple check the system."

"As much as you could? What stopped you from completing the check?"

Crap. Dec rubbed a hand across his brow. He really didn't want to rat out Scott, but the kid had been there and kind of had a motive. He dropped his hand again and, this time, let the sigh out. "Place had a date."

"A date? A woman was there?"

"No, a boy. Young man," he amended. "I'm not sure how old he is. His name is Scott."

Jakes and Diaz shared a look. "Johnson didn't mention anything about this date, and he claims to have handled Place's personal schedule as well as his professional one."

"You'd have to ask him about that, obviously." God, this sucked. Dec felt like he's was getting bogged down in the mud, except this muck was Place's dirty life.

"How is it that you know the date's name?"

"Because the kid works at a local coffee shop I go

to most mornings after I run. That's how Johnson learned about my company. I've been leaving my card around town to drum up business."

"I'd wondered how a guy like Place ended up using you." Again, that lip curled up to a half smile. "No offense."

"None taken." Except that was a lie. Even though he'd wondered the same thing, he bristled at the notion his firm wasn't worthy of the job. That rankled more than the insinuation that somehow Dec had been involved in a murder.

Jakes tapped his pen against his notepad. "Yeah, so anyway, Scott. Why would a man like Place date a barista?" His face scrunched up as if he were perplexed. "Unless it was the kind of date one might pay for."

Dec grit his teeth. "Scott's a good kid. Place was an asshole for all that he was my client and is now dead. I caught him beating on the boy, and not in a mutually kinky way. So, not being a dickhead myself, I put a stop to that shit right then and there."

Jakes lifted his eyebrows. "By killing him?"

"Don't be an ass." Dec's calm shattered in a millisecond. In reaction to his tone and his mood, Pax moved to place her chin on his thigh. He kept his palm on her head, his fingers stroking lightly. He even did some of the breathing exercises Felix had taught him. "Place was alive when we left."

"What's the name of the coffee house this Scott works at?"

The cop acted as if he hadn't just lobbed a verbal hand grenade at him. Police tactics, Dec supposed. Not so different than the ones he and his SEAL team used on suspected terrorists. Always keep them off kilter.

Jakes wrote down the name Dec gave him, then looked up from his notepad. "Back to the new security system you installed. Did that include the lock to the treasure room?"

Chapter Four

The navy SEAL turned private security consultant who was the embodiment of every wet dream Ryan had ever had stared back at him with wide eyes. If his reaction to Ryan's question was staged, he couldn't tell. Everything this man had said, every expression that crossed his face struck Ryan as sincere. It wasn't simply a matter of wishing Declan Hunter had nothing to do with the murder, either. As appealing as the man was, Ryan could hardly ask him out in the middle of a murder investigation, no matter how much his straining dick wished otherwise.

Christ, he had to keep his notebook practically mashed into his crotch to hide his reaction to Hunter. He didn't dare look at Andy again. That one time he had, he'd seen the laughter in his partner's eyes. He knew the score.

Once when they'd gotten shitfaced together, they'd actually talked about sex—girls, boys, and what each of them liked. Andy was totally cool with Ryan's orientation, but they usually steered clear of the topic. That night, though, they'd both needed a release of a different sort, having put to bed a gruesome case involving a man hacking his wife and two kids to death. Alcohol and dick jokes were a good way to purge the poison. So, yeah, Andy knew that Ryan liked his men tall, fair, and as jacked as he was. He liked to hang onto a guy without worrying he'd crush him.

"What the hell are you talking about?" Hunter's deep voice barreled through Ryan's body. He liked a forceful guy, too, someone he could go toe-to-toe with. Someone who could drill Ryan into the mattress all night long. Which, of course, was a totally inappropriate thing for him to notice. He needed to focus on the case.

Leaning forward, he said, "In the back of his bedroom closet, Place had a room filled with art."

Hunter knitted his eyebrows. "The whole fucking place is filled with art."

"Yeah, well, this stuff appears to be the kind you don't show off to just anyone."

"Definitely on the down-low," Andy piped in.

They'd agreed on the way over that Ryan would do most of the questioning, but his partner's voice distracted Hunter enough that Ryan could study his face from a different angle. Still hot as hell and still seemed genuinely surprised. Although Ryan couldn't see it, he knew the guy's hand remained on his dog, petting it probably. Was it for the dog's comfort or his own?

Ryan only knew about the discharge. He couldn't access any details about why Hunter needed a service dog. He had noticed that Hunter tended to keep the left side of his face more toward the person he was talking to. It reminded Ryan of his grandfather who'd lost hearing in one ear during what the old man had referred to as WW two.

Hunter turned his bright blue eyes back to Ryan. "I have no knowledge of this room or the stuff inside it. His closet didn't have any windows, so we never touched it. His previous security firm must have installed the key pad. Johnson would know."

"Johnson said he knew nothing about the room, either." Ryan ignored Andy's sharp glance. Yeah, it didn't make much sense telling Hunter anything about what Johnson said, and yet the words had tripped out of his mouth anyway.

Hunter rubbed his forefinger across his chin, drawing Ryan's gaze to his almost pretty mouth. "Really? For a guy who professes to have been Place's right hand man, he sure doesn't know a lot."

Ryan agreed, although he had come back to his senses long enough not to say anything. He would, however, be interviewing the personal assistant again in the near future. He would bet anything that the guy at least acted as Place's pimp, procuring the boy and undoubtedly others. Maybe this murder had been all about the personal. If Place liked roughing up his "dates," then he might have picked on the wrong one. A decent theory, if not for the missing artwork. He opened his mouth to ask about the companies Hunter used for the security equipment.

The guy cut him off with a thump of his hand against his arm rest. "Were there art pieces missing from Place's house or from that room only?"

Ryan's eyes narrowed. How the hell had Hunter jumped to that conclusion? "Why would you ask that?" he demanded, his voice gruff because he hated to think he'd been wrong about this man, distracted by his masculine beauty and innate sexiness.

Hunter played him out a bit by picking up what had to be cold coffee and taking a long swig. The man had sharp, intelligent eyes. Ryan could see how he'd once been in the most elite fighting force their country had.

He'd bet Hunter would make a great cop, too. Unfortunately, the man had gone the private security route, and Ryan had to remind himself that, not only couldn't he get involved with a potential witness, if not suspect, he also represented a group of people who were a pain in Ryan's ass.

With a sharp exhale of breath that might have been a sigh, Hunter said, "Ever since you told me Place had been killed, my mind immediately went to the threats he received. I never took them as lightly as Place and even Johnson did, but I couldn't force either of them to take my advice about at least reporting the problem to the police."

"You actually recommended they report it instead of taking care of it yourself?" That knowledge surprised him. Private security people were a cocky bunch of assholes, in his experience.

Hunter openly scoffed. "Of course I did. Look, my company exists to provide top notch electronic and physical security. I can keep a guy safe. I expect you, the cops, to find the guys who are after him."

Ryan was nonplussed for a moment. "That's a refreshing attitude."

"Fuck you. You don't know me." The statement was made without heat, although the raw honesty of it shown through nevertheless. Ryan bet Hunter felt that way about a lot of people.

For some reason, Ryan needed to explain himself, as if this man's opinion about him mattered. Damn, it did. "I just meant that private dicks, to use the old vernacular, tend to get in my way, the way of all cops."

"Yeah, I can see how you must hate that." Hunter gave Ryan a wry grin, conveying how little the idea bothered him. "Anyway, with your revelation about the so-called treasure room, I figure the murder must have more to do with theft than a personal grudge. Why would you raise it otherwise?"

"He's got you there, Jakie," Andy added softly.

Ryan glared at his partner for a second, but not so long that he missed the way Hunter's lips twitched at hearing Ryan's nickname. God, did the guy have to be so gorgeous? Even when he made Ryan's blood boil, he still managed to turn him on.

With a quick, small adjustment of his ass to help ease the tension in his groin, Ryan made an attempt to regain control of the interview. "As it happens, you're right. We believe an item is missing. Whether it was stolen and whether it's related to Place's murder remains to be seen. I can't help coming back to the fact that all this happened the moment you finished installing the new security system." Oh, yeah, that got to the big, bad SEAL.

Hunter's eyes narrowed, and his lips flattened into a grim line. "I didn't set up a system so that someone could break into Place's home, kill him, and steal what, a painting or something?"

Ryan just shrugged because, even if he knew what was missing, he'd said too much to Hunter already.

"I'm not a thief and I'm not a murderer. I'm just trying to launch a new business now that I can't be in the Navy anymore." The guy stood up, his large body vibrating with indignation. His dog whined softly, no doubt in tune with its master's moods due to training and necessity.

When the guy leaned over his desk to get more into Ryan's face, all Ryan could concentrate on was the way

Hunter's eyes sparkled an even brighter blue. His broad chest peeked out from the V of his simple cotton shirt. Black jeans hugged his crotch, outlining an impressive package. He was tall, too, six-two according to the info Andy had dug up on him. Damn, Ryan liked guys who were taller than his own six feet.

"Look," Hunter continued, oblivious to Ryan's inappropriate interest. "I know you have a job to do, but this thing happened on my watch. You'll clear me and my team. I'm sure of that because we didn't do anything wrong. But the reputation of my company is on the line. Worse, reading between the few lines you've given me, it seems someone slipped past my security and killed my client. I don't like that. I'm not going to sit idly by while they get away with it, either."

Okay, that pulled Ryan away from his ogling. He stood up, too, not caring if the remnants of his hard-on might be on display. He brought his body right up against Hunter's piece of crap desk and got in his face. "If you're saying you intend to stick your nose into my investigation, think again. What happened to let the police handle finding the threat?"

Hunter didn't back down. He closed the gap between them enough that Ryan could smell the coffee on his breath. He hated that the guy could look down at him, really look down, not figuratively the way that asshat Johnson had done. Hunter's height wasn't so alluring at this point.

"That position ended the moment my client turned up dead."

Ryan gritted his teeth. "You will stay out of this investigation and out of my way, period. You're still a suspect, remember?"

"The hell I am. You know I didn't have anything to do with this."

Ryan arched one brow, a trick he'd learned watching Star Trek reruns. "Do I? A SEAL discharged under a medical with no visible disability yet needs a service dog says PTSD to me. Add to pre-existing emotional instability a failing fledgling business, and I smell desperation. You're not off my list by a long-shot, Mr. Hunter."

Crap. As soon as he'd finished speaking, Ryan regretted his words. Disrespecting a veteran and a wounded one at that, implying that he was a fucked up fuck-up in need of money so much he'd help steal from and kill a man was shamefully low. He thought he heard Andy mutter "ouch" under his breath as well, and that sucked because Andy's opinion of him mattered. The Southie boy in him with the perpetual chip on his shoulder wanted to jut out his chin and double down on the insult. He was trying to be better than that.

Ryan throttled back, physically and emotionally. "Andy, go confirm with Ms. Keyes her meeting with Johnson and lack thereof with Place."

"Sure thing, Jakie." He left quickly, quietly shutting the door again after him.

Ryan waited until they were alone again to apologize to Hunter. "I'm sorry. That was uncalled for. I have nothing but respect and admiration for your service, and I don't think you're some mental case making really poor choices with your life." He took in a deep breath and heaved out a sigh. "My cousin, Jack, he did four tours in Iraq with the marines. He hasn't been the same since he came out."

"His parents named him Jack Jakes?"

Jesus, was that all the guy got out of his lousy apology. "No, it's Jack Murray."

"That's good to hear because no one can fuck you up quite like your parents."

"Is that your way of saying you accept my apology?" Ryan pressed the issue because damn him, it mattered. Regardless of how much Hunter's intentions to stick his nose into the investigation pissed him off, he still didn't want to make the guy feel bad.

"No. But I accept it anyway."

"And, you'll leave Place's murder investigation to me and my partner."

Hunter shook his head. "I didn't say that."

"Christ." Ryan tipped his head back to gaze a moment at the ceiling before staring back at Hunter. "If you interfere in any way, I will arrest you for obstruction."

Hunter's mouth turned up into a broad, if not enthusiastic, grin. "Do what you gotta do, Sergeant Jakes."

Yeah, stupid him. SEALs were known not to have the sense God gave a goose when it came to avoiding trouble. "Right." Flipping his notebook shut, he jammed it back into his pocket and headed for the door. "Thank you for your time, Mr. Hunter."

"You're welcome. Oh, and Sergeant?"

With his hand on the doorknob, Ryan looked over his shoulder.

"You never did confirm exactly where and how Place was killed."

It was Ryan's turn to grin. "No, sir, I did not."

****

"You take the lead on questioning this kid."

71

Andy glanced at Ryan as they walked up the steps of an old, yet not unkempt building in Mission Hill. "You don't think you'd maybe be more relatable to the kid because you're both, you know, gay?"

Ryan pushed the security button for the apartment that, according to the coffee shop, Scott Reilly lived in. "The kid's not necessarily gay. You know that lots of desperate boys are gay for pay. It's one of the main ways runaways make money." When there was no answer, he pressed again.

"Yeah, but there's nothing in the system about a missing child under his name, so I'm thinking the poor guy got kicked out of his house for being gay." He shook his head. "I can't believe how shitty people are. Imagine putting your kid out onto the streets to fend for himself."

"People suck," Ryan agreed because they did. His family had its issues, like any other, but at least they'd accepted his sexual orientation with a hug, or in the case of his brother, a painful noogy. Because there was still no answer, Ryan put his thumb on the button and held it down. "I want you to take the lead because you're a little closer in age to him, and you're way better at disarming witnesses and suspects alike with your boyish charm. I usually come across like an angry bulldog."

Andy grinned. "Aw, you're just smarting over how much you wanted to jump the last guy we interviewed."

"I'm so not going there."

Andy's grin got wider, and Ryan had to look away when he felt his cheeks start to burn with embarrassment.

A tinny voice squawked over the intercom. "What

72

the fuck!"

Finally. "Mr. Reilly, this is the Boston Police Department. We need to speak with you. Please buzz us through, sir," he tacked on because, as young as Reilly was, citizens were always entitled to respect.

A few seconds ticked by. "What's this about?" Even with the shitty quality of the electronics, Ryan could hear the fear lacing the question.

"We'll discuss this face-to-face. Please let us in, son, or we'll be back with a warrant for you and your place." He ignored his inner boy that balked at his thirty-year old self calling Reilly "son," but if Andy was going to play the cool cop, Ryan may as well embrace the persona of the cranky old one. It did the trick, too, because the next thing he knew, the door buzzed open.

Reilly's place was located on the fifth floor. Ryan and Andy took one look at the tiny, rickety box labelled *elevator* and elected to take the stairs instead. The exercise did Ryan a lot of good. It helped him shake off the residual energy from his interview with Hunter.

The image of the man remained firmly branded on his brain, of course, and he figured he'd have to take a long look later, in the privacy of his home, at his ridiculously strong attraction to the man. Maybe he'd do it after sliding into his bed for the night, with the lights out and the quiet of his home wrapped around him. He could slip his hand inside his boxer-briefs, palm his hot and heavy rod, and...

Jesus Christ, what was wrong with him? *Focus on the case, moron.*

The fifth floor looked more like an attic than an actual floor. It held four undoubtedly small apartments, and Reilly's was the last one down the narrow hallway. Ryan had hoped to find the door open, but no such luck.

When they knocked, a voice came through the battered, peeling wood. "Hold up your badges in front of the peephole."

Ryan traded looks with Andy. Apparently, Reilly had learned a thing or two out on the streets about trust. They would have gotten around to it anyway, so they didn't hesitate to comply.

It took a good, long while before the door opened, and shit, the skinny kid on the other side looked like he could be one of Ryan's high school-aged cousin's friends. A little shorter than even Andy's five eight, he wore baggy and threadbare T-shirt and jeans. His white-blond hair, pulled back in a messy ponytail, didn't hide the livid bruise on his pale cheek. Hunter had said Place had been beating on the kid, and here was the proof of that and maybe the motive for murder, much as he hated to think it.

And that face. It could make angels weep, as his Grammy Jakes would say. Jakes bet men paid a lot of money to spend time with this boy. His eyes, though, were old, wary and fuck him, scared. Whether that look came from being guilty of something or just used to life shitting on him regularly, they'd soon find out.

Ryan nudged Andy with a quick jab of his elbow.

His partner stepped forward. "Scott Reilly?" he asked with a quick smile. "I'm Detective Andres Diaz, and this is Detective Sergeant Ryan Jakes. We'd like to come in and ask you a few questions."

The kid swallowed hard, his thin, delicate neck showing every movement. "Like I have a choice." His sullen tone didn't quite mask his obvious fear, but he turned to walk farther into what turned out to be a studio apartment.

Ryan let Andy go first, then closed the door after himself. His quick perusal took in a space to his right that held a dollhouse-sized galley kitchen and a door to his left that was open enough to see what had to be an old closet converted into a bathroom. What the apartment lacked in size, though, it made up for in neat, tidy, and clean.

Reilly flopped down onto a made-up daybed in the far side of the room and crossed his legs. He gestured toward a bean bag chair listing in one corner. It was the only other place to sit. "Sorry, I don't have a lot of furniture. I don't do much entertaining."

Keeping up his good cop routine, Andy shot him a grin and plopped into the squishy chair with more grace than Ryan would have managed. Of course, his partner was wiry while Ryan had always chosen to sacrifice flexibility for muscles. He loved the rhythm of working the weights and the sense of raw power it brought him to bulk up.

He elected to lean against the wall opposite the boy with his arms crossed in front of him. His intent was to look intimidating while Andy disarmed, but frankly, Ryan's heart wasn't into the role. Reilly looked like he could break in two with just a harsh word.

"What is this all about?" the boy demanded the moment Andy's ass hit the chair. Okay, the kid had spine, not as fragile as he appeared.

"We're hoping you can help us out, Scott," Andy said. "Do you mind if I call you Scott?"

"Whatever." Christ, that one dismissive word made him sound more like a teenager than anything else.

Andy chose to treat it like an invitation. "Great. So, we're homicide detectives, not vice. You understand what I mean, Scott?"

Reilly stilled for a moment before shifting his ass, as if getting comfortable. "I guess."

"Good. We're here because we're investigating the murder of Stanford Place. Do you know him?"

Reilly's eyes went wide. "He's dead?"

"I guess that means you do know him," Andy observed, still keeping his tone friendly. "In fact, we know you were with him last night."

Air whooshed out of the kid's lungs, and he shifted his gaze to look out the one small, yet clean, window. "I guess Hunter told you that." He swung his gaze back to Andy, flicked it over to Ryan, before returning to his partner. "He didn't do it."

Andy cocked his head. "Who didn't do what?"

"Mr. Hunter. He didn't kill Stan."

Interesting. The first thing the kid thought to say was that Hunter was in the clear. Why not talk about his own innocence? Shit, was it possible this kid was the killer after all?

"Why do you say that?" Andy asked.

"Because Hunter's a good guy. He's really sweet with his service dog, Pax, and…"

"And he stopped Place from beating you." Ryan couldn't resist inserting himself into the interview.

Andy shot him a look, as if to say butt out. "Is that how you got that bruise on your face?"

Reilly dropped his gaze and nodded.

"Did he do that often…hit you?"

"I guess. Stan could be moody if he'd had a bad day. He liked to work off his stress."

"Is that what you called him, Stan?" Andy's tone was gentle, and Ryan knew it wasn't part of the act. His partner had a soft spot for young victims, and even if Reilly had murdered Place, it didn't change the fact that the boy was a victim of another sort.

"He mostly wanted me to call him Daddy."

Ryan's stomach lurched. Good thing he hadn't had any lunch yet. He'd worked vice long ago and couldn't hack it. On too many cases, his fist had landed on someone's face a few more times than strictly necessary to subdue him. His captain had thought him worthy enough as a cop to reassign him away from the temptation. Child molesters were the worst. A kid like Reilly might be scarred for life.

Andy changed tack because, Christ, what was there to say to that revelation? "What did you do after you and Mr. Hunter left Place's house?"

"I came home. I took Uber, so there's a record of it."

"Did you stay here all night?"

"Yeah, alone, and I haven't been out since then." He pointed to his cheek. "It kind of aches like a bitch, so I called in sick at the coffee shop where I work."

Andy tapped his pen against his thigh. "I see. Did you and Mr. Place spend a lot of time together?"

The kid shrugged. "Once in a while he'd have me over."

"How did you meet? Did he come into the coffee shop where you work?"

Reilly rolled his eyes. "Come on, man. You know that's not how."

"Okay, you're right. Remember when I said we're not vice. We don't care about any business arrangement you and Place had. We want to catch his killer. I need to know the service you work for."

"Why?"

"Well, Scott, I don't really have to explain myself to you, but I will. I need to know if Place used other boys because maybe he had someone come over after you left. You get me?"

The boy shrugged again but also nodded. "Yeah, I get it. I still can't give you a name. I don't want to end up floating in the harbor. *You* get *me*?"

"We'll protect you."

Reilly just snorted at that assertion. "Yeah, right. No one managed to protect Kenny."

"Who's Kenny?" Andy asked, his tone remaining low and soothing. He really was way better than Ryan at this.

"Just I guy I knew who ended up dead a few months ago."

"Did he also date Place?"

"Maybe."

Andy shot Ryan a "what the fuck" look before asking, "Do you think Place killed him?"

"I dunno." Reilly worried his lower lip with his front teeth for a moment. He really was just a kid, and suddenly Ryan hated his job. Place obviously liked his rent boys young, too young even if prostitution were legal.

"How old are you?" He barked out the question before he could think better of it.

Both Reilly and Andy looked up at him, startled.

"Twenty," the boy said before untwisting his legs and getting up. He grabbed a worn leather wallet from a scarred table and, pulling a card out of it, took the few steps necessary to reach Ryan. He held it out. "I got my GED and enrolled this fall at Bunker Hill Community College. I'm hoping to become a vet. You know, veterinarian," he added almost shyly.

Ryan didn't bother to take the school I.D. in hand, just stared at it for a second. "You don't have a driver's license?"

With a huff, Reilly pulled the card back and shoved it into the wallet. "I don't drive." He returned to his seat, and this time, pulled his knees up under his chin. "Look, I didn't have anything to do with Place being killed. I don't know anything about it. And if you want to know who Place might have been seeing other than me, including Kenny, why not ask Johnson?"

Andy glanced at Ryan then back at Reilly. "Did Johnson arrange for your, ah, dates with Place?" All he got was a shrug in response. The fact that the kid even knew the assistant's name gave them enough reason to question the guy again. So, Andy went in for the final question, the money shot, as it were in this weird case. "Did you ever see Place's special art room?"

Once again those almost boney shoulders rose and fell. "Every room in that fucking house is an art room. Place liked to show me stuff, sure, bragging about how successful he was. Like that somehow made him a better lay than he actually was."

The kid looked them both in the eye, first Andy, then Ryan. Although his expression said he told the truth, Ryan wasn't convinced. A kid used to living the kind of hard life Reilly obviously did would have to get good at lying. If nothing else, he'd learn how to stare into a man's eyes and tell him he was, to use the kid's words, a good lay.

"Other than his bedroom," Reilly continued, "I didn't get into any room that I'd think of as private, let alone special."

Andy tapped his pen a few times before standing up. He slipped the pen and his notebook into the inside pocket of his impeccable suit. Ryan always looked like a vagabond next to him, which would have been true for just about any partner he might have. A clothes horse he was not.

Pushing away from the wall, Ryan dropped his arms to his side. They'd gotten as much as they would out of Reilly for the moment.

"Thanks for your time," Andy said. He pulled his card from the same pocket and held it out to Reilly. "If you think of anything else, please give me a call." When the kid made no move to take it, Andy placed it on the table next to Reilly's wallet. "We'll let ourselves out," he added, like their host had made to jump up and walk them to the door.

Neither of them said a word until they were back out on the street. Andy beat Ryan to the punch, saying what they both felt. "Don't you just hate it when you feel like killing the vic yourself?"

Ryan blew out a breath. "Yeah. Place was an asshole, no doubt about it. He might have been smart enough, though, to only fuck boys that looked underage instead of ones that actually were."

Andy snorted. "Like that makes it better."

"Well, it makes it legal. Except for the whole prostitution is illegal in the Commonwealth thing."

"Johnson had to have been procuring for Place. No way a wealthy guy was trolling the internet for rent boys."

"I agree." He headed for the car, Andy at his side. "Let's go get some lunch, then talk to the old security company. Somebody had to have set up the key pad for the treasure room."

"You love calling it that, don't you?" Andy asked as he got into the passenger side.

Ryan buckled up and hit the start button. "I do. I really do."

"Don't you want to have another round with Johnson first?"

Pulling out into traffic, he said, "Nah, let's leave him for last, catch him after a long day, hopefully have the ME's report, too. It might tell us something."

"Something like neither Hunter nor Reilly had anything to do with it? I really don't want either of them to be involved."

"Oh, they're involved all right, if only because we had to interview them. But I'm with you. I don't want either of them to be the killer."

It was a stupid thing to say and stupider thing to want. He had to follow the evidence where it took him. His concern about Reilly the lost boy could be excused. Hunter, though?

He mentally shook his head. He hadn't thought with his dick since his last and most disastrous relationship with fellow cop, Flynn the Fucker Campbell. He'd learned not to get so caught up in a guy's instant hotness that his mind turned to mush. Declan Hunter probably wasn't anything more than he appeared—an innocent bystander to the murder or even a dupe intended to distract the investigators. It was really too soon to make that call.

As long as his head made it and not his lonely cock

and aching balls, he'd be okay.

****

"Dude, a secret treasure room is off the wall awesome."

Dec couldn't say he was surprised at Mal's reaction to the news about the room filled with possibly stolen art not to mention that Place had indeed been killed in his own home. That information came to Dec curtesy of Cindi's internet search. The local and even national press swarmed all over the story, licking up and vomiting back out for mass consumption what little information the City of Boston gave. The mayor, himself, had held a public briefing on the horrific killing of one of the city's most important businesspeople and patron of the arts. It made Hunter a little sick at how the fucker was being lauded in death, given his nastiness in life.

The cause of death hadn't been revealed, but Dec figured if a gun had been used, the sexy Sergeant Jakes would come knocking on his door again looking for a ballistics test of Dec's weapons. Well, let him. He had nothing to hide.

The chance to see the guy again held way too much attraction, excited him to a level he had almost forgotten. Since the cops had left his office, his dick had remained semi-hard, needy to an extent that he'd missed since being blown up. Why, then, did he resent it now? He expected Felix would have all kinds of theories, like maybe the thought of forming an attachment to a real live man scared Dec. Damaged as he was, not so much physically but mentally, the idea of getting close to someone, opening up to and spending time with him was pants-shitting frightening. Who in the world would want to deal with Dec's messy emotions, his night terrors and panic attacks? Maybe, just maybe, a few hours in the sack would be okay. As long as he didn't fall asleep.

And why in the hell was he even encouraging his dick? Jakes was not a dating prospect, not now in the middle of the murder investigation, and not ever. He couldn't even tell if he liked the guy given the more pressing concerns of finding out what happened to Place without Red Cell suffering from negative publicity. Almost certainly, Jakes didn't like him. The blaze in those feral green eyes had warned Dec more than the cop's words that, if Dec crossed the guy, he'd be lucky to survive with just a few scratches.

"Sometimes being a packrat pays off." Mal's voice brought Dec back to the present and the immediate issue at hand. "I figured a lot of this stuff from the old security system might come in handy." The grad student's small one-bedroom apartment looked like some kind of overstock warehouse with boxes overflowing with gadgets and gizmos piled all around.

After the cops left, Dec had immediately called Mal, partly to warn him. Cindi, of course, had already beaten him to the punch. Checking up on Place's previous security firm to see if they'd set up the access to the secret stash of art seemed like the best first step in finding out what had happened. When Mal had told him he'd kept parts from the old system, Dec had come right over, even taking a taxi for speed. The sooner Place's murder case was solved, the better.

Mal rummaged around inside one of them and pulled out part of a key pad. "Yes, here, a bit faded but there's a label on it and a number." He passed it over to

Dec.

"State Street Security," Dec read. Of course. When he'd been researching what he needed to start his own business, he'd looked into existing ones to see what they offered and get some marketing ideas. State Street definitely had popped at the top of his searches, an old company that catered to the very carriage trade Dec aspired to. "I want to pay a little call to their corporate offices and see if I can learn anything."

Mal already had his phone out. His face scrunched up. "Weird, their address is on Federal Street."

"The inherent risk of naming your company after your location, then having to move. Let's go see if we can get someone to talk to us."

"You want me to tag along?" Mal's eager surprise made the decision to include him easy.

"Sure, why not? Like the weapons lessons I've been giving you, it's good for you to learn all aspects of the business. Talking to people, getting information out of them, is sometimes something we'll do."

"Awesome!" Mal grabbed a jacket and slid it onto his slender frame. The temperature was a balmy mid-sixties, but for a boy from India, it was almost like winter.

"We'll take the T. Pax hates taxis."

"Aw, bummer," Mal said, but he patted the dog on their way out.

Because Mal lived in Cambridge, they had to switch from the red line to the green line, giving Dec enough time to formulate how he'd approach the other security company. He knew better than to try to bullshit them with some song and dance to trick them into seeing him and giving him information. He'd sure as shit see through any ruse, so they probably would, too. You didn't stay in the security business for close to fifty years being idiots. Honesty would be the best way to go. He'd try for the head guy, too. No sense in wasting time on a low-level person who wouldn't know anything anyway.

He, Mal, and Pax entered the land of marble floors and tight security, every sound they made from the squeaking of Mal's sneakers to the click-click of Pax's toenails reverberated off the walls. Dec stepped up to the lobby security desk and pulled out his driver's license.

"Excuse me, ma'am," he said to the guard eyeing him from behind the high counter. "We're here to see Mr. Abernathy at State Street Security."

The guard flashed him a bright smile before taking his license and tapping into her screen. "I'm sorry, sir. You're not listed in our system as a visitor today."

"Um, yeah, that's because Mr. Abernathy isn't expecting us." He nodded toward Mal, who also produced his license for her inspection. "We're hoping you could call up and see if he's free to see us." The look the woman gave him said "doubtful," but she picked up her phone anyway. "Please tell him we're from Red Cell Security and it's about Mr. Place."

That last bit caught her attention. Her eyes lit up, and when she spoke into the phone, her voice held more enthusiasm. "Sorry to bother you, Amanda, but there's a Mr. Hunter and"—she scrutinized Mal's license—"a Mr. Srinivasan from Red Cell Security here to see Mr. Abernathy." Pause. "No, I know they don't have an appointment, but they say it's about Mr. Place. Mmmhmm." She glanced up at Dec. "The Mr. Place who was killed last night, right?"

"Yes, ma'am."

"That's the one," she said into the phone. Seconds ticked by, long ones by Dec's reckoning. "All right." Hanging up, the guard handed the I.D.s back. She picked up visitor passes and handed those over, too. "Eighth floor. Mr. Abernathy's admin, Amanda, will be waiting for you."

"Thank you, ma'am." Dec couldn't keep the smile from his face. His heart sped up just a bit, the way it used to do before going into battle. What he was about to do wasn't so different than what he used to do. He was waging a war of a different kind, that's all. The stakes were just as high. His business and reputation were on the line, as were the livelihoods of his team. And, as always, failure was not an option.

Chapter Five

Where the lobby of the building had been loud, the lobby of State Street Security was muted. Dec, with Pax heeling to his right side and Mal flanking him on the left, stepped onto the plush, dark carpet and over to the middle-aged woman in a severe gray suit who stood waiting. Her gaze shifted from Dec's face down to Pax before either he or she had said one word.

The woman's mouth made a mew of disgust. "I'm sorry, sir, company policy prohibits animals in the office."

He gave her what he hoped was an ingratiating smile, well aware that she acted as Abernathy's gatekeeper. "I'm sorry, ma'am, but both the federal and the state Americans with Disabilities Acts trump your policy."

"He's a wounded veteran, ma'am," Mal chimed in, giving the woman what Dec knew to be a disarming smile. Mal's cuteness factor ranked high with women and men alike. Dec didn't like being labeled as a wounded veteran, or rather his ego didn't like it. It was what it was, however, and Mal's extra explanation worked. Not that the admin's expression softened more than an iota.

Still, she nodded. "I see. Thank you for your service, Mr. Hunter, is it?"

"Yes, ma'am." He didn't think her thanks sounded

very genuine. Over the many years of his naval career, he'd heard that thanks delivered by many people, some more sincere than others. He wasn't going to dwell on it, though. The goal was to get in to see Abernathy.

With a slight sniff, the woman turned on her heels. "This way, please. Mr. Abernathy isn't one to take time out of his busy day to meet with unscheduled people. Your mention of poor Mr. Place caught his attention, naturally."

They followed her down the hall and up to the proverbial corner office. The door stood ajar and she knocked once. "Mr. Abernathy? Mr. Hunter and Mr. Srinivasan are here to see you."

Pushing the door more open, she stepped aside to let Dec and company enter a more utilitarian office than Dec would have expected. Two walls of windows gave spectacular views of the city. An older man with white hair and a still-fit body stood from his chair and came toward them. He held out his hand, first to Dec, then to Mal. He gave Pax a cursory glance.

"Gentlemen, please come in and sit down. Thank you, Amanda." He dismissed his admin with a quick nod and returned to his seat while Dec and Mal took theirs.

Pax sat quietly next to Dec's chair within easy reach of his hand if he needed her comfort. He was determined not to show such weakness in front of what he hoped would one day be a competitor. He wrapped his fingers around the armrest to stay any impulse to reach for her. Abernathy's stare reminded him of an admiral's, assessing and with zero tolerance for bullshit.

"Okay, Hunter, you got my attention by dropping

Place's name. Now what the hell is this all about?"

Direct and to the point. "Well, sir, first of all, we appreciate your time." When Abernathy merely grunted, Dec got on with it. "My company, Red Cell Security, was hired a few weeks ago to redo Mr. Place's home security. We saw your company's sticker on one of the key pads, so we know you did the old system."

The man's eyes narrowed. "Yes, we did that system several years ago, and it was state-of-the-art. Nothing that needed replacement."

"I agree with you, sir." Good, that stopped his feathers from ruffling too much. "I said as much to Mr. Johnson and Mr. Place."

Abernathy hmphed. "Johnson." Contempt dripped from his voice, which just meant the guy was a good judge of character. "So, why did they have you redo it?" Then he added before Dec could respond, "Red Cell, you say. Never heard of you."

Dec swallowed his pride and a retort. "That's because we're a new company. Anyway, Place wanted a new system because he was receiving anonymous threats."

Abernathy held up his hand. "Let me guess. He didn't go to the police."

"No, sir, he did not."

The man snorted and shifted his gaze to look out one his amazingly large windows. "He always was a dick." The candor and the vulgarity surprised Dec, although it shouldn't have. Security people usually started out in the military or law enforcement. For all his expensive suit and beautiful office, this guy likely had once run with a rough crowd. "I wish I could say I wept at the news that he was dead." He shook his head.

"A guy doesn't get to be that rich, even with daddy and mommy's money as seed capital, without pissing a lot of people off. I still don't get why you're here. This whole thing happened on your watch, not mine."

Dec squirmed once in his chair before schooling himself to be frostier under the older man's gaze. "Yeah, well, see there's one room we didn't wire and figured maybe you did." Abernathy raised his eyebrows. "Apparently Place had a secret room somewhere in the house in which he kept art he didn't want anyone to see. That room had a key pad entry lock."

The man's eyebrows climbed even higher up his forehead. "Seriously? How did you learn about this?"

"Cops came knocking at my door first thing this morning."

"I bet. Interesting that they haven't come to me yet."

Dec shrugged. "I'm sure they will eventually. They just have hotter leads to follow at the moment. I know because I gave them one." And the thought of sending them after Scott still rankled. Christ, he hoped the kid had nothing to do with the murder or the robbery or whatever the fuck it was they were dealing with. "The lead detective knows what he's doing. He won't leave anything unexplored."

"I assume he doesn't know you're here?"

"Hell no, sir. In fact, I'm sure he'll rip me a new one when he finds out."

Abernathy gave him a rueful smile. "Yeah, don't expect me to cover for you. I have a good relationship with Boston PD, as good as any private security company can have. I'm not going to start playing games with them now."

"I understand, sir. I don't expect you to do anything different. And I've noticed you've not yet answered my question about the room."

The man chuckled. "That's true. I haven't." All mirth left his face. "I run a clean company, Hunter. We put in safes and set up panic rooms all the time, but I don't know anything about this art hideaway. If it had been legit, Place would have had us do it and would have had you redo it."

Dec heaved out a breath. "I agree. You were the first and only place I had to go to for answers. As you said, this happened on my watch, and I'm not going to sit with my thumb up my ass waiting for cops to figure out what happened." He glanced toward the window. "Waiting isn't my strong suit."

Abernathy snorted, a weird sound coming from a guy his age and with his distinction. "I can relate. Hey, you know if your own company doesn't work out, you're welcome to apply here for a job. We're always looking for good operators."

"Thank you, sir. I appreciate the offer, but I have my limitations." He gestured with his head toward Pax.

"Hmm. Well, if that's all? I'm sorry I can't be of any help. I feel for you. I really do." Standing up, he gestured toward his door. "I'm afraid I've given you all the time I can spare. I met you purely as a curtesy to another professional, you understand?"

Dec stood, Mal and Pax following suit. "I do, sir, and I appreciate your time." He made for the door.

Abernathy stopped him. "Wait. You say Place hired you because he was receiving threats, yet you asked me about a secret room of art. Was Place's murder personal or a robbery gone bad?"

Dec looked over his shoulder. "That, sir, is the sixty-four thousand dollar question."

****

Ryan hated downtown buildings. They always made the Southie boy in him want to yell an obscenity just to hear it echo around the cavernous lobby then run away, laughing like a loon. With yet another hit of coffee for lunch, his system hummed along with the right amount of energy to bust someone's balls. Of course, his seething anger over finding out that Hunter had gone to talk to the head of State Street Security before he had fueled much of the spring in his step.

God damn arrogant SEAL, ex-SEAL, as if that really mattered. A cockier bunch of men never existed on this or any other planet. Ryan had warned him off the investigation, and the cocksucker had promptly ignored the order. Well, he'd get his dressing down just as soon as Ryan and Andy took another shot at Johnson.

Fortunately, Place's business office wasn't that far from State Street Security, so he and Andy went from one toney building to the next in quick order. Johnson had tried to put them off until the next day, but fuck that. The first twenty-four hours of an investigation were critical. If the assistant was involved in the murder, Ryan wanted to rattle his cage early and often. He'd leave confronting Hunter for later.

In the meantime, he knew for sure that Place had been killed by one bullet that hit him square in the heart. Dr. Cassidy had said, though, that the other bullet had nicked the heart which would have also proved fatal in a short period of time. The good news, from his perspective even though he didn't want it to be, was that the caliber of the gun used to fire those bullets didn't match any of the weapons that Hunter had registered with the city. Not that that meant anything for sure. The guy could have an unregistered weapon or simply hadn't been the trigger man. Ryan didn't want either of those things to be true, and knowing how he felt just pissed him off even more.

As soon as he and Andy arrived at their destination, they were ushered up to the thirty-third floor, giving them a spectacular view of the harbor. Johnson came out to the lobby to greet them, his face grim.

"Gentlemen, I hope you appreciate how busy I am. This company is in turmoil with Mr. Place's death."

Ryan gave the man a blank look. Getting into a verbal pissing match with him wasn't going to help matters. "I'm sorry, sir. I'm sure you're very busy, but we are trying to find your boss' killer."

"I am aware," came Johnson's haughty reply. "I fail to see how interviewing me again is going to help."

Ryan held his hands out wide. "You never know. Can we take this into your office?"

"No, I have very sensitive business papers out. I'm sure you'll understand that I prefer to do this in the conference room." He nodded toward a set of floor-to-ceiling windows encasing a room with a long table and a whole boat load of brown leather chairs. Without waiting for a reply, the man headed inside.

Ryan and Andy had no choice but to follow. Johnson didn't bother to sit down, so neither did they. Instead, Johnson moved around the massive table, putting it between him and them. He stood with hands clasped in front of him, the shimmering water of the harbor as his background, a put-upon look on his face. "What more do you need from me?"

Shoving his hands into his pants' pockets, Ryan stared the guy down. "We have two issues in particular to circle back on with you. One is the room in the back of the closet."

Johnson clucked his tongue. "Really, Sergeant, I've already told you I know nothing about that."

"Yeah, you did. Here's the thing, we've now been able to confirm that a few of the pieces in that room are on Interpol's list of stolen art."

"I know nothing about that," Johnson repeated in a clipped tone. "I'm as shocked as anyone to hear such a thing." He turned his gaze to the window. "It's as if I never truly knew the man."

"I'm sure it's very disturbing, but someone had to have built that room and set up the security. I've talked to both Red Cell and State Street. Neither of them profess to know anything about it, either. So, who did?"

Johnson returned his gaze to Ryan. "I really couldn't say. How many times do I have to tell you that?"

Ryan moved around the table so that he stood within a few feet of the other man, no table between them now. A slight sheen of moisture shown on Johnson's head where the hair was thinnest. The guy was nervous, and nerves usually meant something interesting was being hidden.

"You said yourself that you handled every aspect of Place's business and personal life."

"Obviously, I was wrong about that, wasn't I?"

"Seems that way. But if you didn't help Place with

that room or its security, then he must have done it himself, don't you think? Or relied on someone else, perhaps?"

A flicker of anger shot through those pale, beady eyes. "He must have made the arrangements himself as there is no one else who handles his affairs."

"So, then maybe he left behind some papers or emails about it?"

"Papers perhaps, but certainly no emails. Mr. Place eschewed electronics for the most part, only grudgingly using a mobile phone for calls, not texts. In many ways, he was a throwback to simpler times, like a nineteenth century man. He liked beauty and elegance in his life as you undoubtedly noticed having been inside his home. His wealth afforded him people like me to deal with the more mundane aspects such as typing, making appointments, researching information."

"Like were to find the best rent boys?" The abrupt switch in topic seemed to stun Johnson into momentary silence. "That's the second issue we're stuck on. Declan Hunter came across Place hitting a boy hired for sex. It seems your late boss had a thing for young men, boys really, and wasn't above venting his daily stress on them."

Fine beads of moisture popped up on Johnson's lower lip. "I was not privy to that aspect of his life, either."

Ryan cracked a smile and hmphed. "Really?" He paced a few steps away before turning back. "So, a guy who didn't use the internet found his own prostitutes by what, using the phone book or the local alternative newspaper's personal adds?" He cocked his head and frowned. "That seems more like nineteen eighties, not eighteen eighties to me. What does strike me as an old-fashioned way of procuring illegal flesh is to have a manservant do it for him." Ryan looked pointedly at Johnson.

"Absolutely not." The denial was issued in a tone dripping with ice and haughtiness, Johnson's obvious default settings.

Ryan paced away again, this time heading to Andy, who'd remained by the door, silently watching the exchange. "Okay then, Place must have a Rolodex or calendar book or something equally non-technical in which he'd put his appointments and contacts that you didn't know about."

"Your point being?"

With his hands still shoved in his pockets, Ryan leaned over the table toward the other man. "My point being that I want to see them."

Johnson's almost pale tongue slipped out to lick his lower lip, another tell that he was nervous. "I'm afraid I'm not authorized to allow that. This company is more than Mr. Place, and I have to answer to the interim president that the board has put in place just this morning in an emergency teleconference."

"So get his or her permission."

"Unfortunately, Mr. Teichman is on a plane from Hong Kong and won't be in Boston until tomorrow. Without his permission, anything in Mr. Place's office, home or here, is potentially company property that I'm not at liberty to show you." He paused with an almost gleeful look. "I'm afraid you'll have to obtain a warrant."

Which they had been working on getting for the better part of the day. More than the usual red tape held them back. Place's standing in the community meant that everyone walked a fine line between wanting his killer caught quickly and not digging up dirt in the process that would sully the man's reputation. The higher ups were already sweating over the confirmation that Place had stolen artwork and liked to pay for not just sex but gay sex. Yeah, they'd come a long way, baby, but guys sticking their dicks into other guys still gave lots of straight men a case of the ewws.

Either of those revelations would normally get them a warrant within an hour. In this case, a lot of feet were dragging. It was as if it were almost better to let the man's murder go unsolved than to have his messy life splash all over the many high-profile people he'd rubbed elbows with over the years. Politicians and art patrons alike had been the beneficiaries of his largess, according to Andy's research, and Place had been generous with his money in a calculated sort of way.

"Sure," Ryan replied, deciding he'd have to settle for rattling the guy's cage and not causing him to collapse under pressure. "We understand completely. We'll be back with that warrant."

He and Andy left at a leisurely pace, looking back once as the elevator doors closed. Johnson watched them from where he stood, not having moved an inch, tracking them the way a prey animal might a predator. Good, Ryan liked having that effect on a suspect, and Johnson definitely fell into that category.

"You know he's just going to spend the night shredding everything."

Ryan sighed. "Yeah, I know. But if he is involved in the murder, he started doing that first thing this morning after we cut him loose. He probably did it even before Place was killed. Hopefully, there's something useful at the house. We may not have a warrant to rifle through Place's home office yet, but at least the house is secure. Anything there from last night is beyond Johnson's reach." He swore softly with a shake of his head. "Who am I kidding? The guy had access to Place's home office constantly. He would have purged stuff there, too."

"If he's involved," Andy reminded him as they stepped off the elevator. "Which I'm kind of inclined to think he is."

"Me, too."

His partner glanced at him from the corner of his eyes. "If we're right, then that leaves the question of whether Hunter was in on it or just being used as a handy dupe—you know timing the break-in and murder right after a new system was put in, implying that Hunter used it himself or gave it to an accomplice."

Ryan rolled his eyes as they stepped out into the relatively warm air of the waning day. "Yes, thanks. I've been doing the math in my head all day." He blew out a breath. "I'm thinking the latter."

"Which of your heads came to that conclusion?" Andy held up his palms in surrender when Ryan bared his teeth. "Sorry, boss, I have to wonder."

Ryan blew out his belligerence with a harsh breath. "Yeah, yeah, I know. I'm attracted to the guy. I admit it freely even though it pisses me off. But I'm not about to let that cloud my judgment. Right now, I'm also pissed that he's stuck his nose into the investigation. And," he added when Andy opened his mouth. "I get that he might be doing that to throw us off the scent."

"You're going to go confront him over it anyway,

tonight, alone." It wasn't even a question.

"Yes, Mom, I am. I promise to be careful. In the meantime, I want you to look into Reilly's story about his friend, Kenny. See what floaters might have turned up in the last six months."

"You think it might have something to do with Place? It's kind of a long shot."

"I think sex workers are at risk for all kinds of violence, and obviously Place wasn't the only guy to hire boys for sex in this town. Still, if he was one of Place's regulars, maybe he saw something that led to his death."

"Like the treasure room?"

Ryan shrugged. "A long shot, but we follow even long-shot leads, you know that."

"Yup, I do. Why do I have the feeling, though, that your assignment for tonight might end up being way better than mine?"

Ryan's answer was a light punch to his partner's arm and an even bigger internal one to his dick. This was going to be a business call to Hunter and nothing more.

****

Pax cocked her head at Dec and let out a low whine. It was as close to begging as she got, and being a total push-over, he tossed the last piece of chicken from his sandwich in her direction. She caught it handily and gulped it down without chewing. Her mouth opened up and her tongue lolled in appreciation.

With a shake of his head, he crumpled up the paper towel he'd used as a plate and tossed it in the waste basket. As usual, he'd eaten his simple dinner standing over the kitchen sink. His sucky day was almost at an end, although the evening still loomed large in the horizon. It was way too early to go to bed, so he resigned himself to a night of mindless television, his brain too keyed up for reading.

The security intercom squawked before he made it to the couch. Who the hell could that be? No one ever visited him at home, not even Cindi or Mal. Pressing the button, he barked, "Yeah?"

"It's Jakes. Buzz me in."

There was no please added, not that Dec would have expected any. He considered for about a half a second not complying, then figured the cop would just find a way to bust in. So, he buzzed him through and opened his apartment door. I didn't take long before he heard the clomp, clomp, clomp of the cop's shoes up the stairs. When the guy loomed in the doorway, a frisson of both wariness and excitement racked Dec's body.

He took a few steps back before turning and heading farther into his living room. "Come in, Sergeant and shut the door."

"Reassure your dog that I'm not a threat."

Dec turned to see Jakes once again leaning down toward Pax so that she could sniff his fingers and get reacquainted with him.

"Why?" Dec couldn't keep the amusement from his tone. Jakes' expression told him well enough that this wasn't a friendly visit, not that there'd been any question about that.

Straightening, the cop gave him a hard stare. "Because I'm about to use my outdoor voice, and I don't want your dog attacking me." Jakes' broad chest already heaved with agitated breaths. This was going to be a party all right.

Because he didn't want Pax or Jakes to get hurt, of course, he said to her, "Friend." Then he gave her the hand signals to lie down on her belly and stay. Unless Jakes physically attacked him, she wouldn't break her position without permission. "What do you want?"

Jakes prowled toward him, his body's stance more at ease than his expression conveyed. He got right up in Dec's face without actually touching him. "You know damn well what this is about. I told you stay out of this investigation, and yet you talked to Abernathy."

Not wanting the cop to think he intimidated him, Dec took a step forward. He took satisfaction from the fact that Jakes had to tilt his head to meet Dec's stare. "And I told you that I can't just sit on the sidelines when a client is killed."

"Just what the hell do you think you can do that I can't? This is my job, for fuck's sake. We're not clearing a village of terrorists, you know. A murder investigation doesn't require the back-up of a Navy SEAL, retired or otherwise."

"Especially one who's fucked up in the head, right?" Dec couldn't help saying. The other man's observation earlier in the day still smarted.

"I apologized for that," Jakes replied through gritted teeth.

"And I accepted your apology, but we both know you meant the dig nevertheless because we both know it's true."

Dec's chest heaved, and the lure of those too-crafty eyes of Jakes' was scarily strong. He broke eye contact and stepped away, not caring that it showed weakness. He just needed some space. His cock already strained against his fly, incessantly demanding attention in a way he'd experienced only during an op.

It was more than mere adrenaline, though. He wanted the cop, and not just with his body. Ever since the guy had turned up at his office, delivering his message of doom, Dec hadn't been able to get him out of his mind. There was more to Jakes that appealed to him than his muscles and his sexual power. For the first time in a long time, maybe for the first time ever, he was interested in another man for more than a one-night fuck. That attraction, alone, coming at the worst possible time in his life, had him running scared. Too bad his apartment was small enough to make physical retreat damn near impossible.

As if sensing his vulnerability, Jakes kept pace with him, coming up to get in his face once more. "It was a shitty thing to say, and I didn't mean it, not really. I'm frustrated, that's all. I have enough on my plate with a high-profile murder without some amateur dogging my heels and tripping me up."

"I may be a private dick, to use your words, but I'm not an amateur. I know what I'm doing. And leaving messes for others to clean up is not my way. That was true even before I joined the SEALs."

Jakes blew out a hot breath, and Dec couldn't help breathing it in with a certain unwanted relish.

"What do I have to say or do to make you back off?" Frustration and, worse, fatigue laced the cop's every word. He'd obviously been going full tilt the whole day, and Dec felt guilty that he'd been the reason for one more stop before Jakes could go home.

He shook his head, ruefully. "Nothing. Sorry, but yeah, nothing."

102

They stared at each other, eerily like lovers, for so long that Dec became convinced Jakes would kiss him. The cop broke the spell, however, not by closing the gap but by widening it. He paced away from Dec, tugging at what was left of his tie knot. "You got any beer?"

Dec blinked at the unexpected question. "Yeah, sure."

He went to the kitchen, grabbed a couple of bottles from the fridge, opened them, and returned to the living room. He handed one over to Jakes who'd made himself comfortable, sort of, in an old recliner. Dec sat to his left on an equally old sofa. Everything in his apartment was hand-me-downs from internet sites.

They both chugged some beer, eyeing each other in the process. Jakes flopped back in the chair, his legs splayed open. With his pants as tight as they were, Dec had no problem seeing the outline of a long, thick cock upright and pressing against the fly. His gaze zoomed in on the sight and stayed there, mesmerized.

Jakes looked at him over the top of his bottle, took a long pull and swallowed audibly. "Yeah, on top of everything else that pisses me off about this case and your involvement in it is this." He pointed his finger at his crotch. Dec's gaze flew to his. Jakes shrugged. "I hope you're not offended."

By way of an answer, Dec lifted the hem of his T-shirt so that his own hard-on became visible.

Jakes took another swig of beer before saying, "Ain't we a pair?"

"I haven't had sex in over two years." Dec heard the confession trip past his lips and did a mental facepalm. What was his problem?

"Is that your way of saying that you'd get hard for any man in your vicinity so I shouldn't take it personally?"

Dec worried the label of his bottle with this thumb, disbelieving that he was having this conversation at all. Felix would say it was because the time was right. As much as he valued the therapist's opinion, he couldn't quite believe that. He figured it was one more version of the kind of self-destructive behavior he thought was behind him.

"No, what I'm really saying is that you're the first guy to make me hard since the injuries that killed my career." There. If that revelation didn't send the man screaming out into the night, nothing would.

Instead, Jakes asked, "What injuries? I mean I know the PTSD, but what else?"

Dec shrugged. "Can't hear out of my right ear and my right knee is kind of shot."

Jakes slugged the rest of his beer back and stood. "Then I'll be sure to talk into your left ear and we'll be careful of your knee."

"Seriously?" Slamming his own bottle down on what served as his battered coffee table, Dec got vertical. "You think our fucking is a good idea?"

"Hell no. It's a spectacularly bad idea, but this"— he waved in the vicinity of his crotch—"isn't going anywhere that I can tell. And, well, I've convinced myself that you're not part of Place's murder. If nothing else, I don't see why you'd make a nuisance of yourself unless you are as innocent as you profess."

"Maybe I'm just really clever and throwing you off the scent." Dec wasn't sure why he wanted to push Jakes away at this point, except the idea of being with another man scared the crap out of him.

Jakes stepped closer. "Maybe. I thought of that, but I don't think so." He grabbed Dec by the back of the head and pulled him down for a kiss.

God, I've missed this. The simple pleasure of another person's touch, lush lips melding with his in a lazy slide of slick skin. How long had it been since he'd been kissed? He couldn't even remember, many of his encounters too fast and hard for such gentle foreplay.

Not that Jakes could be called gentle. His grip tightened on Dec's neck, fingers digging in to keep him in place as if afraid Dec would bolt. Not such a stupid worry. Part of him wanted to push the man away and flee from his embrace. The stronger part of him, or perhaps the needier, overrode the urge. Instead, he wrapped his arms around the cop and pulled him in tight.

Before he could think better of it or at all, Dec pressed his tongue against the seam of Jakes' lips and demanded entrance. The man let him in with a low moan and met him with an equal fervor that had their tongues wrestling inside first Jakes' mouth, then Dec's. Their hard cocks bumped, and Dec slid one hand down to cup Jakes' ass. He mashed their bodies even more tightly together, grinding their pelvises until they both groaned. It was Jakes who broke the kiss, leaving them both gasping for air.

"This is really stupid on all kinds of levels," the cop remarked in a winded voice before he lunged in to nip and suck at Dec's lower lip.

"That mean you want to stop?" Dec's own voice sounded strangled to his ears.

Jakes gave him a hell no look. "Let's take this into

the bedroom. I'm too tired to fuck standing up."

Dec chuckled, still not sure he shouldn't cut the guy loose before they got naked. Grabbing Jakes by the front of his shirt, he hauled him toward the bedroom. Pax's gaze followed them, the dog undoubtedly confused about what was going on. She whined softly as they passed.

"Jesus, your dog's not going to watch us fuck, is she?" Jakes asked on a strangled laugh.

"Not exactly, but I can't close the door, either. She's, ah, shit." Dec stopped and looked Jakes in the eye. "She's trained not to let me out of her sight because one of her functions is to keep me from killing myself."

Okay, there. Although nothing yet had sent the cop to running, maybe this new information would.

Jakes stared at him for a few seconds before kissing him again. This time, he truly was gentle. "I won't let you do that, either."

Dec felt oddly touched that the guy handled the news so well. "I haven't had that urge in a long time. No worries."

"Good." Jakes came in with another quick kiss. He backed his way into the bedroom, dragging Dec with him because he still had that fistful of shirt. "Are you pitching or catching tonight?"

It took Dec a second to understand the question. He imagined feeling comfortable enough to let a man cover him with his body and knew that would be a step too far this first time. "Um, pitching, if you don't mind."

Jakes gave him a cocky grin and twisted free. "Hell, no. It's been a while since a guy's drilled me. I'm looking forward to it."

He began yanking off his clothes, tossing them in a heap in one corner because, really, there was no other place to put them. Dec quickly followed suit. Obviously, neither of them was in the mood for slow and easy. Once his head was clear of his T-shirt, he saw Jakes toss his holster with its service revolver on top of his coat, shirt, and shoes.

"Just so you know, I keep a forty in my nightstand."

The cop looked at him over his shoulder. "I assumed as much."

He kept his gaze on Dec as he unzipped his pants and shoved them down with his underwear. Dec couldn't help but stare at the beautiful muscular body on display. He'd spent his whole career around naked, jacked men, but he'd always been careful not to stare at his teammates. Jakes was different. He was there for Dec to peruse and admire and touch. God, how he wanted to run his hands down all that taut skin. And Jakes cock didn't disappoint. About as long as Dec's, yet thicker, it stood jutting out, redder than the rest of the man's flesh. Dec licked his lips.

Jakes grinned at him. "Come on, Hunter. Let's see the goods."

What? Oh, right. Dec dropped his shirt and undid his jeans. He slid them down with the same speed as Jakes had, and being a former SEAL, he was in the habit of going commando. His dick came popping out for inspection. His balls ached with a new-found need, and a bit of pre-cum already leaked out of his long-unused cock. Primed as he was, he wouldn't last long once he got inside Jakes.

The cop took a couple of steps toward him, a

condom already held by two fingers. Thank God. Dec hadn't considered before how he didn't have any. Hadn't expected to need any. Without taking his eyes off Dec, Jakes tore open the packet and tossed the foil away. He placed the latex on the tip of Dec's cock and slowly rolled it down.

Dec's eyes closed to half-mast. "Fuuuck." He had to grab the base of his dick in a death grip to keep from coming with that touch alone. His chest heaved with labored breath. "Lube," he managed to stutter out.

Jakes' two hands came up to cup the back of Dec's neck, drawing him closer to him and backing up to the bed. "The condom's lubed."

Dec shook his head. "Won't be enough."

"I don't care." Jakes plopped onto the bed, bringing Dec with him, so that he sprawled on top of the man. "Shove it in. I can take it." He punctuated his demand with a searing kiss that left Dec dizzy.

It was all happening so fast, he didn't have time to think it through. Maybe that was the whole point. Given time to consider his decision might make him change his mind. He still wasn't so caught up in the moment, though, that he'd just shove his rod up a guy's ass without some prep. He broke off from the kiss and sucked on a fore and middle finger. Reaching between their slick, hot bodies, he slid the fingers past Jakes' heavy balls and found his hole.

When he breached the puckered ring with just one finger, Jakes arched against him with a moan. "Fuck yeah, give me two."

The second one went in just as easily. Jakes was clearly primed. Dec worked the fingers in and out a few times, sweeping for the prostate.

When he found it, his reward was a gasp and shudder. "Jesus, Hunter, stick it in already."

Because he wanted it, too, Dec pulled out his fingers and lined his cock up in their place. He leveraged himself up on his forearms and stared down at Jakes. The cop gave him a sexy smile as Dec slowly slid his cock into the welcoming heat.

Chapter Six

Ryan gritted his teeth against the burn of being stretched wide for the first time in a long time. He liked it like that, though, fast and hard. Hunter's long, slender cock filled Ryan with one relentless push. Ryan closed his eyes as he shuddered, his body welcoming the invasion with its usual mix of rebellion and almost desperate need. He'd never understand how any man could forego the exquisite pleasure of being fucked. Far from vulnerable or emasculated, he felt powerful.

He wrapped his arms around Hunter's broad shoulders and his legs around the man's tapered waist and dug his heels into that perfectly firm ass. His efforts drove Hunter the final inch necessary to seat him to the hilt.

Hunter's lips found Ryan's, scorching his mouth with a hungry kiss. Ryan grunted when fingers tangled with his short hair and tugged his head to one side so that Hunter's tongue could lunge down his throat. At first, Hunter's body merely rocked into his with shallow thrusts. The angle of the man's cock brushed Ryan's sweet spot with an almost gentle caress.

Ryan moaned and angled his hips to increase the pressure, his heel keeping up a steady drum beat to urge Hunter to move faster. The guy got the hint, making his thrusts longer and faster. Soon, he pounded into Ryan with a ferocious hunger as if he intended to beat the cum out of him.

He could feel the pressure build, but it wasn't going to be enough. He wasn't seventeen anymore. No coming from being fucked alone. He hated having to let go of any of Hunter's smooth and increasingly slick skin. And then, he didn't have to. The man's free hand snaked in between their bodies to grab Ryan's dick with a death grip. His fingers squeezed Ryan's rod as they slid up the shaft to swipe at the head.

Ryan groaned and bucked, goading Hunter to even greater speed and harder thrusts. He couldn't get enough. He wanted more and more, pushing his climax. It had been too long for him to want a leisurely fuck, and Hunter's strength matched his own, making them the perfect pair to take no quarter from each other.

Ryan came first, the orgasm almost catching him off guard, causing him to rear up into Hunter's embrace. His hole clenched tightly around the man's dick. A strangled cry echoed along Ryan's throat, mixing with his own shout as Hunter's cock pulsed inside Ryan's spasming channel. Their hot breaths mingled while they rode their respective orgasms. Hunter kept his grip on Ryan's dick, milking him dry until they both suddenly came to a shuddering halt.

Breaking the kiss, Hunter collapsed on top of Ryan, his chest heaving and one hand still clenching Ryan's hair.

Ryan lowered his legs to place his feet flat on the bed. He kept his arms around Hunter, making lazy circles across the expanse of the man's shoulders. With his eyes closed and his body sated, he could easily fall asleep. It had been way too long since he'd done this particular dance and self-maintenance didn't hold a candle to it.

The stress of his day drained away with his cum, the sticky mess being smooshed between their both equally hard stomachs. He tried not to think about how the only other man he'd fucked who'd been such a perfect physical match for him had been Flynn the Fucker. He'd told himself he would never again get involved with another Alpha male type. Too much ego and jockeying for supremacy made such a relationship impossible. He'd intended to look for a softer kind of guy. One who'd appreciate his natural inclinations to protect and serve and not try to bust his balls every five seconds.

Of course, that hadn't worked out because he wasn't really attracted to the shy and gentle ones. The few dates he'd snuck in over the last year while pulling nightmare hours at work had left him yawning into his Guinness. Sweet guys, flirty guys, guys who'd signaled loud and clear that sucking his dick would be a treat held no interest for him, much as he'd tried. He'd paid the bill and let them down as easily as he could, using his badge as a reason for the early night and no follow-up call. It had made him feel so bad, he'd given up quickly.

The simple truth was he liked men who could go toe-to-toe with him, and didn't that just beat all? Christ, what a relationship Catch 22, or was it a stalemate? Who the hell knew? It was fucked up, that's for sure.

Holding onto a large, heavy body confirmed that he'd been on the wrong path all year. This felt good, felt right—when in bed. Just where did it leave him, though, out of it?

Of course, he was getting ahead of himself. At the

moment, all he had with Hunter was in bed. They might not even get to round two tonight, although Ryan's cock started to rouse with only the fleeting thought crossing his mind.

Hunter stirred, too, except he went from boneless to upright. His abrupt vacating of Ryan's hole made him hiss. Opening his eyes, he watched Hunter stumble out of bed and into the bathroom at the far end of the bedroom.

The sounds of pissing, flushing, and running water floated out of the half-open door. Hunter didn't look at Ryan when he returned, not at first, not really at all. Even after he'd grabbed sweatpants lying across a chair in one corner, he kept his gaze averted.

Ryan pushed up on his elbows, a sinking feeling stealing over him. There wasn't going to be second round, and it seemed like Hunter already regretted the first one. Damn, fucking someone involved in an investigation had been a spectacularly bad idea from the beginning. He'd only risked it because he found Hunter so irresistible. He'd thought the feeling was mutual.

"Um, look, sorry, but I need to take Pax out one last time before we go to bed, which I do kind of early because…" He barked out a laugh. "I'm an old lady or something. Anyway…" He scratched his head, still not looking at Ryan. "I hope you don't mind." He waved his hand vaguely at the pile of Ryan's clothes.

Shoving his legs over the side of the bed, Ryan stood with speed and feigned nonchalance. "Yeah, no worries. I understand completely."

He took up the eye-averting because now he felt awkward, especially given that his thoughts had already strayed into fucking again, maybe with him doing the pitching. Not that Hunter had been privy to those thoughts, thank God.

Ryan dressed quickly, thankful when Hunter left the room. He only bothered to put on his suit coat to hide his service revolver and its harness in case he ran into anyone on the way out. Which actually was likely given that it wasn't even ten o'clock. No way Hunter crapped out for the night this early. He only wanted Ryan gone, and that was okay. It was. Two guys banging, then walking away was the norm. Wanting anything more, expecting it, put him in chickville.

He may have bottomed for Hunter, but he didn't have a pussy. He didn't need pretty words or encouraging smiles or a fucking kiss good-night. He balled up his tie, shoved it into his coat pocket, squared his shoulders, and put a "so long, Charlie" look on his face.

Hunter still didn't look Ryan in the eye. He busied himself with fastening a red vest on Pax. She looked at Ryan, though. He could swear her doggy eyes laughed at him as he passed. He opened the door, intending to walk out without another word.

Instead, he stared at his shoes for a few seconds. "I don't suppose it will do any good for me to once again tell you to butt out of the investigation."

"Not in the least."

Ryan heaved a sigh. "I didn't think so." He left, quietly shutting the door behind him.

All during his drive to his home in Southie, his aching hole served as a reminder of how well Hunter had fucked him. It pissed him off because he knew it had been a one-time event and his body shouldn't get any stupid ideas that it would experience that kind of attention again anytime soon.

Nevertheless, his cock had become semi-hard by the time he pulled into the driveway of the two family house he shared with his brother and his family. He closed the door to his car quietly given the hour and how young his two nieces were even though he really wanted to slam out his frustration. Christ, he even walked with a slight limp now that no one was there to impress with his misplaced pride.

"Hey, Ry," a low voice called out from the backyard.

Ryan turned from his path and followed the sound to find his brother, Sean, standing like an idiot while a golden retriever puppy sniffed the rhododendron.

Shooting his brother a grin, Ryan squatted near the puppy and held out his hand for it to sniff. "Hey yourself, bro. When did you get a dog?"

Sean puffed out a breath. "This afternoon. Jeannie said it was time for the girls to get one, that they're old enough to take care of it. So, that's why I'm the one watching this thing pee on everything, even though he's bone, no pun intended, dry, hoping against hope that he'll finally dump a load out here instead of inside. When I really want to be curled up next to my wife, begging for some before I get my tubes snipped and am out of commission for a while."

Ryan grinned at the puppy while listening to his brother drone on. The adorable little thing found Ryan's shoes intensely interesting, no doubt smelling Hunter's dog. That thought sent a scowl to his face. God damn, why did he have to like the guy and his dog? Why couldn't scratching his itch be his only agenda? He reached out to ruffle the puppy's head. His brother's words finally penetrated his foggy and distracted brain.

He looked up. "Wait, what? You're getting…" He couldn't say the word, just made a scissor motion with two fingers.

Sean grimaced. "Yeah, Jeannie had an ultrasound yesterday, and it's confirmed that the penis has landed." He broke out into a shit-eating grin that proved infectious.

"So, that's it. You're done."

Sean nodded. "Yeah. I mean we were probably going to stop at three no matter what, but… I can't deny I'm happy as fuck that the teams are going to be evenly matched soon in my house."

Ryan frowned. "You're still going to be outgunned, three of them to two of you once the little guy is born."

Sean tossed his head toward the dog. "Murphy is a boy."

"You're counting the dog?"

"I'm a desperate, man. You can't imagine what it's like living in a house of females. Even with Amy starting ice hockey this year, ninety percent of the dinner conversation baffles me."

With a final scratch of the dog, Ryan stood up. "I wouldn't necessarily count on that changing with a having a son." He dropped his gaze. "You don't know, he might turn out like me." It was an uncharacteristically vulnerable thing for him to say, but he felt off kilter at the moment.

"You mean so testosterone-laden that I have to hustle to keep up with *him* instead of the other way around?" his brother teased.

It was the perfect thing to say. Ryan raised his head and grinned. "Yeah, that's what I mean. How come you're the one getting, you know?" He made the scissor motion again, needing to change the topic even though he'd raised it in the first place.

Sean shrugged. "On the assumption that she's going to deliver naturally again, we agreed that it's time for me to step up to the plate. I mean, come on, vasectomies are an office visit. No big deal compared to what they'd have to do for her. Besides, she's done more than enough, you know, bringing forth entirely new human beings into the world." He shook his head. "Man, I'm not looking forward to another labor. Seeing her in such pain, even for a good reason, sucks. I feel so helpless."

Ryan didn't have any words of comfort. He would never go through the experience. Although somewhere in the back of his mind, he had a plan to get married and have a kid or two, he knew he wouldn't have to see his spouse go through that particular kind of pain.

He gestured toward the puppy who'd grown tired of sniffing him and had wandered as far as his leash allowed. "Well, at least the dog is finally getting with the program."

Sean followed his line of vision, and they stood there watching. How weird was that, for two adults to play audience to a dog taking a shit? And yet, that's what they did until finally Murphy returned to Sean, his little tail wagging in excitement because, in the world of dogs, even evacuating one's bowels was a cause for celebration. If only people could be so simple.

Sean reached down and scooped the puppy up, who promptly started licking his face. With a grimace, Sean turned his head. "You're getting home late, as usual."

"Yeah, you know, it's the job. At least I'm not

living at the station the way you do a few days at a time." Sean had gone the firefighter route. "Besides, I caught that Louisburg Square case."

Sean whistled. "I'd say congratulations, but something that high profile must mean the higher-ups are giving you fits."

"Right you are, big bro." At the mention of the murder, fatigue suddenly swamped Ryan. He needed to get to bed. He was on the verge of bidding his brother goodnight, when the guy's too sharp eyes homed in on him.

"Say, is that a well-fucked look I see on your face?"

He almost denied it, then remembered it was Sean, the one guy in the world he could admit anything to. "Yeah," he acknowledged with a sheepish grin.

Sean turned toward the back door. "New boyfriend, I hope." He knew the whole story about Flynn the Fucker.

Ryan followed him. "Nope, just a one-night stand."

Sean tossed a grimace over his shoulder. Since marrying the love of his life, Ryan's older brother wanted everyone to experience the bliss of commitment. "You just need to find the right man." He paused at his back door. "There's this new guy at the station. Six-four, totally jacked, skin like *café au lait*. Could really add some color to our pasty white family," he added with a chuckle. "Hot as hell, too." When Ryan raised his eyebrows at him, Sean held out his hand. "I mean, I guess he is if you're into dudes, which you are."

Ryan shook his head and made for the back door of his unit. The last thing he needed was another alpha male type even though his hole would vehemently disagree, and it was, loudly, with a deep, pulsing ache.

"Thanks bro, but I can find my own men. Good night." He waved and let himself into his empty home. His cock hadn't subsided, so he'd have to do something about that or he'd never get to sleep. Damn, even after a hard fuck, he still had to end the day in his typical fashion—by taking his lonely dick in his equally lonely hand.

****

No amount of pounding pavement could stop the obsessive loop from playing endlessly in his head. Dec could see the flash of hurt cross Jakes' face when he had told him to leave. Even as he studiously avoided looking at the guy, Dec hadn't been able to miss or, apparently, ignore it. He hated himself for putting it there.

No matter how much they clashed over the Place murder, Jakes didn't deserve such callous treatment, not after welcoming Dec inside his body. Even for a man as big and powerful as the cop, it took a certain kind of courage and trust to make oneself so vulnerable. Yet, his reward had been Dec treating him like some sentient form of Dec's fist.

Shameful.

And necessary. Even though, with his body lying flush on top of the other man, Dec had started to think in terms of fucking again and often, maybe with mutual blowjobs thrown into the mix, he knew it wouldn't be. He just couldn't let someone spend the night with him. His nightmares were bad enough to scare the living crap out of even a cop.

Worse, Dec might come out of one in some kind of

Samantha Cayto

fugue state, mistaking Jakes for an enemy and trying to kill him. Probably succeeding given the level of training he had compared to a cop, and all before Pax might be able to work it out in her intelligent, yet still doggy-limited, brain and intervene. Yeah, so not happening.

The irony was that he'd slept better than he had in about two years. No nightmares, only hot dreams of being enveloped in another man's arms. God, how he'd missed the sensations of being with someone. The slide of slick skin, the heat of strong muscles wrapped around his shoulders and waist, the wet warmth of sliding into a slightly resistant hole—he'd missed it all much more than he'd been able to admit. He knew now that he couldn't live the rest of his life without intimacy. It would slowly crush him more than his physical disabilities ever could. He just didn't know how he could ever truly be with another man for more than a quick fuck. Something to discuss with Felix, obviously. First, though, he had a murder to investigate.

He almost sagged with relief when he spotted the familiar white-blond head through the coffee shop window. Scott had returned, and thank God for that. He'd worried the kid would rabbit in fear.

The kid gave him a tired and wary smile but greeted Pax with his usual bowl of water and enthusiasm. Dec stood, catching his breath, giving Scott some time before jumping in with the topic weighing on his mind.

"Are you okay?" Scott asked as he squatted beside Pax.

Dec used the bottom of his T-shirt to wipe at his sweaty brow and gave a rueful laugh. "Damn, you just took the words out of my mouth. Are *you* okay?"

Straightening, the boy shrugged. "I'm fine." The bruise on his cheek had turned from red to more yellow since the last time Dec had seen him. "It doesn't hurt anymore."

"That's good, but I'm also talking about Place's murder. Did the cops come to see you?"

"Sure." Scott returned to behind the counter and started fixing Dec's usual drink.

"I'm sorry I had to give them your name."

"No worries. I know you had to, and it doesn't matter. I was more worried that they suspected you."

"Me? Yeah, well, I guess I was on the possible suspect list. I think I might be off it now," he added, remembering the previous night's activities. Jakes didn't strike him as the type to throw caution to the wind and fuck someone he still thought might have committed murder.

"I assume I'm still on it," Scott said over the sound of milk being aerated. "I went home that night and stayed there. No witnesses to prove it."

"They can't honestly believe you went back and killed Place."

Scott slid Dec's cup across the counter. "I don't know. They didn't hassle me much, even when I refused to name my former escort service. No, it's on me," he said with a wave of his hand when Dec fished out his money. "Least I can do after what you did for me."

"It was nothing," Dec murmured, uncomfortable with the gratitude. As a SEAL, he'd always done his job unsung. It was the SEAL way. He took a sip of his scalding hot coffee. "So, you quit?"

Scott jammed his hands in his apron pockets. "Fired. Place took the time to call and ream out the owner about how unsatisfying I was."

"Fucker," Dec muttered before taking another sip. "Are you okay, you know, money-wise?"

Scott shrugged. "Sure. I mean I have some money saved up, and I can pick up more shifts here. I might not be able to take classes next semester, though."

"College?"

The boy grinned shyly. "Yeah. Being a whore wasn't my original plan."

"But you're out of the life now, for good, or are you looking for another service to go work for?" Dec knew he crossed a line by asking such intrusive questions. Given what had happened, though, he felt invested in the kid's future more than would have been the case if he'd never seen him at Place's.

"I'm out, totally." He stared out the window, and Dec thought that was all the guy was going to say. "At first I had no choice. Do it or starve. Then it became habit, an easy way to make money. Now?" He shook his head. "I can't do it anymore. None of it, not just the kinky stuff."

"Good. But if you're out, why not give the name of the service to the cops? It would maybe get them off your back."

Scott's looked at him intently. "I don't want to end up dead like Kenny."

"Kenny?" Dec's stomach clenched. He just knew he wouldn't like the answer. Even after all the horrors he'd seen, nothing had inured him to children being hurt or killed.

"A guy who worked at the same service for a few

months. He was a really wild kid, into drugs, although we all kinda were. Sometimes, it was all that got you through a date, ya know?"

Dec sort of did. He knew lots of young combat troops turned to drink and drugs to help with the stress. "And this Kenny died how?"

"They said an overdose, and it wasn't such a stretch, except, I don't know. I never got how he ended up falling into the harbor while high. Seemed weird to me."

"You think he was killed."

"Yeah. He had a big mouth and liked to brag about his dates. He was also into some really masochistic stuff. He seemed to like pain, not just tolerate it." A noticeable shiver went through his thin frame. "Anyway, I'm not taking any chances."

"You think he *dated* Place?"

"Maybe."

At that moment, a woman came in, dressed like a leftover back-up dancer from the Let's Get Physical music video. She waved at Scott. "Oh, Scotty, darling, so good to see you. My usual, please."

Scott graced her with a beauteous smile. "Yes, ma'am."

As the boy moved to start the woman's order, Dec slid to the side of the counter, getting out of the way but unwilling to let the matter of the dead rent boy go. He waited patiently, scratching Pax's head to keep himself calm, for the woman to be served and leave.

Once she did, he leaned over the counter to get Scott's attention. "Look, man, I'm not trying to cause you trouble or make you worry, but I think looking into this Kenny guy's death makes sense. Will you please give me the contact info for your former service? I promise I won't let on that I got it from you. I just want to check it out and see what I can learn."

The kid folded his arms across his chest and stared at the floor for a few seconds. "Okay," he said with a huff. "I guess I trust you to do it better than the cops, and maybe Kenny's death is related to Place. It certainly would have made sense for Place to rent him." He grabbed a napkin, wrote something down, and handed it to Dec.

Dec glanced at it. He saw a name, address, and phone number. "Concierge Escort."

"Yeah. It all seems like it's legal, but that's only because Mother Cherry is no fool."

"Mother Cherry?"

Scott just shrugged and left to go help another customer who'd come in.

"Come on, Pax." Dec picked up her leash to head out.

He knew he should call up Jakes and give him the information. Knew the cop's head would explode, and not the one Dec would like, either, if he found out Dec had gone there before him. But not only was his business on the line. He worried Scott's life hung in the balance and maybe Mal's and even his own.

Something big and weird was going on. The death threats, the secret treasure room, and rent boys. Maybe this was the world of wealthy people. What the hell would he know about how the one percent lived? All he did know was that he couldn't sit by and watch the train wreck continue.

Maybe Mother Cherry, God help them all, held some of the answers.

****

The warrant to search all of Place's house came in some time around holy shit o'clock that morning. Not that Ryan had been fast asleep anyway. Despite two jerk-off sessions, his mind had still been racing a mile a minute, playing endless loops of, not the murder investigation, but Dec and the casual way he'd tossed Ryan's naked ass out the door. He didn't want to care. Hell, he'd vowed to take a break on anything more than the occasional one-night stand.

And yet, something about Declan Hunter had seeped under his skin in less than a day. He didn't want to care about the guy, and still, he stood in the foyer of Place's fabulous home and all he could think about was Hunter, almost wishing he'd cross paths with the guy in the near future even though that would mean a civilian continued to trip up his investigation.

"Oh my God," Andy exclaimed. "I think I just saw a dust mote."

"Ha, ha," Ryan deadpanned. He was in no mood for jokes, although he had to admit, with the staff gone, the house had already started to feel less like a museum. "Let's start with the home office." He made for the staircase. "We do every room together. It will help reduce the risk of that asshole personal assistant accusing us of theft."

Keeping pace with him on the wide stairs, Andy said, "You think that's a real worry?"

"I think everything about this case sucks and has the potential of chewing our asses to ribbons." Ryan hoped to God that they would find something useful in the office because otherwise it would take them all day to go through the entire house, maybe longer. They couldn't chance having a larger group help them with the looking, either, for the reason he'd just stated to Andy. It was probably a good thing the warrant didn't cover Place's company.

The judge had balked at taking that final hurdle, at least for now. Too many other, powerful people had their money in that company for the judge to feel comfortable opening up even Place's office there to search. Because Ryan had nothing to tie Place's murder to the business, he would have to live with the restriction.

"I found that boy's death that Reilly mentioned."

Ryan glanced at his partner. "Oh, yeah? What's the story?"

"John Doe, estimated to be late teens, found floating in the harbor. Autopsy pegs drowning as the cause of death, but the kid had a massive amount of heroin in his system. It could have easily killed him, too."

"So, the kid shoots up and goes wandering around the wharfs, because that's what people high on heroin do, wander around instead of lying in a stupor. Then falls into the drink and drowns."

Andy blew out a breath. "Yeah, the coroner raised those issues, but without an I.D. of the vic, no witnesses or anything to go on, it goes into the file as accidental death."

"Even a twenty-year-old prostitute isn't buying that one. No wonder Reilly's so scared."

"We could bring him in," Andy suggested as they arrived at the office. "Lean on him, maybe charge him with solicitation?"

Ryan shook his head. "I hate to be yet another

person exploiting him. Maybe we'll find something useful here to wrap this up." When Andy cocked his eyebrows at him, Ryan sighed. "Yeah, I know wishful thinking never got us anywhere. Let's get started. I'll take the desk. Why don't you begin on the other side of the room?"

Their respective footfalls were muted by a thick area carpet that undoubtedly had been hand woven by ten-year-old girls in some faraway country without labor laws. Not for the first time, he wondered what one had to do to acquire such amazing wealth. Maybe, unlike his own swamp Yankee, Place's ancestors had simply built it up over the generations, although Place himself had contributed a large amount to whatever he inherited by investing wisely and probably in at least some cases, predatorily. Ryan doubted he had enough ruthlessness in his nature to ever achieve anything close to this kind of riches. Wouldn't know what to do with it even if he did.

Place had had no such trouble. Everything in his house was beautiful, even his desk. Mahogany. Gorgeous. Ryan couldn't resist taking a few seconds to admire the craftsmanship, running his hand along the glossy, smooth surface. The edge had a brass inlay that had him practically salivating.

"Hey Jakie, when you're through making love to that desk, you might want to come take a look at this."

Embarrassed that his partner had caught him daydreaming, Ryan pulled his hand back as if scorched and frowned over at Andy. "What?" The guy stood in front of a tall cabinet against the wall directly across from the desk. "A television?"

Andy shook his head and pointed south of where a

smallish flat screen TV stood. On one of the lower shelves, a narrow, black laptop sat. At least that's what it looked like. "Is that what I think it is?"

Andy nodded. "Yup." He pulled it out and held it up. "So much for Place not using computers."

"Bring it over here." Ryan didn't even need to clear a spot on the desk to put the computer because Place had kept a neat and tidy space for himself. Or rather his staff had.

Andy did as told and powered up the sleek machine that looked relatively new. They could not, however, log in. It was password protected, not surprisingly.

"Damn," Ryan said. "It was too much to expect we could just dive right in. We'll have to take it to the CSI computer lab and see if they can crack it open."

"Yeah," Andy agreed. "I don't know enough about the vic to even begin to guess at his passcode. And I'd say check with Johnson, but he supposedly didn't know about this thing existing to begin with."

Ryan grimaced. "Supposedly. I'm becoming more convinced that Place's personal assistant knows a lot more than he's admitting."

"Should we bring him down for formal questioning?" Andy asked as he powered down the computer.

"Not yet. Let's finish our search and see where we are at the end of the day. We can always bring him in. In the meantime," he added, jutting his chin toward the laptop, "take that to one of the uniforms at the door and have them get it to the lab ASAP."

Ryan hated the fact that valuable resources had to be spent guarding the now-infamous house. If the warrant had come in the previous day, they could have returned the house to Place's staff to secure. Of course, that thought made him picture Hunter, which in turn made him frown. He had to ruthlessly push thoughts of that man out of his head to continue with the job at hand.

The desk, however, yielded nothing of interest, not even bank statements. He found a wall safe behind a print of the Charles River, leaving him even more frustrated because he'd have to call in someone to open it. Something he should have anticipated and set up already. Andy returned and continued where he left off with the cabinet.

A scream had Ryan turning toward the other man, his hand reaching for his piece under his arm before he realized it was something playing on the television.

"What the fuck!" He stomped over to stand beside Andy, who stood watching the screen with a sick look on his face.

"Jesus H. Christ, it's the dead kid."

Ryan leaned in closer, making himself look unflinchingly at the teenager featured in this submission to America's Sickest Home Videos. He was being beaten to within an inch of his life by an unseen man, according to the masculine arm wielding a riding crop. "Are you sure?"

Andy turned away. "Yeah. The face in the autopsy photos was bloated from being in the water, but nothing had nibbled at it yet. So..." He blew out a huff as he stared at the beautiful carpet. "I'm going to have to go through all of his DVDs. There's over two dozen of them here, and who knows how many may be stashed elsewhere, like in his bedroom." He turned a sick and weary eye to Ryan. "This thing just got a whole lot uglier."

"Yeah, it did." Mysterious threats—allegedly because nothing Johnson said could be taken at face value—a secret treasure room, and now a dead and maybe other underage prostitutes. Shit, for a victim, Place was looking more like a perp.

"Um, excuse me, Sarge?" A fresh-faced uniform stuck her head in the doorway, her gaze sliding over to the porn channel.

While Andy hastily hit pause, Ryan moved his body to block the view. "Yeah?"

"There's a man here who says he was the victim's brother. He wants to talk to whoever's in charge."

With a certain amount of optimism that he might find out something useful, he gave a curt nod. "Bring him back here, please."

"Yes, sir." The uniform disappeared.

"You want me to stop this?" Andy gestured toward the screen shot of the boy with his mouth open on a scream, back arched, eyes screwed shut.

Going on instinct, Ryan shook his head. "Naw, leave it up. Let's see what this brother knows."

Chapter Seven

No more than a minute passed before the uniform came back, escorting a slender, younger version of the vic. This Place, though, had received the lion share of good looks with jet black hair worn in charming disarray, a pale oval face, and high cheekbones. He wore a black leather jacket that skimmed narrow hips and skinny jeans that would have looked ridiculous on most men, but on this guy was totally hot. He appeared quite a bit younger than the vic, too, and when he approached Ryan, he gave him a smile that must get the man laid on a regular basis.

The man held out his hand. "I'm Elkanah Place. Kane," he amended, deepening his smile.

Ryan took the hand for a firm and warm shake. "Detective Sergeant Ryan Jakes. This is my partner, Detective Andres Diaz."

Place the Second gave Andy the same charming attention before turning to look at the television screen. His eyes narrowed. "Aw, proof that I was right all along. My brother was a total prick."

The surprisingly blunt assessment of the vic threw Ryan for a second. He almost laughed out loud.

When Kane turned his pretty face back to him, the smile had disappeared and been replaced by a look of disgust. "It's not the BDSM, mind you, that revolts me. *Chacun a son goût* as the French would say. I just always had the feeling that Stanford didn't bother with the niceties of contracts and safewords. Besides," he added, turning to the screen again. "I always suspected he liked them too young."

"You knew your brother hired underage prostitutes?"

"Knew?" Kane Place shook his head and sauntered away. There was no other way to describe it. He reminded Ryan of a large cat, sleek and graceful. "Stanford and I were half-brothers, different mothers. Our father had the habit of trading in wives for new models with the same frequency you might trade in a car. There was more than twenty years between us. I hardly knew him, and what I did know, I didn't like. The feeling was quite mutual, I assure you."

He stopped by the window and peered out the heavy drapes. "The media must be wetting their pants with glee over this juicy murder. Who killed the rich and powerful Stanford Place, and who will get all his many millions?"

"Who will?" Ryan asked, closing the distance to see the man's face better.

Place shrugged. "I have no idea. Not me, that's for sure. Like I said, we weren't close."

"Then I don't suppose you know the password to his laptop or the combination to that safe over there?"

Place turned to look in the direction Ryan pointed to. "Hardly. I haven't seen Stanford in over three years, not since our father died. Stanford was pissed when I got the old man's Lalique collection," he added with another devastating smile, as if he enjoyed his brother's ire. "If you want intimate details of Stanford's life, you should ask the ever-loyal Johnson. His head was so far up my brother's ass, there's nothing he didn't know."

"Really?" Ryan frowned. "I would have thought so, too, but he said your brother didn't use computers, and yet we found a laptop in here a short while ago."

Now it was Place's turn to frown. "He said Stanford didn't use computers? How odd. My brother was hardly a troglodyte." He flipped one elegant hand toward the still-paused DVD. "I doubt Johnson held the camera...or maybe he did," he added with a negligent shrug. "Who knows what the two of them were up to? Anyway, I can't imagine why Stanford would have hidden his having a computer from his own assistant." A mischievous grin graced his face. "Unless Johnson lied to you about it."

Ryan tended to agree with the guy, but as he now fell into the category of a possible suspect just because of his relation to the vic, Ryan changed tack instead. "So, you wouldn't know anything about the death threats he received recently?" When Place merely raised his eyebrows, Ryan moved onto the next topic. "Or the room behind his closet filled with at least some stolen art?"

Kane Place fell into one of those categories where he was either a really good actor or genuinely surprised. He stood gaping at Ryan for a few seconds, all trace of suave wiped from his face. Then he burst out laughing. The mirth only lasted for a few seconds but seemed genuine.

The guy wiped at the corners of his eyes. "Classic Stanford. Being able to buy as much art as he wanted legitimately wasn't good enough for him, huh? He was, you know, clinically a psychopath."

"What?" Ryan and Andy said in unison. Now their mouths gaped open a moment or two.

"Seriously?" Ryan shoved his hands in his pocket. "That's a pretty damaging thing to say about your brother, Mr. Place."

"Please call me Kane. Mister never suited me, nor did my full first name. I can't imagine what my parents were thinking of. And yes, it is a horrible thing to say about anyone. Nevertheless, it's true. If I learned anything from my psych one-oh-one class at Brown, it was the abnormal stuff. The signs of psychopathy I remember quite well because for the first time, I had a label for my despised older brother. Fascinating stuff, really. These people are everywhere. Most don't become serial killers. Instead, they hide in board rooms and hospitals and court rooms, even politics. It's all about a total lack of empathy, an inability to even feel real human emotions, let alone something as basic as guilt. If my brother wanted something, he went for it. Rules didn't matter to him. He considered himself above them."

"I see," Ryan said thoughtfully. An idea occurred to him, a risky one perhaps. One that his lieutenant might not approve of. He glanced at Andy, who like the good partner he was, read his mind. He gave a quick nod of assent. "I'd like to show you something, sir, if you don't mind."

"I'm at your disposal, Sergeant. I want this matter closed as quickly as possible. I'm being hounded by the press, so you can imagine how much I want to help regardless of what I felt for my brother."

"I can imagine. Andy, can you continue with this room search?"

"Sure thing, Jakie."

Ryan led the man out of the office and up to the

bedroom. The secret door stood open because no one knew the code. They didn't want to have to break in. The pieces known to be stolen had already been removed by the local FBI. Given that the art had crossed international as well as state lines, it came under their jurisdiction. They hadn't yet tried to wrestle the murder investigation away from the Boston P.D. They would, though, and soon. He could feel it. The dots between the art and the murder were likely enough to make the case for moving jurisdiction. He hated the idea of losing the case, and showing this room and its collection to Kane Place became a calculated risk that could lead him to solving the murder quickly.

He let the man enter the room and take it all in. He didn't lead the guy with questions, merely waited to see what he might say about what he saw. Place prowled the room, eyes narrowed, lips pursed, taking everything in with a pensive silence. He stopped by the chair and sat down. He pointed to the blank space on the wall, the one that had been there when Ryan had first entered. More spots had been emptied by the FBI, yet the brother homed in on the one that mattered.

"Whatever was there would have held the greatest importance to Stanford." He cocked his head at Ryan. "Was this room looted as part of the murder? You've kept a tight enough lid on the details of my brother's death that I'm not even sure where in the house he died."

"His staff found him in a sitting room below. But, to answer your question, there was only one thing missing that morning and you're pointing to where it was. The other removed pieces are the ones known to be stolen. They're in FBI custody."

"There will be more in here that fall under that category, I assure you. Stanford like to show off, another psychopathic trait, so that everyone would admire and envy him. This stuff being locked away only makes sense in the context of illegal activity that he wanted to keep hidden. Psychopaths often have an overblown sense of their own abilities, but my brother wasn't stupid." He nodded toward the spot again. "Getting whatever hung there must have required more than mere money. I bet it involved cunning and daring, an impressive feat."

"But you don't know what that could be?"

Place shook his head and stood up. "Stanford wouldn't have told me anything that I could use against him. He didn't trust me because I didn't see the world the way he did. He viewed me as being hopelessly provincial and maudlin if for no other reason than after completing my residency in plastic surgery, I went to work for an organization that provides free services to people in need, like poor kids in India with cleft palates."

He shook his head again. "As if I should have opened a practice for breast augmentation or something for the rich and/or famous. That was another problem with Stanford. No amount of money was enough for him."

Ryan hid his surprise at hearing that the effete, careless seeming man standing in front of him was a doctor, one who dedicated himself to serving the needy, no less. Hard to believe he and the vic shared any DNA.

Turning on his heel, Ryan walked over the space on the wall and stared at it, as if somehow the paint could talk to him, tell what was missing.

He got nothing, and even though the search of the house had barely begun, he had a feeling he would leave with nothing valuable to the investigation. The computer was their best shot, but that could take days to crack open. He didn't have that kind of time. The trail ran colder and colder with each passing second.

His mind kept turning back to the assistant, Johnson. The guy had to know more than he let on. Not only had he been closer to the vic than anyone else they'd found so far, but he was also the one who had hired Red Cell Security. Yeah, that piece still needed to be analyzed.

Even though he didn't believe Hunter and his crew had anything to do with the murder, the timing still stunk to high heaven. And while he hated to think it, picking a new and inexperienced company for such high-end and delicate work made no sense. No one was that dedicated to hiring veterans. When he thought of Hunter, he not only pictured what they'd done the previous night, he also saw a big red herring.

That all led back to Johnson. Procedure was procedure, though. He had to scour the house first, then he'd lean on the assistant with all he had. Something had to break and break soon, or this thing would be taken away from him. Ryan always finished what he started, and this case wasn't going to be the first one to change that fact.

****

The Concierge Escort service turned out to be located not that far from Dec's own office, making him rethink his decision about leasing the space. Because the elevator had an "out of order" sign, he took the stairs, one painful step after the other. He'd pushed himself too hard on his morning run, trying to flee from his own thoughts. By the time he reached the fourth floor landing, he had a hard time hiding the limp. He didn't want to show any weakness when confronting whomever he met, however. He needed to project power and confidence, and a certain amount of well-to-do-ness. Not that he could picture anybody actually coming to this place. The service had to operate via phone and online. He couldn't imagine a man like Place, or Johnson for that matter, would ever willingly slum it to this degree.

He approached a door that looked like something straight out of a sixties sitcom, cheesy and flimsy. He opened it, expecting to enter into a waiting room to chat up a receptionist in the guise of making an appointment with Mother Cherry. Instead, he found himself inside the madam's actual office, occupied by what he could only assume was the proprietress herself. One look at her told him she'd never been anyone's mother and had undoubtedly lost her cherry long before Dec was born.

With a mobile phone to her ear, she stared at him with narrowed eyes in both appreciation and suspicion. Her heavy make-up and bright red bouffant hairdo reminded him of the type of over the top drag queens who never tried to look like biological women. Throw in the flowery muumuu she wore, and you had an almost comical stereotype. Milton Berle came to mind. Almost laugh-out-loud funny, except Mother Cherry peddled in flesh, some of it underage and all of it exploited. He also reminded himself that she might have been responsible for the murder of at least one boy. Yeah, nothing funny about Mother Cherry.

Switching gears with the speed and grace born

from SEAL straining, Dec gave her his most disarming smile, which wasn't much by his estimation, having no real game to speak of even with men. He was determined to learn something, though, and had put on his nicest business casual, thinking a suit would be too much for a daytime visit with a procurer of flesh.

He shut the door and stood waiting for an invitation to come farther into the room. Pax sat her butt down right beside him as usual, calmly waiting for him to do whatever foolishness he intended. She really was the perfect companion for him. He suspected that even if she understood what he did and could talk to him, she'd still be unflinchingly loyal and supportive.

"Yes," Mother Cherry said in a slow southern drawl, her gaze still on Dec. "Your package will arrive promptly at ten tonight, and I'm sure you won't be disappointed."

Dec mentally rolled his eyes, half expecting to hear something about a *Chinese watch.*

Mother Cherry ended the call and put the phone down on an amazingly clear desk that held only a tablet, a pad of paper, and a cheap pen. "May I help you, suh?" The honey dripping off her tongue was even more affected than her appearance.

Dec smiled broadly and took the question for an invitation. "Yes, ma'am, I'm hoping you can."

Mother Cherry flicked her gaze down to Pax. "I'm sorry, I don't allow animals in my office." She sniffed delicately. "Company policy, I'm afraid."

Dec only broadened his smile while he gave his standard response. "I'm sorry, but the federal and state Americans with Disability Acts would disagree with your policy in my case." He sat down in the one visitor chair, a rickety old wooden one that groaned under his weight.

The madam gave her own tepid smile. "You look perfectly fit to me."

"Like you, there's more to me than meets the eye."

Oh, she didn't like that. Her eyes went back to almost slits, and her hand strayed up to fluff her hair in likely an automatic gesture. "How can I help you, suh?"

"I'm looking for companionship," Dec replied.

"Well, we are an escort service, although we don't have any female escorts, I'm afraid."

"Not a problem as I'm looking for boys, as it happens. I hear you have some lovely ones."

"We do indeed. But most of our clients do their ordering online or over the phone."

"I'm more of a face-to-face kind of guy. I like to see who I'm doing business with, a leftover trait from my years in special operations."

Mother Cherry shimmied in her seat, a spark of interest showing on her face. "Oh, a military man. I should have guessed." She raked him with her eyes.

"I'm a veteran."

"I see. I wouldn't have thought someone as well-put together as yourself would need a service to find dates."

Dec slumped a bit in his seat, feigning the start of boredom. "I haven't had the time to cultivate relationships and frankly have no patience for it or for playing twenty questions. I'm looking to hire companions, and I need specialized attention."

Mother Cherry twirled a lock of her unnatural hair. "What kind of special are you looking for, sugar?"

"After multiple tours of duty in warzones, I've

found that I carry a lot of stress in me. I need someone who can handle games, rough games."

"How rough?" the madam's question came out in a sexy hush.

Leaning forward, he said, "As rough as it gets."

Cherry licked her lips. "Are you a cop?"

Dec barked out a laugh. "Hell no."

Cherry shrugged. "I have to ask, and you have to tell if you are one."

Dec wasn't so sure about that, but he slumped back in his chair and put his hand on Pax's head. His fingers slid through her thick fur. He hoped it looked like an idle gesture rather than the comforting one he needed.

"I'm not a cop," he reiterated in a bored tone.

"How did you hear about us?"

He shrugged. "A friend of a friend. I don't think he'd appreciate my using his name, just in case you're a cop." He grinned and hoped the vague answer would be enough. He'd considered using Place's name, but the timing with the murder plus the unlikelihood of his actually knowing Place seemed too suspicious.

Fortunately, the madam threw back her head and laughed. "Oh, I like a scamp." Her mirth died. "What you're looking for doesn't come cheap, sugar." Her tone was all business.

By way of answer, Dec pulled out of his pocket a clip of money, a one hundred dollar bill wrapped around a bunch of twenties. He hoped it looked like a lot more than it was. "I understand entirely, and it's not a problem."

"Well, then." Mother Cherry picked up her tablet and clicked on the screen. Dec put his money away as she turned the screen toward him. "These are the boys who would be perfect for what you have in mind. Although, I'm afraid that this one is actually no longer available," she added, tapping on long, red nail on the screen.

Dec tried not to look too closely, but he still saw way too much of Scott because that's who she pointed to. Like the other three boys pictured in a skeevy rogue's gallery, he had a head shot, a full body clothed picture, and a full body nude, front and back, for clients to peruse.

"That's too bad, I'm into blonds. I hope that's not Kenny," he added, having decided in advance that if he got this far, he'd take the risk of mentioning the dead boy.

"It's not, although I'm afraid Kenny's also no longer with us," she said with a shuttered expression.

Yeah, in the permanent sense of the word. Smart, though, not to pretend he'd never worked there. Saying he'd left was a safer answer if Dec turned out to be a cop investigating the boy's death. "That's too bad. I heard he liked to party."

The madam said nothing in response, simply sat there waiting for him to make a selection. Dec's tension level started to rise under the scrutiny. When he'd formed his plan, he hoped to get some information, no matter how meager, that would help him connect any dots there might be between Kenny's death and Place's.

Now, he realized too late, his plan for a graceful exit wasn't going to work. Saying he'd think it over and get back to her seemed risky in the light of the fact that he dealt directly with the madam, and not a flunky. She seemed intent on his making a firm commitment, and failing to do so might make her suspicious, more than she already was with Kenny's name coming up. Worst case scenario would be her somehow connecting Scott to Dec's unusual visit, and no way he wanted to jeopardize that kid any more than his association with Place had already.

Christ, he sucked at investigation. He'd never intended to be a private detective, just a security consultant and bodyguard. He was in way over his head, and yet one didn't flake when on a mission. One saw it through no matter how much of a clusterfuck it might have become.

Looking at these boys, too, he couldn't just walk away and let this awful business continue to thrive. Scott might have finally gotten himself out, but these boys hadn't. With a surreptitious deep breath and lot of trepidation, Dec pointed to the one who not only looked the youngest, he looked holy shit young. If he ended up only rescuing one, it should be this one.

"He looks sweet. Jimmy." Joey, Kenny, Jimmy, all the stage names were made to sound like really little boys. His stomach turned. He needed to finish this up quick.

Sensing his mood, as usual, Pax stuck her nose under his hand. He ran his fingers across her muzzle.

Mother Cherry beamed. "An excellent choice. Now, when do you want him?" She tapped her fingers on the tablet. "He's free tonight."

Crap, too soon. "I was hoping for tomorrow night?"

"Hmm. That works. What time?"

With the same mundane effort that one would make to order up a take-out dinner, Dec hired himself a rent boy.

"It's five hundred an hour, two hour minimum."
Mother Cherry held out her hand expectantly. "Paid in
advance, no refunds."

Crap, again. Dec hadn't counted on laying out that
kind of money. His bank roll certainly didn't hold a
thousand dollars. He dug it out anyway while his brain
worked to come up with a way to get out of paying.

The madam saved his ass. "We prefer for you to
charge the fee and take all major credit cards. It's easier
for us to handle our taxes that way. And of course, this
is only for the *agency's* fee. Once the clock has run out
on your date, you and the young man are free to make
whatever arrangements you want. You're all consenting
adults, after all," she added with a toothsome smile.

Relieved, Dec took out his wallet and handed over
his credit card. He shouldn't have been surprised by the
arrangement. The business operated as a legal escort
service, after all. Clients got dates, not the overt
promise of sex. The boys took all the risks, laying out
the price for their real services and taking the cash back
to Mother Cherry. He cringed at the dent the swipe of
his card through the tablet's square would make in his
credit. He had to think of it as an investment in his
company's future. The morass of crime that constituted
Place's life had to be cleared up if he stood any chance
of weathering the storm. Besides, honor dictated it.

"All set." Mother Cherry's mood had improved
with the payment. "I just need your address, Mr.
Hunter."

Five minutes later, and Dec was back on the
sidewalk with a date on his calendar and huge problem.
He'd managed to get himself in deeper than he could
handle on his own. There was really only one thing he

could do, one person he could turn to. The thought of it made him cringe, but there was no other solution.

He checked his watch. It was too early to swallow his pride and seek out Jakes. The cop was undoubtedly busy working his case. He'd try to catch him later when he might be going off duty. In the meantime, he could marshal his thoughts and plan his strategy of attack.

Because seeing Jakes again, confessing what he'd done, then asking for help...that was going to be a battle. He never went into a fight unprepared.

"Come on, girl," he said to Pax. "Let's go see Felix."

****

Dec found Felix where he'd expected, in the basement of a Boston church where he ran a once a week group session for gay at-risk teens. The boys were filing out just as Dec and Pax reached the bottom of the stairs. Some wore the standard sullen expression many kids their age wore while others chatted animatedly with their brethren. Dec figured not all the boys were gay. Felix had a way with everyone, regardless of age or sexual orientation, and an hour with him could help anyone be open to receiving his help.

Dec hadn't been, not at first. He'd only agreed to look Felix up to get the VA doctor off his back. He'd spent the first session acting more defiant than the boys he passed would have. By the third session, he balled like a baby, mourning the loss of his teammates, his physical fitness, and his career. Within six months, he'd found a permanent home in Felix's building, and a year later, he'd set up Red Cell and hired two of Felix's other patients as his admin and comspesh. In his more honest moments, he acknowledged to himself that Felix had taken on the role of a father figure more real than Dec's own father had ever been. Bottom line—he trusted the man's judgment.

Dec found him breaking down the folding chairs. "Hey, Felix."

The older man turned at the greeting and flashed a smile. "Declan, dear boy. What a wonderful surprise."

Dec walked into the room. "I hope it's okay for me to drop in."

"Of course. As you can see, my session has ended. And I always have time for you."

"Thanks." Dec moved to help with the chairs, stacking them back against the wall where they were usually kept. "I need some advice," he admitted once they'd finished the job.

"I'm happy to offer it, always. Come on, since we've put away the chairs, we'll have to make do with the old couch."

Felix led Dec over to the only piece of furniture other than a scarred piano in the room. The man sat delicately on one end and crossed his slender legs."

Dec flopped down on the other end, and Pax sat close to Felix, expecting and getting a lavish amount of attention. Felix and Pax had a love affair going that sometimes left Dec out in the cold.

"So, my dear," Felix drawled in a softer and more elegant version of Mother Cherry's accent.

Noticing that, Dec led with a long-shot question. "Back in your drag days, did you ever come across another performer called Mother Cherry or maybe just Cherry?" The men were about the same age.

"Hmm." Felix pursed his lips and stared off into space. "I do recall a Cherry Blossom. A tiny little thing with an enviable nineteen inch waist. A real live China doll, except," he added with a frown. "I think she was Japanese. Why do you ask?"

Dec shook his head and shot Felix a rueful grin. "Never mind. It was a crazy idea. Anyway..." He suddenly found his thumbnail fascinating. Felix had the patience of Job and would wait until Dec was good and ready to talk. After so long in therapy with the man, Dec didn't allow himself to duck the difficult discussion. Avoiding trouble, wasn't the SEAL way, either. "So, I slept with a guy last night."

Felix's gaze had been fixed on Pax as he scratched and petted and made kissy faces at the dog. Now, his head came up and he beamed at Dec. "Oh, my dear boy, that is good news. Isn't it?"

Dec blew out a breath. "Yeah, sort of. I mean the sex was off the charts hot, and God knows my body waking up and taking interest after almost two years was welcome news."

"But?" Felix prompted.

"But, first of all, it's the lead cop on the Place murder. Who happens to have been my first client and only client, the one who got killed in his home the very night I finished setting up his new security system." He hadn't told Felix the name of his client for privacy reasons, although he'd given the good news about finally having one.

In his shock, Felix abandoned Pax and turned his full attention toward Dec. "Dearest boy, how horrible. Surely, you aren't a suspect?"

"I was. But I don't think I am anymore. If I am, then Detective Sergeant Jakes is a terrible cop for letting me fuck him."

"Oh." Felix waved his hand. "Obviously, you're not a suspect." And because Felix was his therapist and not just a friend, he asked, "How are you feeling about finally getting intimate after all this time?"

"Lousy," Dec admitted. "Guilty. And not because I'm alive while my teammates died." Survivor's guilt was one of his issues he'd been working on. "I feel guilty because I kicked the guy to the curb minutes after we finished."

"Ah. Why was that?"

"You know why." When Felix merely stared and stared, his usual technique, Dec sighed. "Because I was scared shitless I'd have a nightmare and freak him out, or worse, try to kill him in my sleep. Or something."

"And how did you sleep?"

"Better than I have in two years."

"A good orgasm will do that for you," the older man observed.

Dec almost choked on his spit. That's what came from having a therapist who'd lived a flamboyant life once upon a time. "I treated him badly, though. Kicked him out like I was flushing the condom a second time." He shook his head. "He deserved better."

"What do you think he deserved exactly?"

Dec didn't answer right away. He knew what Felix expected him to say, the right answer. The only one. "The truth."

Felix beamed at him, like he'd just said his first word or something. He always looked at Dec that way when he had a breakthrough in therapy. At first, he'd hated it, then he loved it, and now he hated it again. "I don't think I have it in me to explain myself. Not yet, and maybe not with this guy, anyway. I hardly know him. It's not like we're dating or anything."

Felix shrugged, his smile dimming. "I suppose it's easy enough to avoid him, and therefore, the topic entirely. If you truly don't feel ready to face the issue head on."

Dec winced. "Now, there's the problem. I've been looking into the murder myself. I can't just sit it out. The man died on my watch. I owe it to him to find out why. I don't know if my system was compromised by the killer or if it wasn't set. I only know that I left in a huff without double-checking that the client would turn it on." He quickly gave Felix the rundown of that night.

"Oh, that poor boy," he said in response to hearing about Scott. "Please give him my card if the occasion arises."

"Sure, that's a good idea. But in the meantime, I've gotten in way over my head and need help. I have to go to the cops with some new information I've got. Avoidance isn't an option, so what do I do?"

"What do you feel comfortable doing?"

"Honestly? I can't dump my whole psyche on the guy, but I do want to make sure he understands it's me, not him. I'm not ready for anything more than a one-night stand with anyone. Is that enough, though? Am I being a coward for not laying the whole thing out for him?"

Felix gave him a steely look. "What have we discussed about your using words of weakness about your mental health issues?"

"It's not weak to have them, and I have to progress at my own pace. No artificial timetables." Felix had pounded those concepts into his head early and often. Dec still needed to be reminded of them now and again.

"Exactly. Tell this man whatever amount of information is comfortable for you. Then add in a smidge more. Push yourself, but not to the breaking point."

"Right."

They sat there for a few seconds in silence. Felix went back to petting Pax, and Dec got lost in his thoughts.

"It felt really good," he said after a few minutes. "Being with someone, touching him, being touched by him. I hadn't truly realized how much I missed it."

Felix lifted his hand from Pax's head and leaned over to place it on Dec's arm. "Human beings are social animals. We need each other."

Yeah, for a while he'd convinced himself he didn't. Well, that myth had been busted. Memories of sliding into Jakes' heat, being wrapped around him, swamped him suddenly. He dropped his head on the back of the couch and closed his eyes. He relived every moment of their almost frantic coupling.

It was the little details there really got to him, like the look on Jakes' face when Dec first breached his hole. And the staccato grunts the guy made as Dec slammed into his body. The fact that he could take the man fast and hard and the cop had had no problem keeping up with him. Had urged him to go faster and harder until they'd both come in a rush of pleasure that emptied Dec's mind just for a few moments of its usual cacophony of anxiety and guilt and even fear.

If he could have lain in the bliss of Jakes' embrace all night, he would have. But it hadn't taken long for the noise in his head to come back quickly and hard-hitting. For a heart-stopping moment, he'd feared he might cry. He'd jumped up so fast, he'd hurt Jakes. He knew he had, physically and emotionally. Yet, he hadn't had the stomach to explain himself. Still didn't, and Felix's blessing to give the abridged version of his fucked-upedness helped some, yet not completely.

The thought of seeing the cop again wasn't wholly worrisome. His body appreciated the opportunity. Reliving the night before had caused his cock to swell, and his breath hitched. He flicked a glance at Felix. The man smiled back at him knowingly.

"It's all right to be conflicted about seeing the man again." He patted Dec's arm. "Think through what you're going to say. Remember that you do better when you have a plan, but don't obsess about every little word. This isn't a mission, however much your mind might see it as one. Too much planning, and you may end up talking yourself out of seeing him at all."

Dec pushed himself to his feet. "Not seeing him is not an option. I have to because now there's more lives at stake. My problems are nothing compared to what's brewing out there."

With a final pat of Pax's head, Felix got up, too. "You'll do the right thing. I have tremendous faith in you and your abilities. Just be careful, dear boy. I don't know what I'd do without our little chats."

Dec moved in close and gave the man a quick hug. "Felix, you make me feel ten feet tall and right in the head. Thanks."

"Any time, dearest boy. Any time."

Chapter Eight

"Time to call it a night."

Andy paused the latest DVD playing in his computer and shoved the headphones down to his neck. "What?"

Ryan leaned in and said, "Home," with exaggerated clarity. "We've been running twelve hours straight."

Andy puffed out a breath that held the remnants of his cheeseburger dinner. They'd both spent the day subsisting on fast food and coffee and had come up with a big goose egg. "I just want to plow through a couple more of these things. So far, I've identified six different boys, including Kenny and Reilly." He shook his head. "Jesus, no wonder Reilly's so scared. Place was a real sadist with a capital S, for shithead. Other than Kenny, none of the boys looked to be enjoying any part of what Place did to them, and they all looked high or drunk, as well."

"Yeah, I'm sure that's how he got them to tolerate it."

Andy tapped his screen, where the face of a crying boy could be seen lying on a bed. "Look at this kid. He can't be more than fifteen. Where the hell did Place find them?"

Ryan looked away and jammed his hands in his pocket. "With his money, I bet it was all too easy.

Look, if they haven't cracked his laptop open by morning, we'll go lean on Johnson some more. If that doesn't work, we'll have to go back to Reilly. Now that we know for sure the dead boy spent time with Place, we need the name of the service."

"Even though we may be chasing the wrong lead. How would this all fit into Place's murder? Unless it was Reilly or some other kid Place brutalized."

"That theory is still on the table, even though I hate it. But the missing artwork still seems to be the key. Or somehow the two intersect." Pinching the bridge of his nose with thumb and forefinger, Ryan swore. "I'm beat. My brain is no longer functioning. Time to sleep on it and get a fresh start early tomorrow."

Andy held up a finger. "Thirty minutes more, I promise. Then I'll go home."

Ryan clapped his partner on his shoulder. "You better. You're no good to me fried."

With that, he walked away, desperate now to get to his car and to his home. He didn't make it past the desk sergeant.

"Hey, Jakie, someone waiting to see you."

Ryan followed the man's finger and spotted a figure, two of them, actually, sitting in the waiting area of the station. His stomach did a quick roll, and a spark of interest goosed his groin. Even as he admonished himself to knock it the fuck off, he changed direction and made his way quickly to where Hunter and Pax sat.

The SEAL lifted his head from the wall where it had been resting and looked right at Ryan. The intensity of the gaze caused Ryan's feet to get clumsy. He skidded to a halt and tried to plaster a look of indifference on his face. His heartbeat, though, picked up speed. He wondered if the other man could hear it given the way it pounded in his own ears.

With a little yip, Pax greeted him first, padding as far as her leash would allow. Unable to resist the dog, if not the dog's owner, Ryan moved closer so that she could nuzzle his hand. He used the distraction the dog gave him to look away from Hunter and marshal his thoughts. He went with the obvious question.

"What are doing here, Hunter?" He winced inwardly at how confrontational he sounded. The guy hadn't done anything wrong, except, oh yeah, he was sticking his nose into Ryan's business. That was reason enough to be suspicious and hostile. Being drop-kicked to the curb after high-caliber sex had nothing to do with it. Nothing. At. All.

Hunter got slowly to his feet, stretching his neck this way and that as he did so. He looked like Ryan felt. "I'm sorry to bother you." He stuck his thumbs in his front pockets and cocked a hip. His tired gaze met Ryan's.

"I can't say that I was looking forward to doing anything more than going home and to bed."

Hunter's nostrils flared briefly at the mention of getting horizontal.

Oh, no I don't think so, buddy. That's what his brain said. His dick had a different response, one that he held back with difficulty. "How long have you been waiting here?"

"A couple of hours or so."

"Why didn't someone tell me?" Ryan craned his neck around to stare at the desk sergeant, who focused on his computer screen.

"I told him I'd wait. I didn't want to disturb you. I

know how busy you must be."

Ryan rubbed the back of his neck, weighing his next words. Part of him wanted to scream out his frustrations and part wanted to walk into that large body for a hug. Pathetic. "I was, and I am, so I repeat, what do you want?"

"Two things, actually. One is kind of personal." Hunter snorted. "No, very personal. The other is professional. Either way, I'd prefer that we have this conversation somewhere private."

"Do you really?" Ryan didn't even try to keep the snide out of his tone. He really wasn't sure he wanted any part of this conversation. But he was curious enough about the personal and needy enough for the professional that he didn't just turn and walk away. "Did you drive here?"

"Nope. Don't have a car."

"Okay, then, we'll go together." He did turn now and headed for the doors.

Hunter stepped up to pace him on his left, the dog between them. "Where are we going?"

"To the one place I want to be right now, home. It's the most private place I know." And when their little chat ended, Ryan could just flop into bed. Hunter would have to take a taxi or an Uber or something to get back to his own home. Ryan wasn't up for caring at the moment.

They remained silent as they walked to Ryan's car. Hunter joined him in the front while Pax climbed into the back. With rush hour traffic long over, their trip went quickly. By unspoken agreement, they didn't try to make small talk. The quiet should have been awkward, yet for some reason the only tense part was the sexual tension that rose between them.

Ryan was disgusted with himself for being so easy. It had been the same way for a long time with Flynn the Fucker after he'd dumped Ryan. Much as Ryan had been pissed at the guy, Ryan's body had yearned for his touch.

When he pulled into his driveway, Ryan breathed a silent sigh of relief. He didn't see his brother anywhere. He definitely didn't want to add social introductions to the already weird mix. Hunter took in his surroundings with undoubtedly a SEAL trained kind of awareness. For her part, Pax put her nose to the ground, avidly sniffing away. Hunter looked concerned, though.

"What's up, girl?" He gave her some kind of hand signal, and she sat down immediately, looking up at him with her tongue hanging out.

"She probably smells my brother's new puppy, that's all," Ryan said, locking his car and joining them.

"Oh." Hunter gave him a sheepish grin. "Sorry. She was deployed as a bomb-sniffing dog, so I get a little antsy when she's on the trail of something."

Ryan didn't have a response to that. He felt as if Hunter's life kept unfolding in front of him, bits and pieces being revealed with maddening slowness. Not that he needed to know a damn thing, of course. They weren't dating.

He led the way up the backstairs, ignoring the glimpse of his sister-in-law doing something in the kitchen. Shit, he hoped she didn't see them. The thought of his brother getting into his business, wheedling information about Hunter out of him, cramped his brain.

Opening the backdoor, he stood aside and let

Hunter and Pax slip past him. "Straight through to the living room. Make yourself comfortable."

Once they had moved on, he yanked his already loose tie off and went to the fridge. Beer might not be the best idea, but he wanted a cold one, and because his mother had taught him manners, he opened and brought one for Hunter, too.

He found man and dog perched on and in front of the couch, respectively. Hunter carded his fingers through the dog's thick fur, likely a mechanism for dealing with stress. Not that the guy would ever share that information with Ryan. Nope, not that kind of relationship. Not any kind of relationship.

He handed over the beer before flopping down on his recliner. "Okay, spill it." He took a long swig from his bottle, staring at Hunter over the rim.

The man didn't answer right away, just kept his gaze down, the bottle untouched. Then his chest rose and fell on a heavy sigh. "I'd like to start with the personal, if I may?" When Ryan simply shrugged, Hunter lifted his steady gaze on Ryan. "I want to apologize for how last night ended. I didn't mean for it to be so…abrupt."

Ryan drank more beer and said nothing because there was nothing to say. He'd heard sorry plenty of times. Sorries didn't mean jack shit.

"The truth is, I'm not looking for anything more than the occasional fuck. I'm not ready for more."

Oh, yeah, the it's not you it's me line never got old. Oh, wait, it was so fucking old that Ryan felt like Methuselah given how often he'd heard it. Because he was way too tired and frustrated to hear this crap, he broke in to end it.

"Don't sweat yourself, Hunter. You have nothing to apologize for. I'm not looking for anything more than a quick fuck, myself. If you hadn't kicked me out, I would have left anyway in a few minutes." Ryan put his game face on and swigged some more beer.

"Oh, um, good. That's good to hear." Hunter focused his gaze on Pax, his fingers still working through the fur. It looked so relaxing that Ryan wanted to join in, except what he really wanted to do was run his fingers through the head of thick hair on the man instead. And that line of thought was going to lead to nothing but trouble.

"So," he blurted out. "Now that that's out of the way, what is the professional thing?"

Yes, good plan. Ryan had a feeling the next words out of Hunter's mouth would kill Ryan's nascent hard-on.

Hunter finally took a pull of his beer, a long one. A stalling tactic that just ratcheted up Ryan's tension. Hunter flicked his tongue out to catch a drip on his lower lip. Ryan's gaze tracked the movement, derailing his train of thought, a momentary distraction.

"I saw Scott this morning."

What? Oh, right the case. "Reilly, you mean?"

Hunter furrowed his brows. "Is that his last name? I didn't know. Anyway, I managed to get the name of his former escort service."

That got Ryan's attention. "What is it?"

Hunter shook his head. "I need to get this all out before I tell you that."

"Wow, you really know how to piss me off?" *And get me off.*

Hunter held up his palm. "I'm sorry, I know.

Please let me tell this my way. So, I went there, to the office of the service. It's run by someone calling themselves Mother Cherry."

Ryan gaped. "Are you shitting me? Is that a woman or a guy in drag?"

"The latter. Anyway, the place was a dive, but as business is usually conducted via phone or internet, I guess that's not surprising. Mother Cherry has developed a niche service, young guys who will play submissive to their clients, take a beating to be specific. I don't think that's her entire service, but enough of one to attract wealthy guys who are into non-consensual or non-consensual role-playing. It's the only reason I can think of as to why someone like Place would use such a low-rent kind of service."

Images from Andy's computer popped into Ryan's head. "I need the name," he said through gritted teeth.

"I'm not done yet."

"You are if I say you are," Ryan warned.

"Please, let me finish."

God, Ryan was such a sucker. One look into those earnest and pleading blue eyes, and he found himself nodding in assent.

"Thanks. I pretended to be a prospective client looking for that specialty, and long story short, I booked a boy for tomorrow night."

"What!" Popping to his feet, Ryan slammed his beer onto the coffee table. Pax whined, so he dialed back his anger for her sake and his. He didn't want to upset her, and he didn't want to get mauled by triggering her protective instincts. "What?" he asked in a more even tone.

"I didn't think things through, frankly." Hunter

sounded a bit sheepish.

"Ya think?"

"I thought I could nose around without having to go that far. Before I could think my way out of it, I found myself looking at disturbing pictures of boys and being pressed to pick one. I needed to play along and make a date so that Cherry wouldn't be suspicious or maybe trace my visit somehow back to Scott." Hunter licked his lips in obvious nerves. "See, Scott told me about this boy."

"Kenny."

Hunter looked up at him in surprise. "You know about him?"

"Scott mentioned him when I interviewed him. He didn't want to tell us the name of his service because he didn't want to end up dead like Kenny."

"So, he was telling the truth about Kenny being dead?"

"Yeah. We found his file, listed as a John Doe."

"Mother Cherry only said he no longer worked for her."

"You asked her about him?" Wow, Hunter sucked at investigation…or maybe he didn't. Time would tell if mentioning Kenny was a good idea.

"I did. A calculated risk, I know. But she did show me the few boys who she said could help me 'alleviate my stress' as I described it. I figure I couldn't do much for Scott and nothing for this Kenny kid. Maybe I could do something to help one of the other boys. I picked the youngest looking one." He paused. "Jakes, I think the kid is underage."

"Reddish brown hair, green eyes?"

Hunter frowned. "Yes, that's the one. You know of

him?"

"Let's just say Place kept an interesting DVD collection." He facepalmed as soon as the words came out of his mouth. What was wrong with him? He shouldn't be telling this guy anything about the investigation.

Hunter stood up. "He's coming to my apartment tomorrow night at eight. I need you to be there, please. Maybe Mother Cherry's operation has nothing to do with Place's murder. I don't know. I just want something good to come of all this, if only shutting her down and getting those boys some help."

Immobilizing fatigue washed over Ryan. His shoulders slumped, and he brought his palms up to rub the grit out of his eyes. "Shit. I should kick this over to the sex crimes unit. This rent boy stuff probably has nothing to do with the murder. Robbery had to be the motive."

"Except Kenny's dead."

Ryan focused his weary eyes on Hunter. The guy looked back at him with concern, although whether it was for Ryan or the exploited boys, he couldn't tell. "Sex workers get killed all the time, unfortunately. The two murders don't have to be connected in any meaningful way."

"Then Kenny was really murdered? It wasn't an accident?"

"He was killed. I'm sure of that." He gave himself a few seconds to clear his head. "Okay, we'll play this your way. I'll be in your apartment when the kid shows up. If he's underage, that will give me a reason for sure to bring him in. Maybe he knows something that will help the murder investigation, either of them.

Otherwise, we'll kick this over to the sex crimes unit, and they can deal with Mother Cherry. God, I guess we have come a long way, baby. Now gays can be villainous criminals, too. Yay, us." Ryan frowned at Hunter. "I should probably bust your ass for solicitation, regardless of your motive."

Hunter looked startled at first, then remorseful. "I'm sorry. I know I'm treading on your turf. Do what you have to do."

Christ, now the guy was going all noble on him. Bust his ass? Forget that. Ryan, or rather his dick, had other ideas of what he could do with Hunter's ass. The futility of the need made him feel even more tired.

Clasping the back of his neck, Ryan let his chin drop to his chest.

Dec took an involuntary step forward and watched his hand reach out, as if it had a mind of its own. It landed on Jakes' shoulder, right below where the other man's hand still gripped the back of his neck. Jakes started at the contact. His gaze flew to meet Dec's.

Dec stared back, getting lost in the depth of those vivid green eyes. He noticed for the first time amber flecks sprinkled throughout. The effect seemed too pretty for such a classically masculine face.

"What—What are you doing?" Jakes' voice was both slightly breathless and hostile.

The combination made Dec's already wakening cock quickly shake off the last of its slumber. He pressed his fingertips into the tense muscle beneath them, massaging with slow movements. "I'm sorry I'm adding to your already full plate."

"Are you?" Jakes' voice dripped with skepticism, yet he dropped his own hand and closed his eyes with a sigh.

Dec stepped even closer, leaving mere inches between them. He knew intellectually that his actions would only lead to more trouble, possibly obliterating his previous apology. He couldn't help himself. "Yes, I am."

"How sorry?" Jakes asked with his eyes still closed.

"This sorry." It was as if he watched himself from afar, a movie playing for his entertainment, although whether it was going to be a romcom, a tearjerker, or a horror flick, he didn't know. He just couldn't stop himself.

Dec leaned down and planted his lips on Jakes', tentatively at first, expecting a rebuff. When one didn't come, he felt emboldened. He slanted his mouth, sliding over warm and slightly wet skin. With his hand still on Jakes' shoulder, Dec pressed their bodies together. He placed his other hand on Jakes' hip for greater leverage. It didn't stay there, though. It slipped down to cup the man's ass. At the same time that Dec pushed for entrance with his tongue, he pressed against Jakes' groin with his own. A low moan escaped both their mouths as their tongues twined and their hard dicks found each other.

They slipped and slid for long seconds, the intensity increasing with each passing moment. Dec knew this was all a bad idea, he truly knew. Yet, his need to somehow make up for the selfish way he'd used Jakes the night before drove him to want to please the man now. Yeah, that was it, all so altruistic. Not about his need to touch and suck. Suck. Now, that was a great idea. Nothing relaxed a man more than a good blowjob.

If Dec got some benefit from it, too, well no helping that result.

The thought firmly in his mind, he maneuvered Jakes back with subtle pushes of his whole body. Pliant at first, Jakes suddenly broke the kiss and shoved his hands between them. He placed his palms against Dec's chest, stopping the movement.

"What are you doing?" he asked once more.

"Honestly?" Dec murmured. "Acting out the biggest rationalization, I think."

With a final shove, he sent Jakes crashing onto his recliner. Air whooshed out of the guy's lungs, and he looked up at Dec with a mixture of surprise and…hard to say what else. Excitement maybe, or that might be more wishful thinking on Dec's part. He didn't let his stray observations derail his plan. Kicking Jakes' legs apart, he dropped to his knees. He didn't give either of them an opportunity to ponder the wisdom of what he was about to do, or really to think at all.

His hands trembled a bit as he reached for Jakes' fly. He couldn't remember the last time he'd sucked a guy off, typically being on the receiving end in some club's backroom. He licked his lips, this time with anticipation, and watched with mounting excitement as the thick cock he remembered from the night before sprang out. Unable to take his time, to draw out and savor the experience, he lunged forward to envelope the head with his lips.

"Jesus!" The word exploded out of Jakes' mouth, warm breath ruffling Dec's hair. Then fingers drifted down and clenched the strands.

Dec closed his eyes tight and dove down onto the dick in his mouth, taking it deep within his throat. He couldn't hold the position long but managed to swallow before pulling back up. Jakes jerked his hips, trying to keep himself embedded in Dec's mouth. Dec wrapped the fingers of his right hand around the base of Jakes' dick, controlling his movement. When Jakes grunted in frustration, Dec lapped up the shaft and tickled the slit with his tongue. He tasted pre-cum that spurred him to once more take it into his mouth. He held only the head in at first, lavishing it with as much attention as his tongue and teeth could muster. The tiny scrapes he made along the ridge of Jakes' glans made the man jerk and almost whimper. The feel and taste and sounds of him had Dec's own arousal spiking.

Leaning against the chair as he was, he pressed his aching dick into it. It wasn't much, but it gave him some relief.

Jakes bucked again fiercely. "Fuck, swallow me again."

Because Jakes' request came out more as a plea, Dec complied. This time, he took it all the way down, willing his gag reflex back, not stopping until coarse pubic hair tickled his nose. He used tongue to massage the hard flesh filling his mouth, sucking in with Dyson-like power, relishing the way Jakes squirmed and moaned. The man's fingers tightened in Dec's hair, twisting and tugging, and making his eyes water. Dec brought his other hand into play, cupping Jakes' balls and rolling the tight orbs between his fingers.

"Jesus Christ, Hunter, I'm going to..." Jakes' breath exploded out at the exact same moment cum shot down Dec's throat.

Dec swallowed convulsively to take it in, not really tasting it, yet desperate not to spill a drop on Jakes'

Samantha Cayto

pants. At the moment, with his arms leaning on iron hard thighs, he really liked how tight the fabric spread across the thick muscles. He ground his pelvis against the chair front, seeking relief, even as he milked the last of the cum from the dick in his mouth. But he never got a chance to make himself come in his pants for the first time since his teenage years.

In the blink of an eye, he found himself flat on his back, mouth empty and legs splayed open. Shit, when was the last time someone had gotten the drop on him? Maybe during BUDs. He'd always been that good at offense and defense. Yet, he couldn't get too worked up about it given that he'd landed where he wanted to be with Jakes lying on top of him, his tongue invading Dec's mouth while he worked the button fly of Dec's jeans. He brought his arms up to wrap them around Jakes' muscular neck. He came up with a whole lot of nothing because Jakes' quicksilver moves had the man already down by Dec's crotch licking at the newly-freed dick.

Dec's arms flopped against the floor as his eyes rolled into the back of his head. He didn't put up a fight, didn't want to. He just lay there, shuddering under the assault, allowing the climax to build up and escape. He didn't even last a full minute once Jakes sucked him into his hot, wet mouth. With a muted growl, Dec came, the force of his orgasm taking what energy he had left after confessing his sins to the cop, then blowing him. Dec went boneless. As his drained cock flopped out of Jakes' mouth, Jakes lay his head on top of Dec's stomach. His heavy breathing synced up with Dec's.

It was Pax who finally forced them to move. She

whined before nudging Dec's face with her cold, wet nose. He forced his eyes open, realizing way too late that he and Jakes had just given each other head in front of the dog. Thank God, she hadn't misinterpreted what had gone on, only worried about Dec now that he lay like the dead. He rallied enough strength to open his eyes and scratch her ruff.

"It's okay, girl. The nice policeman only gave me a *little* death."

"Ha, ha." Jakes turned his head over so that he could see Dec's face. He looked utterly wasted, which was pretty satisfying actually, so long as he didn't think too hard about how much he'd fucked up—again. "Am I at risk for having my throat ripped out given how I attacked you?"

"Naw," Dec replied, looking into Pax's happy dog eyes. "I think she recognized that I was the aggressor. Besides, she's trained to pick up on my bad moods and self-destructive behavior. And while a good argument could be made that what I started and you finished constitutes a poor choice, it has left me in a really *good* mood."

Jakes chuckled, the vibration doing interesting things to Dec's dick. "Is this the point in the evening where I kick you out?"

Dropping his hand, Dec pushed up on his elbows and looked down his nose at his host. "You'd be perfectly within your rights to do so."

Dec didn't move, however, merely waited for a response. The stupid truth was that he didn't want to leave. He wanted to stay and get another chance at having the cop's ass. It wasn't fair of him, either, and yet he still wanted it. Christ, what was wrong with him?

Samantha Cayto

Too much, apparently. He tried to sit all the way up, but Jakes didn't move.

"I should do it," Jakes muttered. "Neither of us wants anything more than gratuitous sex, and given that we've both come once, that should be enough. We should go to our respective beds, sleep like the dead, and get up again to tackle this miserable case. Not that *you* have a case," he added with a scowl.

Dec bucked, tossing Jakes' head. "So let me get up." He was a little surprised when Jakes complied. As soon as Dec had managed to get vertical, however, with one hand grabbing his waistband, he found himself plastered against the cop's body once more.

Jakes kissed him with the kind of fervor that was more of a hello than a good-bye and good riddance. The guy didn't release Dec's lips until his lungs nearly burst.

He gave Dec a hard look. "Fuck me, but I don't want you to go."

He did let go of Dec long enough to toe off his shoes and kick his slacks and boxers free from his legs. Then he tossed his shirt and tie on the floor. Standing there, with his dick thickening right in front of Dec's eyes, he was too strong a temptation. If Jakes wouldn't shove him away, Dec didn't have the emotional energy to do it himself.

He kept his gaze on the cop as he yanked his own clothing off with jerky movements. "I hope you have condoms."

"As many as you need."

****

In the wee hours of the morning, Dec called upon his SEAL training to dress silently in a room lit only by a narrow shaft of moonlight shining through the blinds. Glowing eyes also anxiously watched him from the hall where he'd made Pax lie down and wait while he fucked Ryan's brains out.

Sometime during the marathon session, they'd switched over to first names, such as *"Shit Ryan, how can you still be so tight?"* and *"Christ Dec, I'm not made of glass; fuck me harder!"* Yeah, difficult to maintain a professional distance when saying those kinds of words.

"Hey," a sleepy voiced called out softly. "You don't have to go."

Damn, he'd woken Ryan. He looked over his shoulder, and the sexily rumpled vision almost tempted him to take off his clothes again. Almost. He'd been careful not to fall asleep and could have stayed up all night if necessary. He knew how to survive on little to no shut-eye. But being wrapped in Ryan's arms made him too comfortable. Sleep had tugged strongly at him, and despite his previous night's experience, he still didn't trust himself not to have a freak out. "Sorry, I really do."

Ryan didn't say anything for a few, long seconds. Then throwing the covers back, he lurched to his feet on the other side of the bed.

"What are you doing?" Dec asked as he watched the man go pull underwear and a T-shirt out of a drawer.

"Driving you home," Ryan replied as he stepped into his boxers.

"You don't have to do that. I'll call a taxi."

"It's after one in the freaking morning." Ryan's voice was muffled by dragging his shirt over his head.

"You'll be waiting forever. I can drive you. It's not the other end of the world." He opened up a closet and pulled jeans off a hanger.

Dec suppressed a sigh, annoyed at himself for robbing the cop of his much needed rest. Unlike Dec, Ryan wouldn't be able to sleep in.

"I can stay," he said, the reluctance audible in his voice.

Ryan cocked his head at him. "No, it's fine. I get it. We're not setting up house here. We're not even dating. We're just fucking, in front of your dog, no less. If I think about that too much, I'm going to end up in therapy." He looked around the room. Snapped his fingers. "Keys and wallet are in the pants in the living room." He strode out of the room, taking a moment to pat Pax on the head as he went by her.

That was one of the things about the guy that Dec really liked. Ryan treated Pax with respect and affection. Shit, how could he not appreciate that? Dec followed him into the hall and picked up the end of Pax's leash. He patted her, too.

"Sorry for the disruption, girl. We're going home now." She gave a low woof in acknowledgment. God only knew how her doggy brain processed everything going on. Dec wasn't sure how he felt about her unwitting voyeurism, either. Unlike Ryan, he already had a therapist. Maybe he'd raise the subject with Felix.

When Ryan rematerialized, shoving his wallet in the back pocket of his jeans and keys jangling in his fist, Dec let him pass. He and an excited Pax followed him. She probably needed to pee.

As soon as they stepped down into the backyard, the dog squatted in the grass. Yup, he'd definitely neglected his dog's needs. That's what happened when you led with your dick, although now that his sex life had been reborn, he had to admit, he'd missed it.

A small ball of fur with big paws came bounding around the corner of the house, tugging a long lead behind it. The puppy stopped and sniffed cautiously at Pax, who'd finished her business and was equally interested in this latest development. As Ryan and Dec watched the puppy sniff and retreat, sniff closer and retreat, an almost carbon copy of Ryan stumbled into view. The man came up short.

"Whoa, Ryan, way to give me a heart attack. What are you doing up so late?" His bleary eyes shifted to focus on Dec. "Oh." His lips turned up into a grin. "That's what."

Ryan blew out a breath, clearly unhappy with this turn of events. "Hey, Sean, this is Declan. Dec, this is my brother, Sean." He pointed to the puppy. "Murphy meet Pax." With a shift of his fingers, he said, "Pax, Murphy. There that's all the introductions you are going to get at this hellish hour of the night."

"Sure thing, bro. Come on, Murphy." The brother shot a wicked smile at Ryan, promising tremendous ribbing in the future with that look. Dec knew it well.

While he had no actual siblings, his teammates had served the role of his brothers. He missed that camaraderie. He missed *them*. With his injuries forcing him out and his emotional problems making him feel unworthy, he'd cut contact with them all. His loss. He really should try to reconnect, at least with those who he'd come to love as much as he would any biological brother.

Ryan flipped Sean the finger and continued to the

car. They rode in silence for the first few minutes before the noise inside Dec's head made him crack. "I'm sorry. You must think I'm a real basket case."

Ryan kept his eyes on the road. "I think we're both idiots. I can't believe I'm fraternizing with someone involved in an active case. IA would have my ass in a sling if they knew."

"But I'm not a suspect. Am I?"

Ryan glanced at him. "I'm not *that* stupid. If I considered you a suspect in Place's murder and still fucked you, I'd turn in my badge."

The city streets were all but deserted, so they sped through the night with few obstacles. There was something peaceful about it. Dec allowed himself to relax. He hadn't done anything horrible. They were grown men, and Ryan wasn't looking for anything more than Dec could offer anyway. Really, the worst thing Dec had done to Ryan was chase after leads in the murder.

"I *am* sorry about butting in and going to see Mother Cherry."

"Yet, I get the feeling that you're not so sorry that you'll butt out from now on?"

"Hmm." Dec shook his head. "I don't think I can make that promise. I'm worried about my people and my business's reputation. And leaving problems to others to solve isn't in my nature."

"I figured you'd say that. Part of me wants to lock your ass up."

"I told you to do what you have to do."

"What I have to do is solve the murder. Locking you up won't accomplish that." He drew in a deep breath and let it out slowly. "I shouldn't be telling you this."

"Then don't," Dec quickly inserted because he didn't want Ryan to put himself out on a limb any more than he had for Dec's sake.

"Maybe another head mulling things over would be helpful. Or that could be my well-fucked ass talking," he added with a wry grin. Dec grinned back. He had plowed Ryan pretty good for two nights straight now. "Anyway, I spoke with Place's brother. Did you ever meet him?"

"No. I didn't even know he had one."

"They were half-brothers and apparently no love lost. I showed him the treasure room just to see his reaction, and he said that whatever is missing would have had to be very meaningful to Place given where it hung. Something hard to get not just because of its cost, but more than that."

"You mean like the Great Train Robbery or something?"

"Yeah, like that, maybe. Something special."

Dec considered the implications of Place acquiring something extraordinary in comparison to all of the other wondrous things he'd filled his house with. How far would someone go to accomplish that, and how long would the thrill of succeeding last? Would having it in and of itself ever be forever satisfying? Wouldn't it be like being an addict, always chasing the next high?

He twisted in his seat enough to look at Ryan's profile. "When you possess a piece of art that required great derring-do, you'd want to show it off once in a while, wouldn't you?"

Ryan gave him a thoughtful look. "I would think so. I mean how long can you spend just staring at it whacking off at your own magnificence?"

"Exactly. But you can't show it to just anybody, or you risk having the police called." Dec felt his fatigue melt away as he considered what might have happened. "So, you show it to a sex worker who's both high as a proverbial kite and in no position to tell the police anything."

Ryan pulled over and threw his car into park. Dec looked around and realized they'd arrived at his apartment building. He'd been so caught up in the skull session, he hadn't noticed where they were.

Ryan turned to him. "If Place showed Kenny the treasure room, and Kenny started talking to other rent boys, who then wanted to see it, too…"

"Place insists perhaps that Kenny is a liar, but now he realizes the kid is a liability. It would be interesting to see Mother Cherry's records to find out if Kenny had a date with Place the night he died."

"A man like Place could get his hands on heroin easily enough, although moving an unconscious person by himself would be difficult."

"Lucky for him he has such a devoted personal assistant." Dec and Ryan sat grinning at each other as the pieces fell into place. "We've made some leaps here," he felt compelled to point out.

"Yeah, but they fit so nicely. Doesn't tell us who killed Place, though."

"You like Johnson for it, don't you?"

"Maybe." Ryan scrubbed his hand down his face, hiding a yawn as he did so.

Dec felt guilty again. "I'm sorry for keeping you out so late."

Trepidation almost stopped him, but Dec decided

he was tired of being afraid. Leaning over, he clasped Ryan's head with one hand and pulled him in for a quick kiss. At least he intended for it to be quick. Ryan had other ideas. He put his hand over Dec's and held him in place, pressing his tongue into Dec's mouth and kissing the breath out of him.

"You. Are. Dangerous," he said before letting Dec go and pulling back. "I'll see you tomorrow night. And, please, for the love of God, stay safe and stay out of my investigation."

Not wanting to lie, Dec exited the car without saying a word. He let Pax out and walked her to the stoop. He turned and watched Ryan drive off, feeling like a part of him had stayed in the car. "Man, am I in trouble."

Pax cocked her head. He thought he saw censure in her eyes. He couldn't blame her if he did. He wasn't being fair to Ryan or himself, yet he couldn't wait for the night to come so he could see the cop again.

Chapter Nine

Ryan shuffled like a zombie into work, nursing the largest cup of coffee he could find. He could only manage a grunt and a wave when the desk sergeant greeted him. He made a bee line for his desk chair with the hopes of collapsing into it before he fell on his face. Andy, damn him, had other ideas. He intercepted Ryan before he got within ten feet of his destination.

"Hey, Jakie, looking a little rough around the edges this morning." Ryan was working up the energy to give his partner the finger when the guy gave him a reason to perk up. "We need to go to the tech lab. Frankie emailed us this morning to say he's cracked the security on Place's laptop."

"Thank God. Maybe we'll catch a break on this case." Ryan gladly turned on his heel and followed Andy to the elevator. Leaning against the back of the cab, he slurped down a large measure of his coffee in the hopes of jump-starting his brain.

Andy's face lit up with a smirk. "Rough night?"

"What makes you ask that?" Ryan looked at Andy suspiciously over the rim of his cup.

"Because I know what time you knocked off last night, and I also heard that you left with someone who'd been waiting for you. Someone with a dog?"

Ryan swore under his breath, debating in a millisecond what to share with his partner. "It was

Hunter," he said just as the doors opened.

"No shit." Andy followed Ryan out of the elevator. "What did he want, besides you, of course?"

Ryan opened his mouth to say that nothing was going on between him and Hunter, then decided that Andy deserved better than that obvious lie. "He's still sticking his nose into our investigation. But the good news is that he realized he'd gotten in over his head and wanted my help."

They rounded into the tech lab. "With what?"

Ryan once again wondered what to share with the man. "It might be nothing and it might be something that could get a cop into trouble for participating. Bottom line is, I'll know better tonight. In the meantime, the less you know, the better."

Andy made a face indicating his displeasure in being kept out of the loop. He didn't get a chance to lay into Ryan about it, though, because they'd arrived at their destination, the desk of Frankie the wonder geek.

The poster boy for nerdy tech guy sat munching on a cronut, peering owlishly up at them from behind his glasses. "Hi, guys."

"Hey, Frankie, whatchu got for us?" Ryan asked, wishing he'd thought of getting something sweet with his caffeine. The sugar might work better on his system.

Licking his fingers, the techie spun in his chair and tapped on the keyboard of Place's laptop. "I cracked through the security of this thing a little while ago. It was more sophisticated than I would have expected for an at-home unit of a regular person. You know, not someone with a high security need. I haven't had time to go through much, but I did find some interesting files."

Ryan sighed. "Don't tell me, you found porn."

Frankie turned his head and pushed his glasses up with his forefinger. "I suppose some people might see it that way."

"You mean people who like underage boys?" Andy piped in.

Frankie blinked a few times. "Ah, no, no kiddie porn. Just art."

"Art?" Ryan took another swig of coffee and shook his head. "I guess given what I know about the vic, that would have been my second guess. What kind of art?"

"Really nice and expensive stuff, I'd say." Frankie tapped a few keys and pictures started popping up, some actual photographs, some hand sketches.

Both Ryan and Andy leaned in to watch the slide show that Frankie gave them, flashing screen after screen of fine art. Paintings and drawings, jewelry, pottery, and assorted valuable knick-knacks, some known to Ryan, many not, lit up the screen. One item in particular caught his attention.

"Hey, wait. Go back." When Frankie back-tracked, Ryan jabbed his finger at the screen. This image was only a hand-drawn sketch, and while it wasn't exactly right, it was damn close. "There, that's one of the things in the room. That Faberge egg. What was it Johnson called it? Hen with Sapphire something or other." He looked at Andy. "I bet everything we found in that room will be on this computer, too."

"Yeah, except why? Because he got all of it on the black market," Andy said, answering his own question. "This is probably his wish list of elusive and illegal artwork."

"Do you guys want to see the rest of the pictures?

There's close to a hundred items."

Ryan nodded at Frankie. "Sure, keep going."

It didn't take long, and by the time the show ended, Ryan and Andy had confirmed that a picture of everything they'd seen in the treasure room had been uploaded onto this computer. That left a crapload more stuff that the dead man probably had been coveting, yet unable to obtain. At least, that was their working supposition.

"If we're right about this," Andy said when the last picture had flashed by, "then one of these items is the missing one."

"Yeah, that's certainly what I'm hoping. Unfortunately, not being an art history major or a patron of any kind of art, I'm clueless about virtually all of it. I mean the only thing I recognized is that weird screaming guy one."

"The Scream," Frankie interjected. "There's more than one copy and I think two of them were stolen several years back."

"It wasn't in Place's room," Ryan said with a shake of his head.

"They've already been recovered."

"Hmm. Can you start trying to identify each piece, concentrating on the pictures only? That's the missing item, I'm sure of it."

"Sure thing." Good old Frankie, nothing fazed him. "I found an email account, too, by the way. So far, I've found some oversees messages and some local social ones."

"Oh yeah?" Ryan drained his coffee cup. "Anything interesting in the messages?"

"Maybe. Some of them cryptically talk about

packages being delivered. Others are about fundraising events."

"We're going to need a print-out of all of them."

"Okay. There's only a couple of hundred."

"Great," Andy remarked with a wry smile. "I know what I'm going to be doing later today."

Ryan shrugged. "Sorry, but yeah. First though, we tackle Johnson again. Now that we know more or less what was on this computer, I want to hear from him again how Place didn't use one. I don't suppose we've received the warrant to search the business office?"

Andy shook his head. "Sorry."

With a sigh, Ryan said, "Too much to hope for. Come on, let's go. Thanks, Frankie," he added with a clasp of the guy's shoulder. "As always, you came through."

Frankie flashed a smile. "No problem."

****

By the time he and Andy reached Place's business address, the caffeine had kicked into high gear within Ryan's system. So had his irritation. He was in absolutely no mood to be shut out by the beautiful, yet officious receptionist, and the scowl on Johnson's face when he came out to meet them only served to crank Ryan's shaft more.

"Gentlemen, while I realize you have an investigation to conduct, this popping by unannounced is bordering on harassment."

Ryan met Johnson's haughty and testy greeting with a sneer. "I haven't even begun, Johnson. You want to us to take this to a private place again?" he asked with a nod at the empty conference room.

"Very well." Johnson narrowed his eyes before

leading them through the glass door. He headed straight to the windows on the far side and clasped his hands behind his back. "What, pray tell, can I help you with? I've told you everything I know about this horrid business."

Ryan shoved his hands in his pants pockets. "Have you now?"

"What are implying?" Johnson asked with an audible sniff.

"I'm saying straight out that I don't think you've been truthful with us. You said Place didn't use a computer and yet we found one in his home office."

"Indeed. I had no idea he possessed one." The man held Ryan's gaze steadily, calmly, and earnestly. Ryan didn't buy the act.

"I find that very hard to believe. You've stressed right from the very beginning that you held a prominent position in your employer's life, and yet you didn't know about his stash of stolen art, his proclivity for hiring and abusing young male prostitutes, and his reliance on technology." Ryan ticked off each thing with an emphatic nod of his head. "In my book, that makes you either a poser or a liar. So which is it?"

The question finally cracked Johnson's haughty façade. The look that flashed in his eyes, just for a second, was one of pure hatred. It revealed a depth of feeling and even strength that the rather effete man hadn't show before.

"Get. Out."

Ryan shook his head with a wry smile that he knew got under the other man's skin enough for him to maybe do violence with a smidge more provocation. "I want to see Teichman."

The abrupt change in topic caused Johnson to freeze. "What do you mean?"

"I mean I want to speak with Teichman. He's the guy you said was in charge now, right? Surely his plane landed a long time ago. The world isn't that big. I want to search Place's office."

"There's nothing there that will help you."

Ryan bet that was true. Johnson had had loads of time to strip out incriminating evidence. "Should I ask the receptionist to get Teichman, or will you?"

Johnson stared at Ryan, tight lipped and obviously seething. "If you'll excuse me, I'll see if Mr. Teichman is free."

Ryan waved at the door with his hand and stepped to one side. "Sure, so long as you understand I need to speak with the man one way or the other."

Johnson minced his way past Ryan and Andy as if he sidestepped dog shit. Once the door shut behind him, Andy and Ryan watched him round the reception desk and disappear.

Andy grimaced at Ryan. "Think he's coming back, or are we going to be standing here with our thumbs up our asses until quitting time?"

"I'll give him five minutes before I start making more noise. We're getting into that office one way or another this morning."

"Do you really think we'll find anything useful?"

"Hell, no. Even if Johnson isn't up to his stiff neck in this mess, I bet he's one of those people so loyal that he'd destroy evidence rather than let Place's memory be soiled with dirt."

Andy scratched the back of his neck. "I think that ship's sailed already."

"I agree, but Johnson's got a lot of pride, and I think a misplaced sense of morals. Image is probably more important than truth, and anything he can do to reduce the fallout for Place's legacy, his own image, and this company's profit margin is fair game."

"Do you think he knew about the laptop?"

"I'd make book on it."

The man in question reappeared with another, older one striding by his side. Neither guy looked happy. Well, too damn bad. Ryan was about to make their day that much worse. He just hoped his lieutenant didn't ream him out for putting the pressure on. Damn, high profile cases. He wished for a moment that some other poor shmoe had caught this case. But, then he wouldn't have met Dec, and while part of him wished that hadn't happened, either, the other part wanted the day to hurry along so he'd have a chance to see the ex-SEAL again.

Yeah, he was fucked, in more ways than one.

****

Dec paced the short length of his living room, checking his watch for the millionth time. It still wasn't quite seven-thirty, the same way it hadn't been two seconds ago. He ignored his knee's protest that he'd already overtaxed it. His jangling nerves took precedence.

Pax lay on her dog bed by the couch, watching his movements with her usual diligence. She knew he was worked up, and while he hated causing her worry, if such a thing were truly possible for a dog to feel, there was no help for it. He'd tried sitting down and watching television. That effort had lasted about five seconds before he turned it off and jumped to his feet again.

His whole day had been off kilter, starting with his

avoiding the coffee shop. He didn't dare see Scott for fear of being pulled into a conversation he didn't want to have about Mother Cherry. No good would come of involving the boy in the morass Dec struggled in. Then Cindi had greeted him at the office with the news that while paying company bills online, she'd found that the last payment for the Place job had landed in the checking account. Not that Dec hadn't earned it, but somehow he felt as if he were being paid hush money or something. He was tempted to return it, and yet, that would have been an empty gesture. He'd done a job, and the fact that his employer turned out to be a creep and dead to boot didn't negate that fact.

He wondered what Ryan would think of it. Ryan, yeah that was really what had stressed Dec out during the long hours of sitting behind his desk. Despite busying himself with searches about Place, Mother Cherry, and stolen art, thoughts of the cop and the time they'd spent together kept racing through his mind. He'd be reading about some great recent heist and images of that hard body spread out for him would pop up. His eyes would lose focus, and he'd relive the feel of hot, rough skin under his greedy hands. Even though he could see every ridge and plane, he'd been like a blind man, dying to touch everything.

And Ryan had not only let him, he'd encouraged him, rising up in undulating waves with each caress. A soft moan would pass lips still moist and swollen from Dec's almost brutal kisses. Low words, almost whispers, egged him on.

Yes. There. Like that. Fuck yeah, just like that.

Strong legs gripped like a vice, forcing him closer, urging him to go faster and faster, making Dec chase down his own release with mounting desperation whether he wanted to or not.

"Shit." Dec almost doubled over as the memories hit him like the proverbial Mack truck. His cock punched up against his fly, and he groaned in frustration and misery. "God, I'm a fucking basket case." Pax cocked her head before laying it on her front paws. "I'm not telling you anything you don't know, huh, girl?"

The sound of the front door buzzer had him reeling around. He looked at his watch and saw that time had finally ticked by. With mounting excitement and trepidation, Dec strode over to the intercom and hit the talk button.

"Yeah?" He couldn't be sure it was Ryan, so he played dumb.

"It's Ryan."

The sound of the man's voice sent Dec's heart racing, and yep, palms were a little sweaty, too. He'd been on more missions than he could count when a SEAL, and never had he been this nervous. "Come on up." He hit the door release button, pulled open his door to the hall, and paced away.

He ran his palms down his thighs to dry them, embarrassed by his own reaction and hoping Ryan wouldn't notice. Footsteps had him turning and Pax rising from her bed. She padded over to his side, waiting and ready as always to assist him if needed. Even before Ryan's big frame entered the doorway, the dog let out a low, happy woof in greeting.

The cop's stern look morphed into a genuine smile, the kind that made him stunningly handsome even to Dec's jaded heart. Or at least he thought of himself that way. His quick heartbeat and fluttering stomach left him in some doubt as to whether he'd somehow turned into a teenage girl.

Ryan loosened his tie as he shut the door behind him. He kept his concentration on Pax first, bending down to give her a quick pat on the head. Then he snagged Dec with a lightening quick move that fused their lips for a quick and sloppy kiss that left Dec breathless. Being a SEAL meant Dec had equally fast reflexes, and yet, he'd done nothing to avoid the embrace.

Quite the contrary, once he found himself within Ryan's arms, he surrendered completely, lifting his arms to circle the guy and pull him in even closer. When they broke apart, they stood eyeing each other, breathing heavily.

"Jesus, what is wrong with me?" Ryan tried to pull back, but Dec wouldn't let go.

"I have no idea. Obviously, we're both idiots or something."

With a shake of his head, Ryan broke free and retreated a few feet. He rubbed the back of his neck, the gesture both one of irritation and fatigue. Dec had a sudden desire to chase that tiredness and stress away. A crazy thought given that in less than a half hour a hired boy would be coming over.

Ryan turned, and his face showed a hint of sadness as well. "I really need to show more self-control around you. Christ, I'm acting like a horny teenager in the middle of a murder investigation."

"If you're asking me to be the gatekeeper, here, you're shit out of luck. I'm no better. I guess I've been out of commission for too long. I don't seem to be able to resist the attraction." Dec shrugged. "Sorry."

Ryan held out his hand. "No. No need for you to apologize. I'm the one who should know better."

"That's bullshit." Because this conversation would get them exactly nowhere, and they needed to gear up for the real purpose of the night, Dec switched topics. "Would you like something to eat or drink?"

Ryan seemed surprised by the change but thankfully went with it. "Ah, no, thanks. I grabbed something on the way over." He looked at his watch. "The kid's coming at eight, right?"

"Right. So, how do you want to play it?"

"I figure I'll hang out in the bedroom until you establish that you're paying for sex, then pop out and take over."

Dec frowned. "You're not going to arrest him, are you?"

Ryan raised his eyebrows. "Seriously? What did you think I was going to do?"

"Question him," Dec bit out.

"That's what I am going to do. Down at the station." He sighed heavily. "Look, Dec, I'm not out to put the kid in jail, but I need leverage to get him to talk. And if he's underage, I've got to kick him over to the system. You know we handle sex trafficking different these days. Even if the guy's a legal adult, we recognize that he may be in the business under duress and in need of help, not punishment." Ryan took a step closer. "Please trust me on this."

Dec took a deep breath and let it out slowly. "I guess I don't have any choice." Whatever else he might have thought to say, the sound of the door buzzer stopped him. Both he and Ryan looked at the intercom.

"Shit, he's early."

"No problem. May as well get the show on the road." So saying, Ryan headed for the bedroom. Dec had left the door to it open, but Ryan tipped it shut enough to hide, yet open enough to hear.

Now that the real point of the night was upon him, Dec went into mission mode. His heartrate dropped, and his sweat dried up. With a steady finger, he pressed the buzzer, not even bothering to ask who was there. He opened the door to the hall and leaned against the doorjamb.

Within a few seconds, a slender young man came walking up the stairs and down the hall. Even at a distance, Dec could see he wore typical teenager clothes—ripped jeans molded tight to his body and a dark T-shirt with some kind of colorful design. The effect made him look really young, which, of course, was the whole point. When the kid spotted Dec waiting, he flashed a smile.

"Hi, I'm Jimmy," he said in a soft voice. He had small, black gauges in each ear and a lip ring. Dec bet his tongue was pierced, too.

He gave the kid a tight smile, trying not to freak him out, even though Dec suddenly felt way the fuck freaked out himself. He'd really waded into the deep end with this whole thing, and unlike his past missions, he didn't have something to blow up or someone to shoot. This was more in the way of a covert op, and those were so not his forte.

"Come on in," he said, stepping to one side.

The boy smiled again, broader this time, as he passed by Dec. He pulled up short, though, when he spied Pax standing just inside the apartment.

Dec followed him in and maneuvered him forward without actually touching him so that he could shut the door. He didn't want the kid rabbiting. "That's my service dog," he said to reassure the boy. "She won't hurt you."

Jimmy sidled away toward the galley kitchen. "Um, okay." His gaze flicked from Pax to Dec. "She's, ah, not going to, you know, join us, is she?" He licked his lips. "'Cause, that's, you know, extra." His voice went up at the end. God, the more he talked, the younger he seemed.

The substance of his question sunk in. Dec barked out a laugh in surprise and disgust. "No. No, she's not."

The boy's body slumped in obvious relief. "Okay, cool." He fluttered his lashes a bit at Dec. "So, what's on the agenda for tonight, Daddy?"

An admonishment not to call him that almost came out before he reminded himself he had a role to play. The sooner he got the kid to say enough to satisfy Ryan, the faster this journey he'd taken into bizarro-world would end. "Did Mother Cherry tell you anything?"

A coy look entered the pretty face. "She told me that you paid for me to keep you company for a couple of hours. That's all. That's all the service does, introduce us, you know?" The kid put his hands on his waist and cocked his narrow hips. "I'm into anything you'd like to do during those hours. Anything at all, Daddy."

Feeling slightly sick, Dec forced a predatory gleam into his eyes. "I like rough games, Jimmy. You know what I mean?"

"Sure, I get you. I'm into those games, too." He winked at Dec, but the bravado didn't meet the kid's eyes and fear lurked there.

Dec hardened his heart and forced the necessary words out of his mouth. "To be clear. I'm going to tie you up, beat you, and fuck you." Something from his internet searches earlier in the day popped into his head. "No safeword. I do what I want, and you take it whether you like it or not. Understand?"

Those lips got licked again, and a small shudder ran through the kid. "I understand," he confirmed in a low voice. "Whatever you want."

When the boy took a step toward him, Dec moved away. The last thing he wanted was physical contact with a guy who had to be too young, and even if he were legal, Dec still didn't want to be one of the guys to exploit him even in a small way.

"How much?" he asked flatly, determined to bring things to an end.

Jimmy's eyes narrowed. "Five hundred an hour, cash." His tone made it clear he expected Dec would know that already. Of course, a man used to buying such services would have assumed all cash at the same rate as the "legitimate" escort services.

Dec didn't get a chance to respond. As soon as the number came out of the boy's mouth, the bedroom door opened wide, and Ryan stepped out. Jimmy started and moved backward until his back hit the wall. With wide eyes, he looked back and forth between Dec and Ryan.

"Wait," he said in a high, stressed tone. "No one said anything about two of you." He swallowed hard enough for it to be heard. His gaze ping-ponged. "It's extra if there's two of you."

Ryan walked closer to him with slow steps, his hands held out in a reassuring gesture. "Take it easy, son."

Jimmy's breath came out in a harsh rush, but he straightened, as if standing his ground and trying not to show his fear. "With two, it's extra," he repeated more firmly.

Stopping a few feet from the boy, Ryan pulled out his badge and held it up. "It's not going to be even one, son," he said in a soothing tone.

The boy gaped at Ryan's badge for few seconds before crumpling to the floor. To Dec's utter horror, the kid began to cry. Dec glared at Ryan, a look totally wasted as the cop's attention remained focused on Jimmy, then he walked over and squatted down by the distraught boy.

"It's okay, Jimmy. No one's going to hurt you. You're not going to jail. Sergeant Jakes just wants to talk to you." He thought he heard a sigh of irritation from behind him. He ignored it.

A cold nose brushed against his hand, Pax trying to insert herself and be of help just as she'd been trained to do. Because he worried the kid wouldn't be able to appreciate her efforts, Dec signaled for her to back off. She huffed as if to say "good luck on your own" before doing as told.

Dec tried to put a hand on the boy's shoulder in comfort but pulled it back when Jimmy raised his head. Despite the tears streaming down his face, he glared up at Dec. "I won't go back. You can't make me. I'll kill myself first."

Whoa, what? Dec looked over his shoulder at Ryan. The cop shrugged. He'd put his badge away and had taken out his handcuffs. "Is that really necessary?"

"Yes, it's procedure. It's safer for me and him." He

stepped closer. "I need you to get up, son." With a nudge of his leg, he tried to get Dec out of the way.

Dec wanted to protest further, verbally and physically, but he trusted Ryan. Maybe he had no reason to, but he did nonetheless. So, he stood up and gave Ryan the room he needed to haul a non-compliant, yet non-resistant, Jimmy back on his feet and to turn him around to face the wall. With efficiency born from a lot of practice no doubt, the cop had the kid cuffed and frisked in less than thirty seconds. The boy kept crying softly with shoulders slumped.

"I'm not going back to them," he said in a quiet voice. "I'm not."

Although Dec didn't fully understand what the kid was talking about, he had an inkling. Regardless, he felt responsible. He moved to block the way out of his apartment and leaned into Jimmy's face.

"You won't have to. I promise you that. Whatever else happens, you won't go back."

"Dec," Ryan warned with exasperation.

Dec glared back at his sometime lover over the boy's head. "I mean it, Ryan."

"Okay, okay. He won't go back. Come on, kid, I have some questions for you."

Snatching up Pax's leash, Dec said, "I'm coming, too."

"No, you're not." Ryan took a moment to frown at him from the doorway.

"Yes, Ryan, I am."

They held a short, silent staring contest before the cop relented. "Fine, but you sit in the back with the kid."

"No problem." Dec figured with Pax sitting

between him and Jimmy, she might be able to help calm the boy down. It was going to be a hell of long night, but at least he felt as if he were doing something. Not just for the Place investigation, either. If he could help this kid get his life back on track, it would be something.

He held onto that hope and tried not to dwell on how easily he was getting his way with Ryan. Christ, he really was starting to think and act like a teenage girl. Pathetic, yet kind of thrilling as well. And who was he kidding? Both he and Ryan were totally becoming more involved. So much for keeping his distance.

****

The caffeine Ryan kept dumping into his system waved a white flag to his fatigue shortly after he delivered poor Cory Hayward, aka Jimmy, into an interview room. So he gave up trying and just kept putting one foot in front of another. He hoped the boy would be able to provide useful information about Place if only the hastily appointed lawyer would give him a chance to question the kid.

And somewhere in the back of his mind was always the knowledge that Dec sat in the visitors area by the front desk, waiting for God only knew what. The guy hadn't been particularly forthcoming. He'd only insisted he wasn't going anywhere and plunked his fine ass down on a plastic chair with his loyal dog by his side.

Damn, Ryan wished he didn't admire the hell out of the man's stick-to-it-ness.

He knocked perfunctorily before opening the door to the interview room. With a nod to the earnest Ms. Brown, who sat next to the kid, he entered and plunked a bottle of cola on the beat-up table. He was gratified that his trip to the vending machine paid off when the boy picked it up, unscrewed the cap, and took a long pull of the cold drink.

"Can we get started?" Ryan asked the lawyer.

"As long as we keep this interview short. It's already past eleven, and I need to get Cory settled for the night."

"Yes, ma'am," Ryan agreed, pulling out a chair and falling into it more than sitting.

Cory fiddled with his bottle cap. "I don't need to be housed with little kids. Just put me in county lock-up." His tears had dried up, replaced by a sneer that failed to hide his fear.

Ms. Brown put a gentle hand on the boy's arm. "You're not even sixteen yet, Cory. No one's putting you in with adults, let alone adult criminals."

The boy took another long swallow of cola. "I hate that name, and I wish those assholes who named me had never had my fingerprints taken. Fucking missing children project."

Brown gave Ryan a meaningful look. "Cory's been cataloging abuse from his family."

"They tied me to a fucking table and prayed over me while they beat me with a strap." Cory's voice caught a bit on the end before he set his lips in a thin, defiant line.

Ryan bit back his own anger. He'd heard this kind of story before. A child running away from abusive parents unable to accept his sexuality and ending up being abused by others. Poor kid hadn't stood a chance, easy prey for someone like Mother Cherry and Stanford Place.

"They're not getting their hands on you again," Ryan vowed, ignoring Brown's warning look. He might not have the power to decide this boy's fate within the system, but he'd be damned if he'd set a trap for the boy to send him to hell. He'd do everything he could to keep him from being sent back to his abusive family. Leaning forward, he rested his arms on his thighs and, in a calculated move, let his fatigue show through.

"I need your help, Jimmy." He deliberately used the name he thought the kid would, if not like, at least hate the least. "I'm trying to figure out who killed Stanford Place. I know," he added with a shake of his head. "The guy was a creep, but it's my job. Sometimes my job sucks. I'm sure you can relate." He gave the boy a rueful smile, letting him know that he understood how the runaway had been forced to grow up quick and earn a living anyway he could. "The thing is, I think you might be able to help me."

With a negligent seeming shrug, the boy said, "I don't know anything about his murder. I didn't do it," he added with a glare.

"I didn't think you did." Ryan took a deep breath and let it out slowly. "What do you think happened to Kenny?"

That got the boy's attention. He stiffened, sitting up straight. "I know he's dead, and that's all."

"Well, I'll tell you, I think he was killed."

A shudder ran through the thin frame. "Yeah, everyone thinks that." His gaze skittered away from Ryan, and he drained the bottle of cola in one long swallow.

"The question is, why? Who did he piss off, or what did he know?"

Cory/Jimmy slumped back in his chair. He shifted his gaze to Brown. "Can we go now? I'm beat."

To her credit, Brown didn't jump right up and pull the kid out. Instead, she looked at Ryan. "I think it would be helpful if you get to the point, Sergeant."

He nodded. "Fair enough. I know that Place hired Kenny the same way he did you, and I also know that Place had secrets. One theory on what happened to Kenny is that Place shared a secret with him that Place later regretted sharing." When Jimmy gave another negligent shrug, Ryan laid it all out. "Kenny had a reputation for shooting his mouth off. What did he learn about Place that he told you about? What secrets did he spill?"

Ryan kept his gaze steady on the boy, willing him to break down and tell all that he knew. The contest of wills only lasted a few seconds. In a new show of just how young he was, Jimmy's eyes filled up with tears again.

He swiped at them angrily and sniffed. "I thought he was a jerk, ya know? Kenny, I mean. Place was a fucking asshole."

Brown winced at the crude language but kept her mouth shut. She'd undoubtedly heard worse and was proving to be far more pragmatic than Ryan had expected.

"Kenny liked to brag about how great he was as an escort, how all the clients liked him." Jimmy made a sound that could have been construed as a laugh. "He actually liked the stuff that Place did to him. Got off on it." His thin frame shuddered again, and he tipped the empty bottle against his lips in a vain hope of there being any cola left. Ryan made a silent promise to buy another one as soon as they were done. "He should have been Place's favorite, except everyone knew Kenny was full of shit. Clients liked Joey best, including Place."

Ryan searched his memory for references to that name and came up empty. "Who's Joey?"

"Just another guy with the service. He rocks this like elven princess look with really pale hair and a face pretty enough to be on a girl. I mean like for real a girl." Jimmy rolled his eyes.

Scott Reilly. Had to be. Ryan made a mental note to ask Dec for more information about the kid. Andy might need to take another run at the boy, too. "So, what exactly did Kenny say about Place in particular?"

Jimmy bit his lower lip and stared at the empty bottle in his hand, as if it held the secrets of the ages. Finally, he sighed. "The old man had some kind of hidden room with stuff in it. Cool stuff, not just art, although there was that, too." He looked at Ryan. "Kenny said something about a mummified hand and Nazi stuff, which I don't think is cool, but Kenny did. Anyway, Place let him hang out there for a while."

Ryan tried not to show his excitement, even though this was exactly what he'd hoped Jimmy would say. "Did Place explain to Kenny why these things were hidden away?"

Jimmy gave a contemptuous look that pegged him as a teenager more than anything else could. "Because it was stuff he wasn't supposed to have. You know, stolen and shit."

"Place told him that specifically?"

"That's what Kenny said. He thought he was something special to be let in on the secret, like Place trusted him or something." The kid smirked. "Like that was a bright idea. Kenny couldn't wait to tell everyone."

"Everyone who, specifically?" All Ryan got was a shrug in response, and the boy's gaze skittered away. Okay, best not to push on that or he might clam up entirely. "Was there anything in particular Place was, you know, proud about, maybe?"

Jimmy considered the question for a few seconds before nodding. "He did say that Place had a big hard-on for one of the paintings. It was like huge and right smack in the middle of one wall, and the old dude had a chair to sit on and just, you know, stare at it."

Ryan's heartrate kicked up in a way no amount of caffeine could have produced that night. "Did Kenny describe it?"

Jimmy screwed up his face in thought. "Something about some biblical dudes in a boat getting the shit tossed out of them in a storm."

"Did he mention the name of the painting or who painted it?" Ryan had a hard time keeping his tone level. This was maybe the best break he could hope for in the case.

Jimmy shook his head. "Naw, like anyone cared. Sounds like a boring room to me." His face turned serious. "But a week later, Kenny disappeared, then the rumors started that he'd been found in the harbor. Mother Cherry said we should forget all about him and keep our mouths shut if we knew what was good for us." His lips quivered a bit. "You don't fuck with Mother, or she'll fuck you up good in return. We don't talk about Kenny anymore, and I'm done with this." He turned to Brown. "Can we go? I'm beat."

Brown gave him a sympathetic smile. "Yes, we can. You did very well here tonight, Jimmy. I'll take care of you now."

The kid didn't look convinced yet stood up when his lawyer did. Ryan stood as well and reached to retrieve the empty bottle Jimmy had left on the table. "Would you like another?"

"No, thanks." Jimmy sounded exhausted, and Ryan felt guilty about that.

"Well, I appreciate your help, Jimmy. I really do. And if you think of anything else Kenny said, please let Ms. Brown know so that I can talk to you again."

"I don't know anything more."

Ryan rather believed him on that point. "Okay. But, ah, please don't say anything to anyone about any of this. That's important. Understand?"

Jimmy gave him another one of those teenager looks, the kind that convey just how stupid you are. "Don't worry. I'm not interested in ending up in the harbor like Kenny."

"No one's going to hurt you," Brown was quick to reassure him.

Jimmy didn't look convinced about that, either, and Ryan couldn't blame him. In his relatively short life, Cory Hayward had learned just how much adults could let him down. Ryan was determined not to be one of them.

Chapter Ten

Dec played a game with himself while he waited for Ryan to re-emerge from the working part of the police station. It was called *how long can I go without looking at my watch?* So far, the longest he'd lasted had been about fifteen minutes. Fifteen agonizingly slow minutes. Never a patient man, he did really badly at the waiting and seeing part of any op. And while he knew he could have left hours ago, he just couldn't do it. He needed to make sure Jimmy was being cared for, and in his more honest moments, he hoped Ryan would let him in on any info he'd learned from the boy. Not that the cop would see it as any of Dec's business and would undoubtedly be breaking a bunch of police rules for sharing. Still. He also wanted to be sure the guy wouldn't feel any fall-out from Dec's legally questionable tactic of hiring Jimmy to begin with.

Really, though, the overriding reason he'd stayed put in the ass-numbing chair was to simply see Ryan again. Other than taking Pax out a couple of times to do what dogs do, he'd stuck to the waiting room, his eyes peeled to the front desk when they weren't glancing at the clock above the desk sergeant's head. Dec hadn't been able to make his feet shuffle for the door and back to his apartment without at least saying goodnight to Ryan. The need to do so had become far stronger than any other, including solving Place's murder or even getting his rocks off.

When the inner door opened and a disheveled Ryan sauntered through, Dec got a funny feeling down low. Not a twitching of his cock, but a quivering of his belly followed by a warmth that quickly spread throughout his body. Man, he was so screwed. In a matter of a few days, he'd gone from being a cloistered monk to an adolescent fan girl.

Beside him, Pax let out a soft whine.

He patted her head as he stood up. "I know how you feel, girl."

It might have been wishful thinking on his part, but he could swear Ryan's dead man walking look morphed into something more hopeful, like he was glad to see that Dec had waited for him. Nah, couldn't be.

Except Ryan walked right up to Dec and gave him a tired smile. He also ruffled Pax's head, and that obvious respect and caring for Dec's dog never failed to get to him in the best possible way. "You didn't have to wait."

"Yeah, I did."

Ryan frowned a bit. "I suppose you're worried about Cory. Jimmy," he amended.

"I am."

"He's fine. We lawyered him up, and she's taking him now to the dorm where social services keeps teenage boys. She's going to advocate that he be put in foster care. Thank God he's from the western part of Massachusetts and not some other state. It will make it easier to keep him out of the hands of his abusive parents."

Dec swore under his breath. "How old is he?"

"Fifteen."

201

"Shit." Dec shook his head. "I wish Place were still alive so I could pound his face into the ground."

Ryan stifled a yawn. "Yeah, I know. Sometimes, my vics are real assholes. I still have a job to do, though." He raised his hand the moment Dec opened his mouth. "I'm not telling you any of the information the kid gave me. You'll have to be satisfied to know that he did give me a good lead." He paused. "Your tactics suck, but thanks anyway. Finding Cory for me turned out to be very helpful, and I'm grateful."

Dec was disappointed that he wouldn't get anything out of Ryan although not surprised. He'd pushed the limits with the guy as it was. Time to stand down, at least where Ryan was concerned.

"I'm glad it turned out to be useful to you, and I understand that you can't let me in on what you learned." He glanced away, suddenly shy to be so physically close to the other man, given how raw his emotions were. He still felt compelled to spill his guts. "I didn't stick around only because I was worried about the kid."

Ryan's eyebrows shot up. "Oh, yeah?"

"Yeah." He leaned forward. "Would the desk sergeant's head explode if I kissed you?"

The cop's eyes went round. "I don't know," he murmured. "I've always been out, so…" His gaze narrowed in on Dec's lips. Ryan's tired eyes closed as Dec pressed forward.

He kept the kiss light and as sweet as anything could get between two alpha male types. No tongue and just a hint of teeth scraping Ryan's lower lip when he pulled back. He heaved a big sigh and stepped back, feeling more relaxed than he had for the last few hours.

Ryan stared back at him with a silly smile on his face. "See, no fireworks unless you count the ones threatening to erupt from my balls."

Yeah, Dec could relate. His dick strained in his pants. He could see the same problem easily inside Ryan's dress slacks. Figuring that prominently displayed hard-ons were more than any of the cops around could handle, he decided it was time to go.

He bent down and grabbed Pax's trailing leash. She stood up happily, just as bored and tired as he, no doubt. "I guess I should be going."

Ryan rolled his eyes. "Seriously? You think I'm going to just send you out to find a taxi or take the T?"

"It's late, Ryan. I'm not going to ask you to drive me home. You look dead on your feet."

"Right back at you, babe. So, let's stop yapping about it." With that, he grabbed Dec's right arm and started yanking him over to the front door.

"Ryan, this is stupid." Dec's protest was kind of weak even to his own ears.

"I'm too tired to argue with you, Dec, and if you think that SEALs have some kind of corner on the stubborn market, then you don't know cops."

Because he wanted to have even a little more time with the guy, Dec gave up his protests and allowed Ryan to lead him to the car. They drove silently through the city, something that was becoming a habit with them. There was a parking spot right in front of Dec's building, its own kind of miracle, and he chose to take it as a sign.

Unbuckling his belt, he turned to Ryan. "Are you hungry?"

Ryan rolled his head to look at Dec. "Am I

supposed to say something clever like do you mean for your cock?"

Dec chuckled. "No, I mean like for a ham sandwich. I'm starving, and I have cold cuts, bread, condiments, you know, food. I figured you could use a bite to eat before going home."

Ryan stared at him a few seconds before switching off the engine. "I could eat."

Dec tried not to get too excited at the idea of Ryan coming home with him. He'd meant what he said. It was to feed the poor guy. It had been hours since either of them had eaten dinner, and he knew trying to get to sleep on an empty stomach sucked.

As soon as he let them all in, he headed to his tiny kitchen, gesturing toward the couch as he did so. "Make yourself at home while I make us sandwiches."

He tossed Pax a treat first and made sure her water bowl was filled with fresh water.

He tried not to focus too much on how Ryan peeled off his suit coat, tie, and holster mere feet away while Dec pulled out cold cuts, mustard, mayo, and seltzer water from the fridge.

"Do you want a glass of lime-flavored seltzer or plain tap? I have beer, too, of course." He unloaded the items in his hands onto the counter and turned around. He nearly choked on his tongue in surprise.

Ryan had unbuttoned his shirt and pulled it from his waistband. Dec had no trouble seeing the man's broad, muscled chest because Ryan had also managed to sneak up on Dec and stood barely a hand's width away from him.

"Jesus, you're quiet and quick," he said in a strangled voice.

Ryan smirked right before he pulled Dec into a far steamier version of the kiss Dec had given him at the station. He attacked Dec's mouth with tongue and teeth, invading the space and conquering every corner. Ryan's fingers gripped Dec's shoulders with brutal strength, shoving him against the counter. With a grunt, Dec returned the hold, sliding his hands down Ryan's back. He made sure to stroke every muscle and count every ridge before landing and curling his palms around Ryan's tight ass.

By mutual effort, their bodies collided, cocks grinding with maddening inefficiency. Dec humped into Ryan in an effort to jerk them both off. There was too much cloth between them. Ryan pulled back from the kiss only to yank Dec's shirt open in a telenovela kind of move that sent buttons flying onto the floor.

Dec gasped and laughed, but only for a moment. When Ryan's mouth attacked the first of his nipples, he barked out a "fuck" before closing his eyes and throwing his head back hard enough to smack into the cabinets.

He didn't care. Rational thought flew out of his head under the assault of Ryan's lips sucking. A quick bite had him swearing even more. He bucked his hips against Ryan's, trying to chase that elusive climax. He tightened his fingers, digging his nails into Ryan's flesh. His reward was a quick laving of first one nipple, then the next.

"Jesus, Ryan," he panted. "I need…"

Ryan's breath tickled his wet pec. "What, baby? What do you need?"

Dec could only moan in response and buck again. Ryan's hand snaked between them, pushing Dec away but then unsnapping his jeans and lowering the zipper.

"Fuck, yeah," Dec moaned again when Ryan took Dec's dick into a tight fist and squeezed. He growled with disappointment when Ryan let him go again.

Ryan chuckled. "Easy, baby. I'm going to take care of you."

The next time Ryan took Dec in hand, he held his own cock, as well. A little spit and pre-cum was all the lube they had, yet Ryan used them to the best advantage as he ground the two dicks together. His fist moved up and down both shafts, squeezing the heads together on the upstroke. He trapped both rods and his hand between the two bodies, pressing into Dec as tightly as he could. His mouth found Dec's stretched neck, where he nibbled and sucked.

Dec panted like a woman in labor as the climax built. He pawed at Ryan's ass, helping to keep them melded together. He undulated his hips in time to Ryan's strokes. The orgasm shimmied up from his balls and pulsed through his cock. Damn, but he could feel an answering wave from Ryan's dick.

They came together with muted shouts. Ryan worked their cocks franticly while he humped Dec against the counter. Warm cum spurted onto Dec's stomach, where Ryan's knuckles coated it across the skin. Dec felt wickedly satisfied at the idea of their cum mingling all over him and Ryan both. By the time their dicks stilled, they both heaved from the effort.

Ryan pulled his hand free and wrapped his arms around Dec's waist. He rested his head on Dec's shoulder, his warm breath tickling the crook of Dec's neck. Dec kept his hands on Ryan's ass because it felt damn good while they came back down to Earth.

Finally, with a chuckle, Ryan pulled back and looked up at Dec.

"I don't think I'm hungry anymore." He grinned sheepishly, and Dec returned the expression. Then Ryan's gaze dropped. "I guess I should be going."

Guilt ate at Dec. Ryan shouldn't have to go. The guy was dead tired. He really shouldn't be even driving. What kind of a selfish prick would Dec be to send Ryan out just because of Dec's fucked-upedness? When Ryan started to move away, Dec held him in place.

"Don't go." His voice came out too soft and unsure, so he cleared his throat and said more forcefully, "Stay the night."

Ryan looked at him skeptically.

"Please."

"You don't do overnights," Ryan reminded him.

"Yeah, well, I'm trying to work on my, ah, issues." He tried for a reassuring smile. "Please stay. I want you to. In fact," he added with a little shove. "Go wash up and get into bed. I'll bring you a sandwich."

Ryan furrowed his brows. "Are you sure?"

"Absolutely. Go." Dec turned to grab some paper towels and do a quick clean-up of himself. He couldn't help smiling when he heard Ryan head into the bedroom.

By the time Dec joined Ryan, a plate stacked with two big, thick sandwiches and the bottle of seltzer, which he figured they could take turns chugging, Ryan was sprawled gloriously naked on his bed. Fast asleep.

Dec quietly put the plate and bottle on the nightstand and stripped off his clothes. He climbed onto the bed beside Ryan and looked down at him. Relaxed, Ryan's face really was a thing of beauty. Feeling like a voyeur and not caring a bit, Dec grabbed one of the sandwiches and watched his lover sleep.

He could do this. He just had to stay awake for the night. No big deal, he'd done it a million times. He'd lie down, pull Ryan into his arms, and watch over him, the knowledge that the other man slept peacefully plenty good enough for Dec. It would also give him lots of time to obsess over how, in just a few days, he'd not only woken up sexually, he'd started to get emotionally involved.

God help him, and God help Ryan, too.

****

"Report! God damn it, Carter, what's the status? Who's been hit? Fuck, I can't hear you!"

Ryan bolted upright, torn from a deep sleep by the shouting and flailing beside him. His fuzzy brain took a few seconds to recognize his surroundings and realize he was in Dec's bed, and that the commotion was coming from his lover. He twisted onto his knees, tossing aside the blanket covering them both. He knew instinctively to keep out of the former SEALs reach. Caught up in a nightmare as the guy obviously was, he might mistake Ryan for an enemy. Ryan's confidence in his fighting ability did not extend to coming out on the winning side of a struggle with an elite fighter.

"Dec," he called softly. Shit, he didn't want to startle the guy awake, yet couldn't sit idly by while a nightmare tortured Dec.

A flash of two bright eyes streaking toward the bed startled Ryan until he realized it was Pax. The dog leaped onto the bed and Dec. She covered her master with her body and began licking his face, as if it were a doggy ice cream cone. Ryan figured the extra weight on

Dec would increase the man's panic. Instead, he almost instantly started to calm down. In the darkness of the room, Ryan could make out Dec's arms encircling the dog, hugging her tight as his words trailed off into silence.

For long seconds, all that could be heard was the heavy breathing of all three of them. Ryan ran his hand across the top of his head in an effort to calm himself. He felt helpless in the wake of Dec's nightmare. He wanted to help but didn't know what to do. Thank God, Pax did. He could understand now more than ever why a service dog would be invaluable to someone suffering from PTSD. Not knowing what he should or could do, he knelt on one side of the bed, willing his heartrate to subside and dithering over what his next move should be.

Dec solved the problem for him. "Ryan?"

"Yeah, right here, buddy."

"Fuck." The swear held no real heat, more like regret.

Dec must have given Pax some kind of silent command because she jumped off the bed and disappeared from sight. Lying down, probably. Dec switched on the lamp on his nightstand.

Ryan blinked at the sudden light and squinted down at Dec. "Are you okay?" Man, what a lame question, yet nothing else came to mind.

"Yeah." Dec wearily pulled himself up to a sitting position, knees bent, arms dangling on top of them, and with his head hanging down. He looked so lost Ryan really wanted to reach over and pull him into his arms. He sensed, though, that Dec wouldn't be receptive to any show of pity, so he kept his hands to himself.

"Sorry. I hope I didn't scare too much crap out of you."

"Seriously? You're apologizing for having a nightmare?" Ryan tried to keep his tone light.

Dec turned haunted eyes—there was no other word to adequately describe them—on Ryan. "Yeah, I am." He swallowed hard. "I'm just glad I didn't hurt you."

Ryan shook his head. "There was no chance of that." When Dec simply stared him down, Ryan got more real. "Okay, there was a little chance of that. I mean it did occur to me that you could do some damage if you mistook me for a terrorist or something. I was trying to figure out what to do when Pax came to save the day."

Dec smiled ruefully. "Yeah, she's great that way. I don't know what I would do without her." He swiped a palm across his brow and stared at a point across the room. "This is why I don't do sleepovers anymore. Not that there have been any opportunities other than you these last couple of years."

Ah, Jesus. Now he felt bad for all of the crappy things he'd thought about Dec each time they fucked and Dec pushed him away. It hadn't been indifference. It had been fear and embarrassment. "Christ, Dec, why didn't you just tell me?"

The guy turned his skeptical eyes on Ryan. "Why didn't I tell the first man in two years that I was attracted to that I'm a basket case who wakes up screaming like a girl?"

Blowing out a breath, Ryan shifted to sit cross-legged on the bed, realizing for the first time they were both naked. He had a vague memory of plopping down on the bed after cleaning up, waiting for a sandwich. He could see one sitting on a plate on the nightstand beside

Dec. Obviously, Dec had found him fast asleep and had let him be. It must have been a hard thing for Dec to decide to let Ryan sleep over, and the fact that he had gave Ryan hope for the first time that what was happening between the two of them went both ways and was far more than just an occasional fuck.

"First of all," he began, levelling his gaze at Dec. "That's sexist. Second, I appreciate how you let me sleep here instead of kicking me out again. That took some guts and, I hope, some trust on your part."

Dec looked away and placed his chin on his knee. "I couldn't bear the idea of making you get back in your car. You were so exhausted, and I figured I could stay awake all night."

Ryan gave him the fisheye. "You were going to stay awake all night, and what…stare at me?"

The first real ghost of a smile crossed Dec's lips. "You're pretty adorable when you're asleep."

"Adorable?" Ryan sputtered. "I am many things, but not that."

Dec cocked his head in Ryan's direction. "I beg to differ. When you smile and when you're asleep, you go from hot to beautiful."

Ryan tried not to be so pleased with the simple compliment, but it made him ridiculously happy. He dipped his head shyly—so not like him. "Now I know you're not right in the head." The import of his careless words hit him like an anvil. He shot his head up. "Shit, I'm sorry. That was a dick thing to say."

To Ryan's surprise, Dec merely laughed. "No, it was the perfect thing to say. I hate having people tip-toe around me like I'm made of glass."

They lapsed into silence with that comment, Ryan

feeling more relaxed, yet worried still about Dec's emotional state. Even though he seemed calm, surely that kind of violent nightmare couldn't be left unaddressed. They might not be in a relationship, they might never be in one, but Ryan wanted to help. He'd been tamping down his burgeoning feelings for Dec for fear of getting hurt again. Now, with Dec's own vulnerability out in the open, Ryan couldn't pretend that he didn't care about the guy.

He cleared his throat. "Um, do you want to, you know, talk about it?"

Dec narrowed his eyes. "Talk about what...my freak-out?"

Ryan frowned. "You act as if having a nightmare is something to be ashamed about. I know you SEALs like to think you're supermen, but come on."

Dec flopped back onto his pillow, keeping his knees up in a provocative pose. Ryan reminded his cock that his lover needed a sympathetic ear, nothing else at the moment.

"You know what the most critical characteristic of a SEAL is, the thing that most indicates whether someone will survive BUDs training?" When Ryan shook his head, Dec answered his own question. "Stubbornness. We never give up."

"I expect that's a good trait to have during a mission."

Dec stared up at the ceiling. "It is, except when the mission is over, and it's gone to shit, and your career is over because you're never going to fully recover from your wounds, you still don't want to give up."

Ryan shifted his body again, lying on his side to face Dec. He propped his head on his hand. "Accepting reality isn't giving up."

Dec heaved a big sigh. "What part of stubborn didn't you get?" He turned his head to Ryan and gave him a tired smile. "It may not be sensible or realistic, but I still can't accept that my last mission didn't just leave me disabled. It left two guys dead, one a good friend and one a kid on only his third mission." He looked away again. "Shit."

Ryan tamped down his sympathy. Dec didn't need sentiment so much as a non-judgmental ear. "Was that Carter?"

"What?" Dec chuckled. "No. Carter was a member of the Cultural Support Team, women trained to accompany us on missions so that we could access village women. It was a great program, really helped. It just added an extra layer of worry because they weren't part of the Teams, not really. They hadn't gone through BUDs, been trained and tested as a SEAL. I worried about her more than the others."

Dec chuckled again. "Talk about sexism." He stared at Ryan again, and Ryan worked to stay focused on Dec's words and not how easy it was to lose himself in those blue eyes. "There I am, writhing on the ground, trying to get a status report when I can't hear a damn thing, and insurgents start firing on us. The woman I was worried about, the one with less training than I had, returned fire while she dragged me behind a rock for cover. I owe her my life."

Ryan wanted to ask the guy if he knew Carter's full name and address so Ryan could send her flowers of thanks or something. He didn't dare say anything more, however, not wanting to stop the flow of Dec's mental purging.

It didn't matter, he was done anyway. "I'm sorry I woke you. You should probably go on home."

The dismissal rankled Ryan even though he sensed it was done out of insecurity. He pushed up to see the clock on the bedside table. "It's only a little after five. We can go back to sleep for another couple of hours, and I'll still have time to jump home for a change of clothes before I need to be back in the office."

Dec moaned and slid his legs out straight. "Sorry. I can't get back to sleep after one of these nightmare induced panic attacks. You're welcome to stay, of course. I just, um, figured you'd like to leave."

"Fuck that, and fuck you for thinking it," Ryan replied without too much heat, although he was a little miffed that Dec would think he'd run at the first sign of trouble. "You're not the only one in this bed carrying around baggage, you know."

He scratched the back of his neck while considering how much of his own backstory to dump on the guy. Compared to what Dec had just told him, Ryan's broken heart seemed pretty penny-ante.

"I'll admit my feelings were kind of hurt the first time we fucked and you booted me out right after. That was mostly ego because it felt like I hadn't made a good enough impression on you."

"That wasn't it," Dec jumped in. "Fucking you was sweet. I was too afraid of letting you stay and, well, experiencing what you just did."

"I get that now. The thing is, I wasn't looking for anything more than a one-night stand myself. I've been keeping it cool dating-wise since my last boyfriend broke up with me last year." Ryan bared his teeth with the memory. "He's a cop, which was my first mistake.

Gave me the old 'it's me, not you' speech. I wanted to punch him in the face, but intimate partner violence is wrong, so I settled for encasing my heart in ice instead."

When Dec simply raised his eyebrows, Ryan sighed. "I know, I'm being really melodramatic, but it really hurt. I had started to think in terms of rings and weddings, and, shit, forever." He shook his head. "I fell hard."

Dec reached over and placed his hand on Ryan's knee. The simple gesture, the subtle warmth of the touch made Ryan's heart do a slow roll. Damn, he was getting in deep too fast—again. The thought should have scared the shit out of him, especially in light of the story he told about Flynn the Fucker. It didn't. He wasn't even sure Flynn deserved his alliterative title anymore. Or, more to the point, his anger at the guy had started to wane all of a sudden.

"I guess we both have reasons why being involved with each other is a bad idea, even putting aside the murder investigation," Dec observed.

"Yup. And yet, we still seem to end up in bed together. We're going to have to figure out what to do about that. What we want to do about it." Even as he said the words, his heart was already trying to weigh in. He ruthlessly smacked it down. No good decisions were made at this time of day. "We should probably get some more sleep first."

Dec grimaced. "Sorry. That doesn't work for me. Not after a nightmare. I've tried, believe me."

"Maybe you just haven't tried the right remedy to fall back to sleep," Ryan observed with a sly grin. Before Dec could process what he meant, Ryan slid and rolled himself on top of Dec's lower half. He kneed open the other man's legs enough to fit between them.

Dec eyed him through heavy lids. "What are you doing?"

"This." Ryan licked a stripe down the length of Dec's flaccid cock. The reaction was immediate. The rod filled with blood in response, hardening right in front of Ryan's eyes. He licked it some more, encouraging it to grow and sucking it into his mouth when it did. Dec moaned, and his legs moved restlessly against Ryan's body.

There was no more talking after that. Ryan swallowed the dick down, laving the hardness and biting just a bit. He worked the shaft vigorously, intent on bringing Dec up and over quickly, hoping the quickness and intensity would wring the guy out so that he could go back to sleep. To that end, he worked his finger into his mouth alongside the cock to wet it. Then he rubbed it against Dec's hole. Dec groaned and bucked his hips in encouragement. The moment Ryan slipped the finger past the tight ring, he crooked it to find and stroke Dec's prostate.

God, the guy was so tight. He clenched against Ryan's finger, milking it with the same devotion that Ryan did Dec's dick. Ryan couldn't help but wonder how sweet it would be to replace his finger with his cock. Just the thought of fucking Dec made him hard. He humped the bed, sending perfect sparks of pleasure through his groin. It wouldn't be enough to come and that was fine. This was all about relaxing Dec.

The cock in Ryan's mouth swelled and twitched, the only warning he had before Dec spilled cum down his throat. He swallowed it all like the good boy he was.

When the spasms stopped, he let the softening rod plop out while he removed his finger with a slow drag. Pushing up, he gathered a slightly resistant Dec in his arms.

"Your turn," Dec said sleepily into Ryan's chest.

"Later, baby. Sleep now."

And amazingly, Dec did. With the rhythm of his lover's breathing overlaying Ryan's heartbeat, he closed his eyes and willed himself back to sleep.

Chapter Eleven

The moment Dec realized he was actually whistling on his way to work, he mentally slapped himself. One night of awesome sex and heart-to-heart confessions did not a relationship make. He was way too happy given the circumstances. It was as if his physical and emotional dam had broken and now he couldn't stop the rush of his needs from pouring out and threatening to swamp him and Ryan both.

He needed to talk to Felix in the near future to help him cope with his burgeoning social life. If he didn't stop to consider what he was doing, he ran the risk of going to yet another extreme. Ryan deserved better. The last thing Dec wanted to do was be another heartbreak to the cop. Not that he believed Ryan loved him or anything. That would be absurd given how short a time they'd known each other.

Too bad Dec's heart wasn't buying that logic.

When he arrived at work, he found Cindi and Mal sitting behind Cindi's desk, giggling over something on her computer. They took a second to greet Dec before returning to whatever held their interest. He gave them their space, liking that his staff, small as it was, got along so well.

Grabbing a mug of coffee, he continued into his private office and settled behind his desk. He didn't bother to shut the door, enjoying the company. There wasn't anything for him to do anyway. His first and only client was dead, and so far there were no other takers.

No more than a minute passed before his team joined him with a perfunctory knock on the doorjamb.

"Mind if we come in, boss?" Cindi asked.

Dec waved them in. "Sure, not like I'm busy or anything." Cindi and Mal took a visitor seat each, their own coffee in hand, and stared at him expectantly. "What?"

"We're hoping for an update on the Place murder," Mal said.

Dec rolled his eyes. "I don't have much to tell." He filled them in on how the night had gone with Jimmy.

Cindi's eyes got dewy. "That poor boy. They won't send him back to his awful family, will they?"

"Ryan doesn't think so." He inwardly winced at the casual reference to the cop.

Cindi and Mal shared a look before she said, "Ryan, huh? He's hot. So is his partner."

Dec narrowed his eyes. "Your point being."

Cindi merely shrugged and took a sip of her coffee.

"So, what's our next move?" Mal asked.

Dec leaned his head back on his chair and stared up at the ceiling. "I don't know. I came close to fucking things up going half-cocked after the escort service. A private detective I am not, it seems."

"We can't just give up," Mal scoffed. "Our reputations are on the line."

"Such as they are," Dec intoned. He shoved aside any irritation over Mal's insistence, too. The guy was right, after all, and wasn't saying anything Dec hadn't said to himself a thousand times over.

"I've been mulling our next move this entire morning." He didn't qualify his statement by adding that he hadn't been thinking of the case or anything else really as he'd fucked Ryan in the shower. "I think the key to the murder lies in the secret stash of art. Whatever else might have been going on in Place's life that might have led to murder, it doesn't change the fact that something was stolen. Whoever took it must have wanted one specific thing, otherwise more would have been taken. At least, that's the theory I think the police are working on and it makes sense."

Cindi piped in. "Yeah, but how does that help us? What do we know about stolen art?"

That's what he'd been turning over in his mind for the last hour or so. "The one thing I know is that people buy it. There's a market for it, meaning supply and demand. Where there's a market for something, there has to be some kind of advertisement. How else do buyers and sellers connect?"

Mal sat up straighter, a gleam in his eye. "Oh, man, you're talking about the darknet."

Cindi turned and blinked at him. "The what?"

"The part of the internet that most of the world doesn't see. We all, upstanding citizens, connect on the clearnet. We search and interact on public websites. The darknet can only be accessed using certain software and connections. That's where people meet up cyber-wise to do mostly illegal things."

Cindi wrinkled her nose. "That doesn't sound like a very nice place."

"It isn't," Dec replied. "But if we want to know where and how we can find illegal artwork for sale in the Boston area, it's where we'll learn it." He looked at

Mal. "Can you access that info?"

Mal held up his hands. "Not me, man. That stuff can be nasty, like child pornography, murder for hire, drugs. I don't play that way."

Shit, of course not. Mal was a good kid. He wouldn't so much as download a pirated copy of a song. A thought occurred to Dec. "I bet you might know someone, though. All those brilliant minds at MIT, surely someone there likes the challenge of cracking. Not black hats, necessarily…"

While Mal squirmed a bit in his chair, Cindi refocused on Dec. "Black hats?"

"People who hack, or rather crack, computers for bad reasons. Sometimes talented people like to try their hand at it just for the thrill of seeing if they can succeed. Not because they intend to do something bad."

Cindi turned back to Mal. "But you do the opposite. You set up security systems so they're secure and test them to make sure they are." She smiled brightly. "Does that make you a white hat?"

Mal smiled sheepishly in return. "Yes, actually it does." His smile died, and he looked at Dec. "I might know someone who can help us."

Dec tried not to show too much enthusiasm, sensing Mal had conflicted feelings about maybe ratting out a friend. This was exactly what he hoped for. "You know I'm not trying to get anyone in trouble. I just want to scope out any underground art auctions."

"What do we do if we find one that's being held?" Cindi asked.

Dec grimaced. "That's the tricky part. I want to try to go and see if I can figure out who might have had a hand in any of the art Place collected."

Mal sipped at his coffee and shook his head. "Even if my guy is willing to help and we get info on it, no way they'll let just anyone get in there. It will be by invitation only and security will be tight. It's a long-shot, Dec."

"I know." He concentrated on his own coffee, marshalling his thoughts about how to approach the next phase of his almost plan. "I thought maybe you could lay down a false background I.D. on me to make me look like a player."

Instead of glaring back in horror at the idea, Mal's lips curled up in a smile. "Really?" His tone contained a whole lot of excitement. "I could do that. Easy."

Cindi, however, frowned. "I don't get it. Wouldn't that be in the black hat category?"

Mal shrugged. "Naw. Given the reason behind it, I figure it's more in the gray hat area."

"Is that really a thing?"

"It is now," Mal replied with a wiggle of his brows.

Guilt pricked at Dec. "Seriously, Mal. Please don't do this if it makes you uncomfortable."

"Nah, I'm good. We need to catch these fuckers, and it would mean coloring outside the lines just a little bit."

"Sergeant Hottie won't like it," Cindi reminded them.

Dec groaned. "Tell me about it. I'll handle him."

Even as he said the words, he cringed inwardly at the unintended double-entendre. Not that his cock minded in the least. Of course, he had no intention of telling Ryan anything about this plan, which made him feel even guiltier.

"One thing, boss," Cindi said. "Assuming we find

this illegal art auction, don't you think you and Pax might stand out in a bad way?"

"Hmm." He hadn't really considered that.

"Seems to me that you'd do better with a woman for extra cover. You know Mr. and Mrs. We're Too Rich To Give A Fuck About The Law. Who would suspect them?"

Dec eyed her with mounting trepidation. "Oh, no. No," he repeated with emphasis. "I'm not dragging you into something that might prove dangerous."

A mutinous look settled on Cindi's kewpie doll face. "So what, I'm just good enough to make coffee and take your calls? You don't trust a *girl* to hold her own?"

"Jesus Christ," he muttered into his coffee cup.

"She's right, boss," Mal interjected. "If my friend finds an auction, and if I manage to create a convincing profile, it would be much more believable if you've got a woman with you. No offense, but you look like a narc."

Cindi beamed at her co-worker and friend. Dec knew he was spitting into the wind on this with the two of them forming a united front. Shit, they were also right.

"Okay, fine." He pointed a finger at Mal. "First, you see if this friend of yours can help us. Then we'll see about the rest."

And eventually if this crazy idea actually worked, he'd have to confess yet one more sin to Ryan. How many more chances would the cop give him? When he thought about giving up his investigation and leaving it to Ryan, he just couldn't do it. This might be his only chance to save his business, and not even his growing affection for the cop could force him to give up.

****

Ryan hurried into the observation room, intent on hearing the interview of the infamous Mother Cherry. Andy had informed him the moment he arrived at his desk that the sex crimes unit had already raided the escort service and had hauled its owner in for questioning. His feet stumbled to a halt, and his heart did a quick skip when he saw that the arresting officer was none other than Flynn the Fucker.

Of course. He should have anticipated that. Flynn had gone into sex crimes the minute he got a chance. The guy had a crusade going in that area for reasons Ryan had never been able to tease out of him. That had been his first clue that his relationship with the man was doomed. Flynn had never been inclined to bare his soul to Ryan.

Not like Dec. That little confab they'd shared in the wee hours had been a real eye-opener. Knowing intellectually that the former SEAL suffered from PTSD and hearing it from his own lips made all the difference. That he'd let Ryan stay and had been willing to share some of his secrets did more to propel them into relationship land in just a few days than anything that had happened in the year that Ryan had spent dating Flynn. Just Flynn. Definitely time to drop the Fucker part.

As he stood by the observation window and took a good look at his ex-lover, Ryan realized it didn't hurt nearly so much as he would have expected. He could move on. The fact he had Dec in his life now—maybe—helped. But he could also be man enough to face the fact that he'd always been way more into Flynn than the man had been into him.

The guy still caught Ryan's eye. Hard not to appreciate the grace and beauty of the man. He'd always put Ryan in mind of a great cat, all sleek and silent as he circled his prey. Not as tall as Ryan, yet lean and sexy, he rocked that whole black Irish look with dark hair and vivid blue eyes. Ryan let himself have one more second of remembering how wonderful it was to get lost in them, then he let the past go and concentrated on the here and now.

The ridiculously named Mother Cherry sat on a hard interview chair, bright red hair frizzled and sticking out every which way. The make-up had started to run with the sweat on the perp's face, and beady eyes tracked Flynn's every movement. Neither of them said anything for long seconds.

Leaning against the wall, Ryan sipped at his coffee and waited. He knew the drill. Flynn could string along someone in interview all day. The man had the patience of Job.

"You have no basis for holding me here. I run a perfectly respectable business." Cherry huffed and made a show of looking away from Flynn.

Flynn stopped his pacing and folded his arms. "We both know that's a big, fat lie, Lyle."

At the use of his undoubtedly real name, Cherry's mouth flatlined and fire shot from his eyeballs. "Given that you've seized my records, illegally I might add, you'll see that my company arranges for legitimate escort services."

Flynn sighed and dropped his arms to his side. He took a step toward the table where Cherry sat. The perp flinched with whatever he saw in the cop's eyes. Ryan chuckled under his breath. He hated pedophiles and pimps and loved the way Flynn could cut them to ribbons.

"What I'll find is what I already know. You provided boys, some underage, all desperate, to wealthy men with no moral compasses whatsoever."

Cherry's—or rather Lyle's—double chin quivered with indignation. "Now, that's a lie. All of my boys are of legal age." He shrugged. "Well, I suppose it's possible that some of them lied to me about that. If so, I didn't know. Twinks excel at looking deceptively young. It's part of their charm. And if any of those scamps had side deals with their clients, well…" The perp shrugged again.

If Ryan had been in that room, he would have been sorely tempted to knock that smug look off the guy's face. That's why he worked homicide now. Flynn had always been able to keep it cool. Un-fucking-flappable. You had to be in order to bring down scum like Lyle Cherry. Or Cherry Lyle. Whatever.

Flynn shook his head, his lips curling in a derisive smile. "Seriously, Lyle. I got a warrant to search your office, your computer, your home, and to arrest you. You think I don't have enough to put you away already?" Leaning even more forward, he slapped his palms onto the table. "You peddle young boys to old pervs, and one of those kids ended up dead."

A look of fear crossed Lyle's face. "I don't know what you're talking about." His chin quivered once more, and sweat ran rivulets down his cheeks.

Flynn pulled back and grabbed up a folder sitting on the table. He pulled out and held up a photo. Ryan didn't need to see it to know whose picture it was.

"I understand this poor kid went by Kenny. We don't have an I.D. on him, may never be able to figure out who he really was. But you know something about him, don't you? He was one of your boys."

For the first time since Ryan started watching, Lyle's face took on an expression other than smug, belligerent, or fearful. He almost looked regretful. "He was." He heaved a big sigh. "Unfortunately, the poor boy had a heroin habit. I tried to overlook it. He told me he'd gotten clean. Obviously, he hadn't."

"He didn't die of an overdose, as well you know, Lyle. He drowned in the harbor." Flynn paced away. "Weird thing about that. His body contained a lot of very pure heroin, and yet we're supposed to believe that, after shooting up, he went for a stroll. Addicts don't take heroin for energy. I'm sure you know that already."

"I wouldn't know, actually. Other than weed and the occasional poppers in my club days, I don't do drugs. I don't get your point, in any event."

Flynn turned on the man with another feral look. "The point is that he was murdered, Lyle. I want to know why."

Even though Flynn's interview with the perp had moved into Ryan's territory, he didn't feel compelled to join in. He might not trust Flynn with his heart anymore, but he did trust him to grill a suspect.

"I don't know anything about that." Lyle's voice rose and his tone had become shrill to put it mildly.

"Bullshit. Kenny had a rep for shooting off his mouth. What did he learn and what did he say that got him dead?"

Lyle folded his arms around a chest big enough to

actually have a bra size. "Kenny did have a big mouth, that's true enough. I counseled him on a number of occasions about how our clients expected their escorts to be discreet. Frankly, if he hadn't died, I would have had to fire him for his unprofessional conduct. And," he added with a huff, "that's all I have to say about any of it. I want my lawyer."

Flynn kept at the man for a few minutes more before leaving the interview room with his file in hand and nothing more, like a confession or useful information. Too bad, although more often than not, when dealing with white-collar criminals, they knew to lawyer up and did so fast.

Draining his coffee, Ryan dumped the empty container in the trash before exiting his own room to intercept Flynn. The cop had stopped in the hall, waiting for him.

He gave Ryan a wary smile. "Hey, Jakie. Glad you could make the interview. Sorry it didn't prove more useful."

Ryan worked his lips up into what he hoped was a reassuring response. He didn't want Flynn to think their meeting over a work matter had to be awkward. Or at least not *really* awkward. "Don't sweat it. I appreciate your giving Andy the heads-up so I could observe. I didn't expect Cherry to roll on anything, let alone admit that he murdered Kenny or Place, for that matter. I'm not even convinced the guy did so directly. He strikes me more as the snitch type, ratting someone else out and letting others do the real dirty work."

"I'm inclined to agree from what his record of solicitation, petty theft, and fraud indicate." Flynn moved down the hall, and Ryan kept pace with him. "I haven't had a chance to interview Cory. I read your notes from last night, though. Sounds like the kid could be a solid witness to the pimping charges."

"Yeah, I'd really rather you build a case without having to drag the kid in to testify."

Flynn nodded. "So would I, but you know that's not how this is likely to go down. I've had a quick look at the company's computer records and looks like Lyle doesn't keep records and wipes clean his emails every day. This is one procurer who's learned from others. Keeps no "little black book" on clients and jobs. The most we have are the kids' profiles and call records that are probably going to lead to drop phones. Lyle is smarter than he looks."

They got into the elevator together and pushed their respective floor buttons. Ryan blew out a breath. "I bet Frankie can retrieve whatever there is. There's credit card statements, too. They charge the clients for the time and have the boys take in the cash for the illegal services."

Flynn gave him a sideways look. "I really should ask you how all this fell into your lap, but I have a feeling I don't want to know."

Ryan thought of Dec and the desire to protect him more than himself loomed large. "You don't. You really don't. Another reason it would help if you find enough evidence to at least get him to plea bargain is so there's no trial."

The elevator stopped, and Flynn stepped forward to get off. Pausing mid-stride, he held the door open and gave Ryan another smile. This one kind of sweet, kind of sad. "You look good, Jakie. Everything going okay with you?"

Ryan gave his ex-lover a big, genuine smile in return. "Yeah, actually it is. You?"

The look in Flynn's eyes told the story, but the guy lied anyway. "I'm good, thanks. See you around." He released the doors and walked away.

Ryan gave himself one more second to dwell on Flynn before turning his full attention back to his case. He found Andy sitting at his desk and planted his ass on the corner of it. "So, Flynn got a big nothing out of Mother Cherry, aka Lyle something or other."

"No surprise there." Andy's eyes lit up. "I think I figured out what's missing from Place's treasure room."

"Fuck me." Ryan's mood perked right up. "What, and how did you figure it out?"

Andy looked around the room before sliding his chair in closer to Ryan. His voice dipped low. "I think it was Rembrandt's *The Storm on the Sea of Galilee.* It's one of the Gardner heist paintings."

"Ah, fuck," Ryan swore under his breath.

If Andy was right, then the FBI would definitely take over the murder investigation. They were already handling the theft from the Isabella Stewart Gardner Museum. Even after more than twenty-five years, none of the stolen works had been recovered. If Place's murder was somehow linked to that infamous heist, the FBI would claim jurisdiction.

"Are you sure?"

Andy winced, understanding the implications if he was right. "Pretty sure. I took the Cory kid's interview description of what Kenny had supposedly seen and went down to review Place's laptop list and found that Rembrandt picture. The description fits and when I compare the dimensions of the painting to the photo's I took of the empty spot in the treasure room, they line up nicely. Sorry."

With a deep sigh, Ryan pinched the bridge of his nose with finger and thumb. "No, don't apologize. This is a really important break in the case."

"If it's true."

"Yeah, if. But things match up awfully good. I believe Cory's description, and I think Kenny saw the thing and shot his mouth off. Place must have gotten wind of it. Maybe Lyle Cherry told him, although that seems short-sighted of him. Why risk alienating a good client? Anyway, however it happened, Place might have moved to silence Kenny. Having something from the Gardner heist is huge. They've managed to get away with it for so long, and I know the FBI thinks they've traced the stolen works through Pennsylvania. I don't think they realize at least one piece stayed here in Boston."

"If Place killed Kenny, why didn't he go after Cory or any of the other boys, too? Wouldn't he worry about word spreading even with Kenny dead?"

"You'd think. Except the more bodies piling up, the more police take notice. If Kenny was the only boy to actually see the painting, anything else would be hearsay. And, of course, it doesn't explain why Place was killed. If you're right about the painting, then the murder has to be tied to that. Nothing else makes sense."

"So, where does that leave us?"

"Fuck if I know. I just want a little bit more time to work the case ourselves before we let this theory out and hand it over to the FBI."

Andy grimaced. "Well, it's just a theory. I mean

we can't know for sure this is the missing painting. It's really just supposition."

Ryan appreciated what his partner was trying to do. For a few seconds, his conscience warred with his strong need to continue with his own investigation and his confidence in his ability to solve the case. Rightly or wrongly, his conscience lost the fight—for now.

He stood up and cracked his neck. "Okay, we put this part of it aside and concentrate on finding our killer. We do that, we'll find the painting and maybe uncover more."

Andy gave him a shit-eating grin, clearly happy with the call. "Right. So what's our next lead?"

"We start back from the beginning. My money is on Johnson knowing more than he's said. I'd make bet he's involved up to his receding hairline."

"His alibi checked out."

"I'm sure it did. He doesn't strike me as someone who gets his hands dirty. We dig into him deeper. I want to know everything we can about him from the time he came out of the womb until the day after Place was murdered."

"You got it." Andy pulled up to his desk and started clicking at his computer.

Ryan headed to his own desk, mulling over his next move. He silently gave himself a few more days. If they hadn't made any headway by then, he'd take what they had to his captain, including the idea about the identity of the painting, and live with the possibility of being shut out of the investigation. Really, if he couldn't solve the case within a week's time, he wasn't sure he deserved to keep it anyway.

****

Mal's black hat computer cracker looked like an elf with shaggy electric blue hair. If he hadn't been sitting in a dorm room at MIT, Dec would have pegged him for some kind of brain-dead gamer. According to Mal, though, the kid made most of the other students at the renowned college seem like blithering idiots.

As he sat staring at Dec and Mal over the rim of his amazingly large cup of soda, slurping noisily on a straw, Dec found that assessment hard to believe. He was desperate enough to try, though, and Mal was a good judge of talent.

"So, you think you can do that for us?" Mal asked.

The kid, Breckin Wolf if one could believe that, shrugged and pulled his cupid-bow lips off the straw. "Sure, I mean it sounds easy enough. I can find anything on the darknet. What's in it for me?"

Dec's wallet let out a yelp, but he shushed it. This was too important.

"How much?" he demanded in a flat, no-nonsense tone he hoped conveyed both his willingness to pay and that he wasn't a complete pushover.

The kid took another pull of his drink before answering. He had freaky violet eyes that oddly complimented his blue hair. "I'm not interested in money, man."

Dec glanced around the room. It was packed with electronics. "Really? This stuff looks expensive."

Breckin shrugged again. "I get a lot of stuff in trade. Money, even in precious metal form, has no intrinsic value, so what's the point of amassing it? I trade my services for things I can really use. If you knew what I know about the banking system, you'd be doing the same."

"If the zombie apocalypse happens, I'm pretty sure the grid will be the first to go down."

"That's why I have a cache of batteries, man."

"Of course you do. So, if not money, what do you want?" The boy's gaze slid to Pax. Dec scoffed. "No fucking way, kid. She's my service dog."

Breckin gave Dec an appraising look. "You seem pretty fit to me."

Dec strove for patience. They needed this info, and if Mal said this annoying twink was the answer, he needed to play along. "I won't bore you with my litany of problems, but I need to make a different bargain."

"Okay. I'll do it on credit."

"Meaning?"

"Meaning, you'll owe me one. I'll collect someday when I think of something you can do for me."

It sounded like a devil's bargain. Dec took it anyway. "Fine, so long as it's nothing illegal."

"You mean like having me troll the darknet for an auction of stolen art?"

"Point taken." He held out his hand. "It's a deal."

Dec figured he could always renege later if the kid asked for something too outlandish. Yeah, and then watch the guy wipe out Dec's bank accounts and trash his credit in retaliation. Damn, he'd worry about that if and when it happened.

Ignoring Dec's offer to shake, the kid twirled around to face his computer screen. "Once I find what you're looking for, under what name should I insert you into that community?"

"Um." Shit, he obviously couldn't use his real name.

Mal had it covered, though. "Hunter Williams."

When Dec looked pointedly at him, he explained. "Cindi came up with it. It's easier to answer to a fake name if it's somewhat familiar to you. She's going to be your wife, Paris Fox-Williams. She wanted to use something that really popped and figures she's used to answering to a new name so won't screw up."

"I'm surprised she didn't keep her maiden name," Dec deadpanned, starting to regret the whole idea. Going undercover hadn't proved to be his strong suit so far.

"She thought of it, then decided to hyphenate instead. You know because you're such an alpha male and she loves you and all," he added with a grin.

Dec closed his eyes briefly. "Right."

"Anyway, I'm going to go back to my place now and lay a false trail for both of you that will impress anyone who chooses to look. You're going to be a trust fund baby with a taste for art and the thrill of adventure."

"I love the new me already." Christ, he better not fuck this up, and he didn't even want to think how Ryan would feel about this new venture into his case. Better not to tell him, obviously.

Not that he expected to see the cop again any time soon. They weren't exactly dating, and the guy had a case to solve. If they never saw each other again, it shouldn't surprise Dec. It would hurt, however, and there was no denying that. Not anymore.

"I'll head back to the office. Thanks, both of you."

The elf was already deeply immersed in the 'net and not paying attention to their leaving. But Mal shot him a quick grin as they parted ways.

Dec just hoped he was doing the right thing.

Samantha Cayto

****

Sitting behind his desk for the rest of the day and waiting for something to happen drove Dec nuts. It didn't help how Cindi practically danced around the office with excitement. She'd force-fed him their back story to fill the time, having given a lot of thought to it. He didn't see why it mattered. Even if they managed to worm their way into an auction, he couldn't imagine that people at those things chatted about themselves. Everyone would be on the down-low, not swapping life stories.

Cindi had a point, though. If they were going to go undercover, they needed to have consistent answers should the questions arise. He also had to admit she'd put some real thought into it. Even he had started to believe they were the kind of couple that, while young, were greedy and self-absorbed enough to be interested in buying high-end stolen art.

Nearing six o'clock, he gave up any hope that Breckin would succeed in his quest that day. As there was no reason for him to stay late or have Cindi do so, he was just about to tell her to knock off for the day when she rapped once and stuck her head inside the office.

She battered her eyelashes at him. "Sergeant Jakes is here to see you, boss. If you're free," she added with a wink.

His body flushed with excitement, both freezing his lungs and goosing his heart. Christ, he really had turned into a teenage girl with her first crush. He started to answer but turned bright red when his voice caught. Then cleared his throat to try again.

"Send him in." His voice was steady, but the

236

damage had been done.

With laughing eyes, Cindi opened the door more fully and stepped to one side. "Please come in, Sergeant."

The sight of Ryan, with his tousled hair, rumpled suit, and loosened tie, made him salivate. His cock had remained in check all day, yet now woke up almost violently. He couldn't keep a grin from popping up. "Hey, Ryan. This is a surprise."

There, he sounded almost normal, like this visit wasn't important to him. He couldn't miss, though, how Cindi rolled her eyes as she shut the door behind Ryan. Yeah, he wasn't fooling anyone, probably. He just hadn't expected the guy to show up so soon and not at his office.

His grin died as an ugly thought popped up. "Is something wrong? Are you here to arrest me or something?"

Ryan had already squatted down to greet Pax. His eyebrows shot up. "What?" He barked out a laugh. "No. Why would you even ask something like that?" His expression turned fierce. "Have you done something to deserve getting arrested?"

Dec thought of Breckin searching the darknet and Mal creating a false profile online for him. Technically, he might have done something to deserve being locked up, but maybe not quite yet.

With a modicum of guilt, he went with the partial truth. "Yeah, I hired an under-age prostitute, remember?"

Ryan scratched Pax's head before standing up again. "Oh, that. Don't worry, the lead investigator is an old, um, friend of mine. You know, the guy I mentioned last night." He plopped down on a visitors' chair and absolutely reeked of exhaustion.

"Ouch." Dec could only imagine how hard it was to have to work with an ex, even if it was only rarely.

Ryan shrugged. "Nah, it's fine, actually. He's a good guy and a great cop. He's not looking too closely at how this whole thing unfolded. He'll be careful with the kid, too."

"That's good. I don't suppose you can tell me what's happening with Mother Cherry?"

Ryan made a face. "Sorry, I've been indiscreet as it is." He heaved a big sigh. "I actually was hoping I could take you to dinner, and we could, you know, set this whole thing aside for a few hours."

It took Dec a moment to absorb what Ryan was saying. "Are you asking me out on like a date?"

Ryan gave him a sheepish grin. "Yeah, I am." He glanced away, and Dec could see the vulnerability in his expression. "Unless you want to keep this strictly to a fucking relationship."

Dec felt oddly touched. He would have said yes to that last bit only a few days ago. Now, he kind of wanted more. Crazy as it might be. "Dinner sounds nice, actually," he replied, suddenly feeling a bit shy of all things.

The broad smile Ryan gave him in response eased any doubts Dec might have had lurking in the back of his mind. "Great. Can you leave now?"

"Sure." Dec stood up, happier than he would have thought possible. He gave what he'd hoped was a subtle tug to his jeans to easy the tightness in his groin. Ryan's gaze tracked the movement, though.

"I've got a similar problem," he confessed,

standing up himself. His tight slacks couldn't hide the bulge. "Let's try to get through a meal before jumping each other. Whadda you say?"

"I'd like to think we can," Dec replied, grabbing up Pax's leash and vest. He fitted her up, and she gave him a doggie smile. She obviously liked hanging with Ryan. "So, where to?"

"You like Italian?"

"Who doesn't?" He started for the door.

Ryan stepped up to follow. "Awesome. I know this nice little place. Cozy." He managed to reach the door before Dec and open it for him. "Romantic," he added with another grin, a sexier one that held a world of promise.

Yeah, Dec was definitely getting in deep here. Funny, but the idea didn't frighten him quite as much as he would have expected.

Chapter Twelve

The hostess at the intimate restaurant in the North End greeted Ryan warmly even though he hadn't stepped foot in the place since Flynn had broken up with him. It wasn't shadowed in bad memories, either. Instead, he saw a bright potential future in the candle lit glow of the room. The hostess gave Dec a sideways glance before grinning knowingly at Ryan. She also gave Pax a friendly pat, which earned her bonus points all around.

It was still relatively early, so there were plenty of tables. Ryan specifically asked for one in the corner by the front window, hoping Dec would appreciate both having his back to the wall and a clear view of anyone coming in the restaurant. It provided a nice spot for Pax to lie down in as well. The utter serenity of the service dog amazed him.

"Thanks," Dec murmured when the hostess handed him a menu but didn't open it right away. Instead, he sat back and surveyed the restaurant with an intense interest. His gaze landed back on Ryan. "Sorry. Habit." He opened the menu.

Ryan reached over and placed his hand on Dec's arm. "You don't have to apologize to me for doing what you need to in order to feel comfortable."

Dec flashed him a smile. "Thanks. I guess I'm a bit nervous and unsure of how to act around you. I haven't been on a date in like forever."

Leaning back in his chair, Ryan gave Dec a level gaze. "You don't have to act any particular way around me, either. I don't scare off easily. And I'm glad I'm the first guy to take you out in a while," he added with as much of a smoldering look at he could manage.

Dec laughed and shook his head. "You also don't have to act in a particular way around me." He refocused his attention on the menu. "I mean you had me at 'hello.'"

"I did?" Ryan felt ridiculously pleased by that declaration.

"Yeah," Dec confirmed on a sigh. Before Ryan could bask further in the news, the waiter came over to take their drink orders. Ryan looked at Dec. "I'm just going to stick to water, thanks."

That sounded like a good idea to Ryan. He wanted the evening to end on a high note, and as tired as he was, alcohol could easily put him down too early. "We'll have a bottle of San Pellegrino, please."

The waiter took off with a nod. Surprisingly, Dec picked up where he'd left off. He cleared his throat, and Ryan could swear he saw a blush on the man's face even in the dim light. "Yeah, I couldn't quite ignore how gorgeous you were when you smiled at Cindi, and of course, your clothes leave nothing to the imagination." He kept his gaze plastered on the menu before him.

It was Ryan's turn to blush. He could feel the heat crawling up his face. "Yeah, well I've spent the last year bulking up. After getting dumped, I figured I could drown my sorrows in food and drink or spend more hours at the gym working out my frustration."

Dec glanced up. "The gym was a very good call."

Ryan wiggled his shoulders. "Except now almost all of my clothes are too tight. Time to go shopping, I guess."

"Don't hurry on my account." Dec closed his menu. "I'm terrible at deciding what food to order at a new place. Why don't you order for me?"

The idea of picking out Dec's meal pressed Ryan's caretaking and possessive buttons. It was the next best thing to cooking for him, something Ryan actually liked doing for his boyfriends. Not that he could call Dec that yet, maybe not ever. He needed to take things slowly with this man. He suspected Dec needed time and space, and that didn't have anything to do with his PTSD.

"Are you sure?" Ryan asked just as the waiter returned with their water.

"Yup. I'll eat anything."

"Okay." Ryan waited until the young man filled their glasses before ordering. "We'll both have a bowl of the lentil soup, we'll split a *caprese* salad, and we'll each have the fusilli Bolognese with meat sauce."

"Very good, sir."

Ryan busied himself drinking some water, and Dec did the same. The silence was nice, companionable, but eventually Ryan broke it by asking the usual first date questions. As much as he'd learned about Dec before interviewing him that first time, he really didn't know much at all.

"So, you're from Boston originally?"

Dec sat back and fiddled with his glass. "Yeah, Somerville, actually. I always wanted to join the navy and was fortunate enough to get into Annapolis after I graduated from high school. When my career ended, it seemed like the thing to do to come back this way." He hesitated, and Ryan could tell he was about to say something difficult. "I couldn't stand staying in Coronado with the SEAL community. Not being able to be one of them anymore hurt way too much."

"I can imagine. Are your folks still in the area?"

Dec shrugged. "My mother died when I was ten. Lung cancer, 'cause smoking two packs a day will do that to a person."

"I'm sorry," Ryan said, knowing it was always a paltry thing to say.

Dec shrugged as if losing his mother was no big deal. "She wasn't that attentive before she died, so I can't say my life changed much after. I suppose my father's still alive. I haven't heard he died or anything." He picked up his glass and drained it. "I haven't seen or spoken to him since I left for the navy."

Ryan reached over to pick up the bottle of water and refilled Dec's glass. "I take it he wasn't any better at parenting than your mother."

"You would be correct about that." Dec's tone was light, yet Ryan heard the hurt underlying it.

He was contemplating on poking more at Dec's past when the soup came and took both their attentions.

Dec moaned in appreciation. "This is terrific."

"Yeah, it's all homemade stuff. Nothing like it on a cold day. Not that this fall has been particularly cold." Christ. He mentally smacked himself. Was he really talking about the weather? He sucked down some more soup and changed topics. "My family's been in Boston since the late nineteenth century. And there's like a gazillion of us."

"The potato famine?" Dec asked around a mouthful of lentils.

"You got it."

"I take it, then, that you've got a lot of siblings."

Ryan made a face. "Just my brother that you met the other night. My parents wanted more kids, but that turned out to be impossible for my mother. Having me almost killed her, actually. Sean told me that with the kind of evil glee only an older brother can have."

Dec laughed, and the way his face lit up did funny things to Ryan's insides. "That was dickish of him."

"Yup, Sean excels at that. He's also my biggest supporter and protector. He and his wife own the two-family we all live in. I rent my unit from them."

"Nice of them, or nice of you?"

Ryan shrugged. "It suits us both, although their third child is coming in a few months and they're probably going to need to convert the whole house into a single family."

Dec scraped the last of his soup out of the bowl. Ryan was gratified to see how much the other man liked what Ryan had ordered. "What will you do then?"

Ryan finished his own soup. "I've been saving to get my own place."

"In Boston?"

Ryan grinned. "Yeah, I'm a Southie boy. Besides, Boston cops are supposed to live in Boston."

The waiter came again, cleared their bowls and put down the plate of sliced tomatoes, mozzarella and basil. Ryan took the serving fork and spoon and divided up the salad between them on the plates left by the waiter. The homeliness of it all served to relax Ryan and helped him put aside the stress of the case.

They downed their salads in silence, but once those plates were cleared, Ryan couldn't help returning to Dec's family story. It mattered to him to know the how and why of what made Dec tick besides the lost SEAL career and the PTSD.

Leaning forward, he folded his arms on the table and stared into Dec's eyes. "My family is important to me, and I always know they're there for me. Do you have anyone, Dec? Family, I mean besides your parents. I could tell from the little time I spent with them that Cindi and Malcolm are very loyal to you. But there's no substitute for family."

Dec didn't answer right away, although he dropped his hand by his side. Pax immediately came up on her front paws and tucked her head under his hand. Dec's fingers played over the dog's head in slow strokes. Ryan instantly regretted his probing question. Stressing Dec was so not the way he intended this date to go.

He pulled back to give the man space. "I'm sorry. I'm being a nosy prick."

Dec gave him kind of a shy grin. "Naw, it's okay. We're on our first date, even though we've fucked a few times. Talking about ourselves is what you do." With a final pat, he pulled his hand back and must have given Pax some kind of signal because she plopped back down to the floor.

Dec fiddled with his glass of water, but he did look Ryan in the eye when he said, "I'm an only child of self-centered people who came from long lines of the same type of person. I have only a vague memory of meeting one of my grandmothers, and that's because getting slapped in the face for taking a cookie is the kind of thing that sticks in your mind. After my mom died, my father started drinking even more heavily than he had been before. If I was lucky, he ignored me."

Unfortunately, the waiter came back with their main course. The steaming plates wafted an amazing smell to each of them. Dec sniffed and smiled. "Smells delicious."

"It's my favorite dish here," Ryan admitted and picked up his fork.

Dec did the same, put a manful-sized amount of fusilli in his mouth, chewed, and swallowed. "That's outstanding." He ate more and washed it down with water. "The truth is that when I left what nominally was my home, I couldn't wait to show my father my back. As far as I'm concerned, I'm an orphan, and having seen what the world can be like for other kids, I refuse to feel sorry for myself." He looked pointedly at Ryan over another forkful of pasta. "And I don't want anyone else to, either."

"Point taken." Ryan felt compelled to add after a few moments of silent chewing, "I don't feel sorry for you, just so you know. I understand about the injuries and the PTSD, and now the shitty parents. When I look at you, though, all I see is a guy who rings my bell in a major way."

The scalding gaze Dec sent him across the table made Ryan's insides melt. "Is that so?" Ryan could only nod, his voice suddenly choked off. "Well, then, I guess I won't order dessert. Wouldn't want to get overly full now, would I?"

Ryan shook his head and broke eye contact. The amazing fusilli didn't stand a chance against the delicious enticement of spending the night being fucked by Dec. They finished their meal within minutes, both being big guys with a lot of incentive. After a brief wrestle over the check, which Ryan won, they stepped outside to a still relatively warm fall night and a sidewalk bustling with pedestrians.

"Shall we head to your place?" Ryan asked.

"No, let's go to yours." When Ryan raised his eyebrows at the unexpected answer, Dec shrugged. "If you're worried about my comfort zone, your place is just as good as mine. I can't guaranty I'll have a night free of nightmares regardless, so we may as well be at a more convenient location for you tomorrow morning. I don't have to answer to a boss, after all."

"Okay," Ryan agreed, feeling guilty even though he knew Dec's reasoning made sense. "If you're sure?"

"Definitely."

"Wait, what about Pax? Doesn't she need dinner?"

"No, she only needs to eat once a day in the morning, although I usually can't resist giving her treats at night."

"I bet I can bum a few puppy-sized ones off Sean."

"You don't have to go to the trouble. I do love how nice you are to her, though."

Oddly touched, Ryan ran a hand down both Dec's arm and Pax's head. "Dogs are easy. People are harder," he added with a wry grin.

They merged into the stream of people walking down the sidewalk, with Ryan leading the way back to his car. He so wanted to hang by Dec's right side, to be his ear and brace him if his knee gave out. That job belonged to Pax, however, and envying the dog her job was a really low and childish feeling, yet there it was. He felt protective of the man, even knowing that if Dec could know Ryan's thoughts, he wouldn't appreciate them. The guy didn't need coddling. He did more than fine on his own.

When they reached the car, Ryan let them all in and took off for the relatively short ride back to his house. The sexual tension only mounted once they were sitting in a private place, speeding toward the opportunity to jump each other. Ryan tried to concentrate on the driving and not the way his pants pinched his stiffening cock. From the way Dec kept squirming in his seat, the guy had to be having a similar problem.

"Just a few more minutes," Ryan murmured as much to reassure himself as Dec.

From the corner of his eye, he saw Dec's mouth open. Before the man said anything, though, his phone chimed with a message. He pulled it out and read it. A flash of something, excitement maybe, crossed his face before it was gone in an instant. Dec typed in a return message and stuffed the phone back into his pocket.

"Everything all right?"

"Huh?" Dec seemed distracted. "Oh, ah, sure. It's fine. Just some work stuff. Nothing that can't wait."

"Okay. Good." A funny feeling stole over Ryan. He sensed he didn't want to know more about what was going on with Dec. The damn case had brought them together, yet it remained a bone of contention. He so wanted to ask if Dec was finally staying out of it, except he really didn't want the answer. If they stood any chance of a relationship, they needed to stay clear of the case while they were together. It would be over soon anyway, either because he and Andy would solve it or the FBI would take over the whole thing.

Putting the matter out of his mind, he whisked

them over to Southie and his home. He parked and met Dec over on the other side just as he was letting Pax out of the back seat. Ryan couldn't wait another moment. He grabbed Dec by one arm and, swinging him around, pressed him against the car. He had to go up on his toes a bit to reach Dec's lips, but oh, how sweet it was. Wasting no time, he dove his tongue inside Dec's willing mouth.

Dec had stiffened for only a second when Ryan took hold of him. That had been instinct and the leftover effect of his service. Yet his body had also known instantly that this was Ryan. He relaxed almost as quickly and allowed himself to be squished between the car and Ryan's hard body. He dropped Pax leash, knowing she'd stay put and wanting desperately to finally get his hands on all those muscles Ryan had been pumping up in the last year.

Resisting the urge to paw at the guy while in the restaurant had been difficult. He'd never really been on a date before. The most he'd done was sit at a bar with a guy while they sized each other up. How did people do it all the time? Sitting quietly while the person of your wet dreams ate within reach was pure torture. No matter. There was no holding them back now.

Dec wrapped his arms around Ryan's broad back and pulled him closer. He tipped his head down, too, to make it easier for them both to slant their lips and wrestle with their tongues. It felt as if each of them had about eight hands because of all of the rubbing and groping. Dec couldn't land on feeling up just one part of Ryan's ripped body. He wanted all of it, every hot, hard inch in his grasp.

Already stoked, he nearly came when Ryan ground

his pelvis against Dec's straining dick. He gasped at the same time Ryan moaned, their breaths mingling past their fused lips.

Ryan pulled back first, puffing like the proverbial locomotive. "We need to take this inside," he panted out. "If one of my nieces wakes up and gets an eyeful out of their bedroom window, my ass will be grass."

Even though his dick screamed at him to jump Ryan and be done with it, Dec got himself under control. It was physically painful. That's what he got for his prolonged celibacy. He allowed Ryan to pull him by the arm around to the back of the house. He had sense enough to make sure Pax followed and paused at the door to give her time to pee on the lawn. Poor girl. He wondered what she made of all of this sudden back and forth between homes, let alone his new interest in another human.

Ryan flicked on the lights to the kitchen and waited for Dec and Pax to join him before locking up again. Dec took a moment to release the dog from her leash, and as he did so, his gaze landed on the small kitchen table. He hadn't paid it much mind before. Now, as revved up as he was, he could still admire the craftsmanship of the piece of furniture.

Straightening, he ran his fingers across the smooth surface. It looked like oak with a simple line of a darker wood inlaid all around the perimeter.

Ryan stepped up behind him and slipped his arm around Dec's waist. He laid his chin on Dec's shoulder. "Are you going to make love to my table or me?" The tone was laced with wryness and tiredness.

Dec turned within the embrace and managed to switch their positions so that Ryan faced the table and

Dec stood behind him. He used his tongue to trace the shell of one of Ryan's ears. "How sturdy is this thing?"

Ryan shivered at the touch. "Very. I made it myself."

"Really?" Surprised by the news, Dec's intention to seduce got sidetracked. "That's amazing. It's beautiful."

Ryan pushed his ass back into Dec. "Thanks, but can we talk woodworking later? I'm kind of on a mission here."

Dec gave a throaty laugh. "And what would that be?"

"To get fucked by you, obviously."

Dec liked the sound of that. "Fair enough."

He slid his hand up to the back of Ryan's neck and pushed him down until Ryan's upper body lay sprawled against the table. He maneuvered his other hand around to Ryan's waist in order to undo his belt, then his pants.

Ryan remained pliant, allowing Dec to do what he wanted, his only independent movement was the sharp rise and fall of his back with each harsh breath. Dec used both hands to expose Ryan's fine ass, not bothering to undress him fully and leaving the pants and underwear stretched halfway down Ryan's thighs. Dec liked the idea of keeping them both mostly dressed while they fucked.

He slid his palms across the Ryan's muscular ass, enjoying the way the flesh quivered and the man moaned. A sudden impulse had him kneeling so that he could first kiss one taut buttock cheek, then scrape his teeth along it. Ryan hissed and writhed. Dec kept his hold firm, not allowing Ryan much movement at all while Dec kissed and bit. He lapped over the skin he tortured with long, wet strokes before sliding it into Ryan's crease.

"Christ, Dec," Ryan groaned and pushed his ass toward Dec in invitation.

Dec had never rimmed a guy. Had never wanted to. Now, it seemed the most natural thing in the world to want a special taste of Ryan. Tightening his grip on the ass cheeks, he pried them apart to expose Ryan's dusky hole. He didn't hesitate to delve in.

Ryan squirmed and swore. Dec took that as a good sign and increased his efforts. He licked around the puckered skin before making a point of his tongue and stabbing at the hole. Ryan opened for him immediately, allowing him to enter into a slightly bitter and musky world. To Dec, it was exciting and humbling. It took a certain kind of trust to allow such intimacy. He loved the way his tongue and saliva slicked the path his cock would soon take.

When he judged Ryan to be open and wet enough to accommodate him, Dec pulled his tongue back. He rose while fumbling with his own jeans, working the snap open and the zipper down. His cock sprang out, also wet and ready. Tugging a newly-purchased condom out of his wallet, opening it with his shaky hands, and managing to slide it onto his jumpy dick was like torture. By the time he was ready to mount Ryan, he worried he'd taken too long. So, he willed himself to slow down, coated a couple of fingers with spit and probed the entrance to Ryan's hole.

The guy was still slick and relaxed. He took Dec's fingers with a low moan and a quick shove back to meet them halfway. He lay on the table just as Dec had placed him and with his head turned to one side, his eyes shut. "Shit, Dec, fuck me already. I'm so damn worked up from that rimming, I'm ready to explode."

Dec could relate. When he went to replace his fingers with his cock, it took him a few tries to get it lined up right. With his legs trembling in an effort to control himself, he pressed his cock and surged in right to the hilt. Ryan gave a muted cry. Dec's eyes slammed shut, and he held himself seated up against Ryan's ass for a few seconds. Holy shit, being inside Ryan felt perfect. Strong muscles gripped along the length of Dec's rod, welcoming him in, demanding more.

"Come on, motherfucker," Ryan groaned. "Move!"

Dec could have easily remained sheathed in Ryan's ass forever, but he heard the man's desperation and because it mirrored his own, he gave them both what they really wanted. He pulled almost all the way out and slammed home again. Not pausing for a moment, he began to thrust, fast and urgent, as if speed alone was the goal.

Far from passive, Ryan picked up the rhythm and shot his ass back each time to meet Dec's next thrust. Dec dug his fingers into Ryan's hips to force him to rock that ass even faster and harder. The sound of wood scraping against linoleum reached his ears, and he vaguely worried they were damaging Ryan's beautiful table. No worries. He'd buy him a new one. Hell, he'd make him a new one.

Ryan grunted in time to the thrusting. "Oh. My. God. Dec. Coming. Help me."

The words penetrated the focus on Dec's building climax. He understood what Ryan needed and cursed himself for being too self-centered. Pealing one of his hands from Ryan's hip, he bent over to grab Ryan's dick. It jumped at his touch and was already slick from pre-cum. Dec squeezed it while tugging up the length.

That's all it took to send Ryan over. He reared up at the first splash of his cum over Dec's hand. Dec had him pinned to the table, though, so there was nowhere for Ryan to go except back to the table top with a loud thunk. Dec forced his eyes to fully open. He wanted to see the effect he had on Ryan. Wanted to see as well as feel the way the man writhed in the throes of his orgasm.

The sight of it, the sensation of Ryan's hole clenching and spasming around Dec's dick, brought him off with blinding force. He gritted his teeth and shut his eyes once more as the waves of pleasure crashed over him. There's was nothing gentle about it. With almost brutal intensity, he filled the condom. A primitive part of him wished he filled Ryan's ass instead. The vision of it had him convulsing again with a second, dryer orgasm. Good God, when had that ever happened before? Never.

Dec collapsed on top of Ryan's back, utterly spent and dizzy with it.

Eventually, he let go of Ryan's softening dick and came to his senses in time to pull his own dick out without losing the condom. He staggered around to find a trashcan, grateful when he realized Pax had slunk off to lie in the hall. Someone had to keep their wits about them, and it sure as shit wasn't going to be Dec. Or Ryan, either, apparently. The guy remained sprawled across the table, unmoving. Dec thought he might have fallen asleep. No matter. Dec would carry him to bed if he had to. He would take care of Ryan.

He paused mid-stride, mid-thought. He would take

care of Ryan, however he needed it. The certainty of it, the fierceness of his intent scared the crap out of him.

Ryan rallied enough to work the rest of his clothes off, brush his teeth, and land face down in his bed. Dec took a little bit more time, grateful that Ryan had a spare tooth brush, and made sure Pax was settled for the night before joining his lover in bed. He lay awake for a long time, though, turning over and over in his mind whether he was willing to proceed with the plan he'd started in motion earlier in the day.

On the ride over, he'd received a text from Mal confirming that Breckin had found what Dec was looking for. Mal was asking Dec to green light the kid making inquiries as the fictitious Hunter Williams. The false identities were ready to go. Dec trusted that his wizkid employee had done a good job, and that they would pass any scrutiny. Dec had texted him back, telling him to wait.

The only thing holding Dec back from giving that green light was lying peacefully beside him. He knew how Ryan would feel about this whole thing. Yet, Dec couldn't rest until Place's murder was solved and his company firmly put in the clear. Felix would say it was just another manifestation of his newly-acquired OCD. Dec knew better. It was his SEAL stubbornness and pride driving him.

With more than a little guilt, he quietly reached for his phone and sent Mal a reply.

****

Nothing could wipe the grin off of Dec's face the next morning. He ruthlessly pushed down his worries about the Place situation and let the glow of a quiet night, followed by a quick shower blowjob, buoy him until he reached first home to change clothes and feed Pax, then the office. He hadn't even missed doing his morning run. Sex with Ryan was workout enough.

Cindi had gotten there before him, as usual, even though he'd risen early in deference to Ryan's schedule. He swore sometimes his admin must have some kind of ESP and knew when he was on his way. She never failed to greet him with a pot of coffee and a cheery disposition. This day was no different, except an extra gleam showed through her eyes.

"Hey, Dec." Cindi handed him a mug of coffee before grabbing him by the arm and yanking him into his office. "Mal's here."

Dec allowed himself to be propelled through the doorway and went straight to his desk. Mal sat in a visitors chair with his laptop. He barely looked up.

"Dec, go log into your email. I've forwarded you a few messages from the dummy account I set up for Hunter Williams."

Dec did as told, his good mood not spoiled, yet his battle edge coming to the fore. He gulped at his coffee while he waited for his computer to boot up. Sensing his sudden tension, Pax sat by his side, her chin resting on his thigh. He absentmindedly stroked her head before logging into his email with one hand. "What am I looking at?"

"Breckin found a site that promotes available art pieces on the down low. They do private sales, special procurement and auctions. He sent a message posing as you, or rather Williams, giving the return address that I had set up. Once we got the first response, I took over."

Dec nodded and opened the first of a few messages. He scanned each one quickly before rocking back in his chair and staring at Mal over the rim of his mug. "It can't be this easy."

Mal raised an eyebrow, a la Mr. Spock. "You think finding these guys was easy? Breckin had to do some serious cracking. And I spent hours laying down a false identity for you and Cindi. None of this was easy."

Sitting on the other visitor chair, Cindi smiled brightly. "He even photo-shopped some pictures of us to make it look like we went to these really cool events for rich people." She was having way too much fun with this.

Dec took a few more big swallows of his coffee as he considered how deep they'd gotten into this whole mess in such a short period of time. The wonderful buzz from his night with Ryan was wearing off. "So, these people, whoever they are, have actually bought our cover?"

Now a rare look of arrogance stole over Mal's face. "I just pretended that I was like this man in my village who is from a high caste and lords it over everyone. With every message I sent on your behalf, I mimicked his tone. And I gave them just enough information about your financials to prove your bona fides without seeming eager to provide them with such intimate information."

"Hmm." Dec reread the last message Mal had forwarded. It was an invitation to an auction this coming Friday. It said that if he and Mrs. Williams were interested in attending, they'd be sent the location an hour before the auction was due to begin along with a passcode to enter. They would need government issued picture I.D.s and as much cash as they intended to spend. Cash equivalents, such as gold, would also be accepted, subject to current market rates.

Christ.

He looked up at his colleagues. Their excitement over the prospect was obvious, and while he had his doubts, he also knew this might be the best chance he had to figure out why Place was killed and maybe by whom. If nothing else, he'd have information about stolen art for Ryan.

Shit, Ryan. Dec winced inwardly when he thought of his lover. If Dec went through with this harebrained scheme, it might well end his burgeoning relationship with the cop. There was only so many times Ryan would overlook the illegality of Dec's dubious efforts.

Yet, even with that knowledge, something drove him forward. Maybe it was simply a matter of the need to recapture the life he used to live as a SEAL. When he'd been in the Teams, every day he'd had the chance to make a real difference in the world. What he'd done mattered.

And what had Mal said about coloring outside the lines? Yeah, that was also kind of the SEAL way. Sometimes, you had to put the rule book away, get creative, and hope the whole thing didn't turn to shit. His feelings about the Place murder and his ability to solve it might be misplaced. He still had to try, and he'd bet, even a good cop like Ryan probably sometimes crossed his own lines. Maybe he'd be understanding if he found out. When he found out.

"Okay," he said with a nod. "Send a message saying we would love to come or however a spoiled rich guy would say it."

Mal flashed his straight, white teeth. "You got it, boss." He bowed over his laptop and typed furiously.

Dec reached for Pax. Her head still lay on his thigh. He buried his fingers in her fur, calming himself, except he really didn't need it. From this point on, he was heading into a mission. He'd never felt nervous before one, and now was no different. Nerves got you killed. So did doubt.

"You know what we have to do?" Cindi asked suddenly. When Dec simply looked at her, baffled by what she meant, she said, "Shop."

"Seriously?"

Cindi rolled her eyes. "Of course. If we're going to pretend to be rich, we need better clothes."

"Crap." Dec hated shopping. And expensive-looking clothes were going to be expensive. His bank account would be taking another hit. Couldn't be helped. "Fine. Where?"

"Now it's my turn. Seriously? Newbury Street."

Of course. Probably the most expensive shopping area of the whole of Boston. He sighed. "That's what I was afraid of."

****

Ryan found himself actually whistling as he entered the station. The previous night's dinner date, followed by being rimmed and fucked on his kitchen table had put him in a very good mood. The peaceful night with Dec had helped as well. He'd been really glad for his lover's sake that there'd been no nightmares. The wet and wild blowjob that morning hadn't hurt, either. His case might be giving him fits, but his love life had taken an awesome turn for the better. And, yeah, perhaps he was getting ahead of himself, but it did feel like a love life and not just a sex life.

Samantha Cayto

His good mood died a hard death when he saw Andy standing by his desk with a whole lot of grim on his face. "Captain wants to see us."

"Aw, fuck." That could only mean one thing. Ryan dumped his coffee and bagel on his desk before following his partner to the meeting of doom.

They entered Captain Dixon's office, and it felt like a meat locker. Not that the actual temperature was way down, but the icy silence that greeted them gave the same effect. Normally, Dixon was a fair guy and not one prone to anger. The set of his jaw and the narrowing of his gaze told Ryan that the man was in a rare pissed mood. His other visitor probably had something to do with it, although Ryan felt the iceberg moving toward him from the moment he and Andy walked in.

"Jakes, Diaz, I'm sure you know Special Agent Chan."

Both of them nodded toward the woman who sat in one of the visitor chairs. "Ma'am," they said in unison. They knew her. Of course, they did. She was the FBI agent in charge of the Place stolen art investigation. She nodded briskly. As the captain didn't invite them to also sit, they stood awkwardly for a few seconds, waiting like naughty school boys for whatever was coming their way.

"Gentlemen," the captain intoned. "Agent Chan and her people have been keeping track of the murder investigation, including the lead through the escort service. She thinks she's found an interesting piece of the puzzle that you seem to have missed."

Ryan stiffened a fraction. Shit, he knew what was coming, but like a smart school boy, he didn't confess

260

to anything. "I see, sir. What would that be, may I ask?"

Chan turned her head slightly to look at him more fully. "I listened to the interview with Cory Hayward, and I believe he described one of the pieces stolen from the Gardner Museum."

Sweat itched the back of his neck. "Is that so? I know of the heist, of course, but I'm not that familiar with the pieces involved." That was technically true.

"Well, I am," Chan said. "And if this murder of Stanford Place is connected to that robbery, it's FBI jurisdiction."

"I can appreciate that, ma'am, but we don't know enough to make that leap."

"I disagree," Chan said with a frown.

"So, do I," the captain chimed in.

Seeing the case slipping away from him, Ryan tried to hold onto it. "Sir, the investigation is in the early stages yet. I'd like to hold onto it."

"I'm sure you would, Jakes. Do you have any real leads?"

He hated answering the question. "Nothing solid, sir. But I think Place's personal assistant is worth looking at again."

"Based on what?"

Ryan suppressed a wince. "My gut, actually, sir."

The captain made a noise that clearly dismissed Ryan's gut. "The FBI has formally requested that the matter be turned over to them. The commissioner has agreed. You will turn over all files and notes you have on the Place murder to Special Agent Chan right away." When neither Ryan nor Andy said anything, the man stared pointedly at them. "Do you understand, gentlemen?"

"Yes, sir," they said once more with one voice. What else was there to say?

"Dismissed."

Ryan left without another word and without looking at Chan again. He held it together until they were well away from the office. "Son-of-a-God-damn-bitch!"

"Yeah, it sucks." Andy was always a cooler head than Ryan. "Let's get this transfer over as soon as possible. We can work some cold cases until something hot comes in."

"The hell with that," Ryan practically spat. "We'll give her what we have, but we're going to keep working this case ourselves."

Grabbing Ryan's arm, Andy pulled him up short. "Are you out of your fucking mind?" When a passing uniform looked at him, Andy lowered his voice. "Did you not hear Nixon just now? The FBI is yanking it, man. It's over."

"I heard, and no fucking way is this over. This is our case. The FBI are interested in the stolen art. I want to find the killer."

"They're linked, man, you know that."

"No, I think that's true, but I don't know that for sure." He fumed for a few moments, aware that his partner was right, yet unwilling to let the case go. "I can't shake the feeling that Johnson is the key."

"I'm with you on that, but how does that change things?"

"It doesn't. I just want to pursue this avenue for a while longer."

"We can't interview him again because we're off the case."

"I know," Ryan replied testily, then rubbed his forehead. Where had all that post-sex afterglow gone? "We can follow him, though. See where he leads us. If enough time goes by and the FBI don't pursue him as a suspect, he might let his guard down."

"That could take days, even weeks."

"Let's start with days. We don't have another case. If we catch one, then we let this go. In the meantime, it's as good a way to spend our time as any."

Andy didn't look convinced. He was a good partner, though, so he relented. "Okay, if you think it's worth it. I trust you." He gave Ryan a tentative smile.

Ryan grinned back and punched him in the arm. "Thanks, man. I knew I could count on you. Let's get the docu-dump to the FBI done and start planning out our tail."

It was a shot in the dark and would lead to long hours in the car. It would also mean maybe not seeing Dec much in the next few days or not at all. Shit, after a year-long dry spell, he hated to slow down on his newly-forming relationship, but he'd be better company once this damn case was solved.

That's what he told himself, anyway.

Chapter Thirteen

Ryan's ass had gone numb hours ago. No amount of shifting or squirming helped. His stomach rebelled at the ingestion of any more caffeine while his eyes all but crossed with fatigue.

A few days of tailing Johnson had yielded only boredom and discomfort, and Andy had almost reached the breaking point given that this endless stakeout was based on a feeling, not any real evidence. Plus, they had to do it all themselves. Hard to ask for help when they were supposed to be doing something else, anything else, and not still be pursuing a case that had been handed over to the FBI. Make that yanked by the FBI. He still seethed at the high-handed way the feds had coopted the murder case.

Over in the passenger's seat, Andy sighed and put his forehead in his palm. They were outside Johnson's condo on Battery Wharf. The neighborhood wasn't quite as toney as Place's had been, yet well beyond Ryan's cop's salary. Maybe he should rethink his career choice and become the personal assistant to a rich asshole who had nothing but contempt for the law. Yeah, sure that was a plan.

"I'm sorry, man." Andy's voice dragged him out of his reverie. "You know I have the utmost respect for your gut feelings. In this case, I'm beginning to think this lead isn't going to pan out." He turned to look at

Ryan, his eyes rimmed by dark circles from lack of sleep. "I don't know how much longer I can keep up this pace."

Ryan grimaced at the confession. He understood. There were limits to everything. As much as he believed they were on the right track, he couldn't say he was going to be able to stay with the program. The only reason they had so much time to devote to this was because they hadn't yet caught another case.

That would change soon. Although Boston's murder rate might not be the biggest in the country, it was hardly a sleepy, little town. Right at the moment, someone was undoubtedly killing someone else, and Ryan and Andy's number would be up along with the victim's.

What was he trying to prove, anyway? He had unsolved cases like every other murder cop. So what if he let this one go. The FBI would technically be the ones to solve it or not anyway. And if he gave up this pursuit that was beginning to border on an obsession, he'd have more time to spend with Dec, to see where their relationship might take them. If nothing else, he should be grateful that the case had brought him into the man's orbit and vice versa.

They hadn't met up in the last few days. With the stakeout, Ryan hadn't had time. Dec had said he was busy, too, and while there was something a little cagey about the guy's interaction with Ryan in texts and when they'd had phone sex, Ryan didn't ask any questions. He didn't want to know. He really didn't. One of the things that he and the guy shared was single-minded determination. He truly hoped Dec had dropped his investigation. Unfortunately, he didn't believe it for a moment.

Nothing he could do about Dec. He flashed an apologetic smile at his partner, though. "I'm sorry, man. I know this sucks." He blew out a breath. "And it is probably a colossal waste of time. Let's just give it this one more night."

Andy nodded. "You got it, man. One more night, and hey, it's Friday. What else have we got to do?"

That last bit was sarcasm as Ryan well knew. Andy had a very active social life, even though he rarely had what would be called a girlfriend. No doubt Ryan was cock-blocking his partner.

They both sat up straighter when Johnson sauntered out of his building's front door and climbed into a private car that had been idling in front for a few minutes. They'd seen this routine before. Johnson seemed to use a livery service to get around town. No taxis for him, or even Uber. Lots of people in his building appeared to do the same, so there'd been no reason to expect that car in particular was for him.

Ryan was pathetically grateful to be on the move. At least the scenery would change, and who knew? Maybe this would be the night in which Johnson would do something more interesting than taking his girlfriend out or meeting friends.

Ryan started the car and slipped into traffic to follow at a discreet distance. So far, none of Johnson's drivers had tried to lose them. Ryan was damn good at tailing, if he said so himself. Plus, he and Andy had switched cars every day to make sure Johnson wouldn't realize he was being followed. When Johnson's car took an unexpected turn to head to the warehouse district instead of Downtown or the Back Bay, Ryan's heartbeat ticked up a little.

"Damn," Andy said for both of them. "This could be interesting."

For sure, it was different. Ryan became extra cautious, although his car blended in with the existing traffic better than Johnson's. Unfortunately, that traffic thinned as they wended their way further into blocks filled with large, sometimes empty, buildings. It was already dark, as well, so Ryan had to have his headlights on. He made the decision to turn them back to running lights and hoped no black and white saw and pulled them over.

Johnson's car took a sudden turn down a narrow road that was really an alley between two quiet and unlit buildings. Ryan had no choice but to keep driving past. He pulled over at the first opportunity. By unspoken agreement, he and Andy jumped out of the car and ran toward where Johnson had turned. They slowed down within a few feet of the turn-off and, plastering themselves against a building, inched their way to the mouth of the alley.

Ryan stuck his head out just enough to take a peek. Johnson's car was parked at what looked like a loading dock. Nothing and no one moved, so with a jerk of his head at Andy, he darted in. He kept low. There was little cover to be had. He slid in behind a battered and rusty dumpster. Andy came right on his heels. They crouched and listened. The only sound was their suddenly harsh breathing.

Another peek confirmed there was a jut to the building that would allow them to get closer and still have a tiny amount of cover if they were very careful and made themselves very thin. Still, nothing stirred.

So, pulling his revolver out for extra measure, he made the next move. He'd just reached his destination, adrenaline pumping, and mashed his body against the wall when he heard something that made his heart stop.

A shot rang out behind him. He whirled around in time to see Andy, gun at the ready, crumpling to the pavement. It took his confused brain a couple of seconds to process what he was seeing. Another man stood at the mouth of the alley, also with a gun drawn. But that startling sight was completely overtaken by the way Andy's body twisted in an unnatural position, gun hand slack, eyes closed, and blood already seeping through his white shirt. All Ryan could think for a moment was how meticulous his partner dressed and how much he'd hate to ruin a shirt.

A second later, his brain overrode his shock. "No!" The shout tore out of his mouth as he raised his own weapon to fire at Andy's attacker.

He never got a chance to shoot. Blinding pain exploded through his head. Darkness consumed him. The last thing he saw was Andy's still, bloody body.

****

Dec had to admit he felt like a million bucks in his fancy new clothes. With what he'd spent on them, he better. The car he'd hired, driven by Mal in his own spiffy dark suit, had set him back some as well. The real show-stopper, however, was Cindi.

As they got out in front of what looked like an old warehouse screaming to be condemned, she captured the attention of the security loitering by the door. And as well she should. Even a gay guy could appreciate what a knockout she was in a strapless red silk dress that hugged her curves.

She stood in her mile-high strappy, black shoes, waiting for him to give her his arm. The smile she shot him was every bit as sparkly as the gems she wore at her ears, throat, wrist, and fingers. Fortunately, the jewelry wasn't as genuine as her excitement. Even Pax looked lovely, having been washed and groomed that morning and wearing a collar that could be set with real diamonds but, of course, wasn't. Cindi had assured him that as long as the clothes were decent, everyone would assume all the gems were real.

He sincerely hoped she was right. He'd almost wiped out the profit from the Place engagement with the trappings for the evening. If it turned into a bust, it would have all been for nothing. He'd be no closer to solving Place's murder while also risking alienating the one man who'd captured his interest in forever.

Thoughts of Ryan only served to make him sweat, however, so he made himself put the cop out of his mind. There was no way of even telling if Ryan shared his interest no matter how much they'd enjoyed each other's company so far. One date and a few fucks hardly made for a relationship, let alone anything more.

With Cindi clasping his left arm and Pax at his right, as usual, he walked up to the door with the kind of arrogance he figured someone like Hunter Williams would wear.

One of the security guards smiled at them when they arrived. "Good evening, sir. Ma'am," he added with a nod at Cindi.

She flashed him that weaponized smile of hers. The guy looked like he would kill without compunction, and he and his friend certainly were carrying under their long, leather jackets. And yet, the guard's olive cheeks turned dusky. There was no doubt that bringing Cindi along gave Dec an advantage. It almost made up for the fact that he'd had to leave his own gun at home. The invitation he'd received stressed that weapons of any kind were strictly prohibited.

"Name, sir?" The other guard held a clipboard of all things. Well, paper was easier to destroy than electronic records.

"Williams." Dec made his voice clipped, slightly impatient. "Mr. and Mrs. Hunter and Paris Fox." Then he said the code word supplied in the last email he'd received.

The first guard waited until the second one looked through his list and nodded. With a bit of a flourish that was meant undoubtedly for Cindi's benefit, he opened the door and ushered them in.

The initial interior was only slightly lighter than the outside, although farther in, behind a black curtain hanging across the wide expanse almost up to the ceiling, light could be seen. There were the murmurs of voices beyond there, too. They had to get past the second security check point first, though.

This one was manned by a half-dozen men. Their guns were out in the open. A couple of men were being processed past a metal detector. Dec wasn't surprised by this. It's why he hadn't tried to sneak in even so much as a knife. He didn't think this fact-finding mission would require any defensive maneuvering. If it did, he could simply relieve one of these men of his weapon. Whatever their training had been, it hadn't been better than his. Maybe one or more of them was ex-special forces. He hoped not for a variety of reasons, but even if he was wrong about that, he still knew they wouldn't be better at anything than he was.

The head man gave them a less effusive welcome and seemed more immune to Cindi's charms. He double-checked their names, then eyed Pax.

"She's my service dog," Dec said before the question could be asked. He stared down his nose at the guy, much the way the clerk on Newbury Street had when Dec had come in to buy his current suit of clothing. "She's under firm control, I assure you," he added, holding up her leash.

The guy didn't look convinced but didn't argue the point. "Please go through the detector, ma'am."

Cindi tottered through, handed her bag over for a visual inspection, then pouted when her phone was confiscated. Again, this had been known because the invitation said as much. Still, Cindi played her part of a spoiled princess and postured about while she waited for Dec to send Pax through, then himself.

Finally, they were allowed past the curtain and entered into the bizarre world of an old warehouse turned into a plush auction house. There was a stage, rows of cushy chairs, and waitstaff weaving among the patrons with trays of flutes of champagne and finger food. The crowd wasn't very big, no more than a couple of dozen people, really, but how did such an operation exist within the city limits without detection? Obviously, money and threats kept things under wraps.

Cindi grabbed two glasses of champagne and hurriedly handed one to Dec before she snagged a stuffed mushroom. "Hmm," she said through her mouthful. "This is amazing." From another server, she plucked up a cracker covered with some kind of cream and what looked like even to Dec's untrained eye, caviar.

He couldn't help but smile at her enthusiasm. If nothing else, he'd be showing her a great night out. She didn't seem to date much. Being a straight trans woman and pre-op to boot, she lived in a kind of delicate space. It would take an understanding straight man, and he doubted many of those existed even in a fairly cosmopolitan place like Boston.

"Come on, let's look around before the auction starts." By pre-agreement, they avoided mingling with the other people. They had memorized their cover, but nothing would change the fact they didn't actually move in the same circles as these other people. They couldn't afford to be drawn into any "oh, you must know so-and-so" types of conversations.

They stuck to the perimeter. The space was entirely enclosed by the same long, black curtains that they'd walked through. Yet the staff came and went from and to parts unknown by ducking through breaks in the fabric.

Dec led Cindi leisurely around the circuit a couple of times, sipping at the champagne and letting her stop every so often to take more of the food constantly being offered. Given how small the group was and how much he and Cindi stood out because of Pax, he didn't think he could just sneak out and scout the rest of the building. Prudence dictated staying put, going through the auction, then leaving with whatever information they had. While that virtue had its place in the world, SEALs also knew that sometimes one had to take chances.

He stopped the next waitperson who came near them. "Excuse me. Is there a restroom?"

The middle aged woman stopped and frowned. "There's a portable one set up for the staff, sir. I'm afraid we don't expect clients to need one given the short stay."

He cleared his throat delicately and leaned in. "I'm afraid I have a medical condition." He shot a look at Pax. "I really am in need of facilities. I don't mind a portable one if you'd be so kind."

Cindi huffed. "Really, Hunter. I would have thought you'd have been more careful before leaving the house." She looked away in obvious embarrassment and tipped her glass dry.

At that moment, Dec realized he was really under-utilizing his admin. This idea for recon hadn't been discussed earlier. Cindi was doing all of this on the fly, the same as he was. She'd make an awesome special operator.

"I'm sorry, dear. It can't be helped." He hoped he did as good a job at conveying irritation and his own embarrassment.

"I'm sure no one will mind given the circumstances," the woman said. She led Dec through a slit in the curtain. "It's right over there, sir."

He followed her finger and saw a small flight of steps leading to a portable toilet. A really nice one compared to what he was used to. He flashed her a smile. "Thank you so much."

He slipped her a twenty, too, and the woman returned to the auction area. He walked to the facilities, turned at the base of the stairs, and seeing no one, slipped away.

****

Ryan came to with a start, head pounding, stomach

churning. He knew instantly that he was bound to a chair, mostly naked, and totally fucked. Jesus Christ, what had happened?

Andy had been killed, for one. The fresh pain from that realization cut more deeply than whatever bound his arms and legs. He nearly threw up right then and there. He'd led his partner into an ambush, his pride not allowing him to let go of the case, so the feds could do it right. Now, not only had Andy died, Ryan had been taken alive. There could only be one reason for that.

"Open your eyes, Sergeant." Johnson's cold, smug voice riled Ryan enough that he complied.

The cavernous room they had him in wasn't very brightly lit, thankfully. Opening his eyes didn't cause him the world of pain he'd expected. They did indeed have him tied to an old wooden chair that creaked when he shifted. He had been stripped down to his underwear, although there seemed little point to that until he spied what looked like a cattle prod in the hand of one of the other three men ranged around him. Oh, yeah, direct skin contact with that baby was really going to hurt.

Johnson stepped closer, his eyes narrow and a vicious sneer on his face. "I was told by the FBI that they'd taken over the case." As it wasn't even posed as a question, Ryan didn't waste any energy responding. "You've been a pain in my ass, Jakes. Now, I'm going to return the favor unless you tell me what I want to know."

Ryan couldn't resist. "You sound like you're auditioning for a really bad movie."

One of the goons walked past Johnson and casually backhanded Ryan with his fist. Ryan tasted blood. Of course, he did. None of his teeth felt loose, though. That would change soon.

Johnson didn't even flinch at the show of violence. "Such a smart mouth you have, Southie trash. You're going to tell me what I want to know."

"Which is what, exactly?" Ryan sneered.

"Everything you know about me, Place's murder, the stolen art. In short, I want to know why the FBI said you were off the case, yet you followed me tonight. What does the FBI know, and what is their game?"

Ryan barked out a rueful laugh. He couldn't help himself. "You want a lot, Johnson. My question back to you is why do you think I'm going to tell you anything? You've already killed my partner. You're going to kill me. I like the idea of your not knowing a fucking thing."

Johnson's face twisted. "I'm sure you do, and you're right. We are going to kill you just like we did your partner. But he died quickly and relatively painlessly, I would imagine." He grinned. "You won't unless you give me the answers I want."

Ryan sighed. "Yeah, I figured you'd say that. But I know that no matter what I say, you're going to torture me anyway to make sure I've spilled all my secrets. I'll stay with my original plan, thanks, and say a big *fuck you*."

"Well, perhaps you're smarter than I've thought so far." He nodded his head at the backhander and stepped to one side.

****

It felt like old times. Slinking in and around the staff, their gear, and what he assumed was the artwork covered in sheets was no different than doing recon on a village. More than anything he'd done so far in his investigation, Dec stood on firm ground. He knew what he was doing.

Pax did, too. Her military experience made her the perfect companion. He used hand signals exclusively, keeping her close. She stuck to his side, sat when he stopped, and lay down when he crouched. That's why when she nuzzled his hand suddenly and let out a small whine, he turned in surprise. He signaled her to silence and to get down again when he saw she'd stood up. Instead of obeying him, she turned and took off.

With a curse, Dec followed her. His new shoes were blessedly quiet, the effect he supposed of being made of fine Italian leather. What the hell had gotten into her doggie brain? Something had overridden every bit of training she'd had as both a bomb sniffer and a service dog. He vowed to get her into a refresher course the very next day.

She led him farther into the warehouse. The murmurs of the staff couldn't be heard anymore, and he worried that soon someone would realize that the new buyer with the dog had abandoned his wife. Cindi could end up in danger without him there to protect her.

What a clusterfuck.

Pax stopped suddenly and swerved behind a bunch of crates. Then she did the weirdest thing of all—she alerted. Oh shit. Dec approached her quietly and peered around the crates, expecting to see explosives or ammunition of some sort. Made sense. No point in having a place for just illegal art auctions. There must be a lot of dubious uses for this warehouse.

He didn't see what he expected to, though. Oh, no, this was much worse. His heart skipped a beat, and he grabbed Pax's collar as much to hold himself in place as her.

In an open area, four men stood around a figure tied to a chair. Johnson, that fucker, was one of them. The others weren't familiar to him. He only recognized the man in the chair. Even at a distance and in profile, Dec could tell that the tied up man was Ryan. His head hung to his chest. One of the goons working him over pulled it up by Ryan's hair. His face was a bloody mess already.

Johnson stood with his arms behind his back, as if he were making a presentation at a fucking board meeting. "This is getting tedious, Jakes. Tell me what I want to know, and this can end quickly. Surely, you're tired of the pain by now."

Dec couldn't hear Ryan's response, but another man walked up and stuck a cane of some sort against Ryan's stomach. The scream Ryan let out was like a bullet to Dec's heart. Pax let out another low whine. Dec silenced her with a shaky gesture. His breathing had become more labored. Blood pounded in his head like a hammer, and his chest tightened. Oh, no. He knew the onset of a panic attack.

He lurched toward Pax, gripped her fur with both hands, and leaned close enough to press his face against hers. He breathed in her shampooed doggie smell with even breaths. He would not do this. He would not lose his shit when it mattered most to keep it together. Ryan would die. Cindi might also.

With more strength than he thought he possessed, he beat back the panic and steeled himself to go into action. He was a Goddamn SEAL. Taking on and out a bunch of rank amateurs was his best skill. Inhaling a final cleansing breath, he let go of Pax. He signaled her to stay put and hoped like hell her training would keep her from racing to Ryan's rescue. He needed weapons and knew just where to find them.

On quick, quiet steps, he returned to where he'd last seen a guard posted. He had the man in a headlock and knocked out within seconds. Then he dragged him over to yet more crates and tied him up with the laces to his fancy shoes and his obscenely expensive silk tie. He used the matching pocket square to gag the guy. Killing him would have been faster and safer, yet he didn't want to end up being grilled by the police and maybe arrested for manslaughter or even murder. The rules of engagement in the civilian world were different. Besides, he wanted a chance at a long and happy life with Ryan.

He paused a moment to consider how strong and clear his feelings had become while he palmed the guard's Glock and extra clip. Yeah, okay, he loved Ryan. That's all. No big deal. Just the first time he'd ever fallen in love and in just a few, short days. In an instant, he pictured rings, a house, kids even. Shit. Way to take his head out of the game just as the mission was heating up.

He toed off his laceless shoes and ran back to rescue his man.

****

"Jesus, Mary, and Joseph, what the hell is this all about?"

The thick brogue penetrated the fog in Ryan's head. He opened the one eye he could still see through and watched a shortish, older man stride up. He had to be the head of the goon squad, his jeans and leather jacket a sharp contrast to Johnson's well-tailored suit. The man looked and sounded pissed, and Johnson's face lost a trace of its smugness. Whoever the new arrival was, he must scare the effete personal assistant some.

"He's the cop in charge of Place's murder investigation," Johnson replied. He tugged at the collar of his shirt. Stupid moron didn't even know enough to check any tells of his nervousness.

The new guy stopped a few feet from Johnson and shoved his hands on his hips. "You brought a cop here? Are you out of your fucking mind?"

Whatever Johnson saw in the guy's eyes had him taking a half-step back. "He was following me. Kruger spotted him while he was driving me here. We led them to another building a few blocks away and ambushed them." He smiled. "It was easy. They never saw it coming, and Kruger killed the other one."

The mention of Andy's murder caused a fresh wave of pain to wash over Ryan. It hurt far more than anything they'd done to him so far. He screamed internally at his stupidity. This Kruger asshole may have pulled the trigger, but Ryan knew he'd been the one to get Andy killed. And he would get off lucky because it wouldn't be much longer before they killed him, too, and he'd be eternally rid of his guilt.

The idea of the peace, of having his pain removed, appealed to a big part of him. Yet, the other part mourned that he'd never have a chance to see Dec again and to express how much he'd fallen in love with the man. Love at first sight was for teenage girls, perhaps. Still, at that moment, with pain and imminent death roaring in his face, he could admit that he'd started falling in love with Declan Hunter the first time he laid eyes on him.

The Irish guy was talking again. Sputtering really. "And why would you be doing such a foolish thing? Killing a cop was a stupid risk to take but bringing a live one here takes the cake, boyo."

"I wanted to find out how much he knows," Johnson fumed.

"Did it never occur to you that even this far from the auction, a man's screams might be heard? It's what alerted me, you stupid fucker. I bet you've learned nothing. Look at him." The man flung his hand in Ryan's direction. "You don't get to looking like that without working through pain."

Johnson crossed his arms, sulking like a chastised child. "We've just started."

"Now, you're finished." The man pulled a gun with a silencer from the back of his waist, giving Ryan a clear look at his own death. "I'm going to have to clear up this mess the same way I did Place's after he showed that slut his private collection. The same way I did with Place himself when it became obvious he couldn't be trusted not to make the same mistake again."

Even with his brain rattled from blows, Ryan saw what was coming before Johnson did. A neat, red hole formed in the man's forehead before he could even register that Irish's gun was pointed at Johnson, not Ryan. Ryan watched the personal assistant join his former master in what Ryan hoped was hell. Never a true believer, he sincerely hoped Father O'Malley's sermons had been correct. Then, he had no more thoughts of anyone except himself when the gun swung in his direction. In the second he had left on this Earth,

Ryan thought of his family and how much his death would hurt them. Of the nephew he'd never get to meet. Of Dec.

Just as he started to close his eye, a streak of black and brown fur passed his line of vision. Irish screamed as bright, sharp teeth sank into his arm. The man tumbled down, his gun falling from his grip to go skittering across the floor. A gun shot sounded to Ryan's left. One of the goon squad who had been reaching for his own weapon went down as well. As did the guy wielding the cattle prod before he could do more than make an aborted move for his gun.

Knowing there was one more man positioned now behind him, Ryan did the only thing he could think of to take himself out of the equation. With what little strength he had left, he rocked hard to his right. The old chair didn't fight his intention, crashing to the floor with him still in it. His bones rattled with the impact, and he grunted. But he'd accomplished his goal. With him down, Dec had a clear shot at the last man standing.

With the echo of every shot fired still ringing in his ears, he panted through his pain and watched Dec call Pax off the Irish man she'd been wrestling with. Dec took the man out with a single punch to the head. Pax then sat next to the guy, effectively making sure he stayed put.

Down on one knee, Dec gazed at Ryan. The depth of emotion Ryan saw in his lover's expression almost undid him. For the first time since he and Andy had been ambushed, Ryan felt tears prick the back of his eyes, threatening to spill over. Dec had miraculously arrived to save Ryan's ass. The man had killed for him with such efficient lethality it made Ryan shudder just thinking about it. He worried, too, that he'd given his man a new reason to have nightmares.

Overriding everything, though, was the love he saw in that intense stare. Ryan poured everything he had in his returning gaze. He wanted Dec to see his love reflected back instead of the bloody vision he must make. They made cow eyes at each other for only a few seconds before Dec sprang up and toward him. He skidded to a halt and changed course for a moment.

When he finally knelt beside Ryan, he held a small knife in his hand. He sawed through Ryan's bindings with practiced ease. "Holy, shit, Ryan." That's all he said before he pulled Ryan out of the chair and into his arms.

Ryan hated bloodying Dec's nice suit, had a million questions about what the guy was doing there, but in the end, he couldn't resist the comforting warmth of pressing up against his lover. He shuddered with shock and cold. He couldn't hold back an embarrassing whimper when Dec pulled him away long enough to shrug out of his suit coat. He tucked Ryan's pins and needle arms into the sleeves, as if Ryan were a two-year-old. He didn't care. It was Dec. He could be vulnerable in front of this man. His man.

He snuggled into the warmth. "Nice jacket," he murmured.

"For two thousand dollars, it should be," Dec replied.

That raised the critical question. "How is it that you—"

"Police! Nobody move!"

Dec didn't release his hold on Ryan, but he did

swing his head back. "Pax, down. Friendlies."

Blue uniforms swarmed into the space, weapons drawn, loaded for bear. One by one, they stopped, stared, and lowered their weapons.

"Jakes!"

Ryan shifted in Dec's arms enough to see his captain storming in. What the fuck? "Sir?"

Dixon rushed over and peered down at him. "Thank God, you're alive." He looked over his shoulder. "Get the EMTs in here, now!" He turned narrow eyes on Dec. "Who the hell are you?"

"Declan Hunter."

"My boyfriend," Ryan chimed in. He managed a smile for Dec, who was looking down at him with his mouth slightly open. "He saved me from imminent death, sir. He and his dog. But for them, I'd be dead. The unconscious one killed Place's assistant over there. He's got a lot to say, I'd imagine, if we can get him to talk."

Dixon shook his head. "I'm going to need a lot of explanation about this, Jakes."

"Yes, sir."

The captain shook his head. "My God, if a black and white hadn't spotted the location of the car with the plate number Diaz called in, we'd still be sitting around scratching our heads over where they'd taken you."

"Andy's alive?" Jakes sat up straight. Or rather tried to. Dec tightened his grip to hold him steady.

"Probably still in surgery, but the prognosis was good going into it."

Ryan wheezed, the air trapped in his lungs. "I thought he'd been killed."

"From what I hear, apparently, he played possum

283

when he got hit. He yelled the house down as they loaded him into the ambulance, worried about you."

Ryan forced a breath in. "Thank God, he was able to fake it. Otherwise, they would have shot him again for sure."

His vision clouded with tears. Andy had survived the ambush. Although he blinked them back to keep from being a real baby about matters, he also leaned into Dec more heavily. He didn't care who saw him taking comfort from his man. And, more importantly, Dec didn't seem to mind. His grip tightened around Ryan even more.

His voice sounded above Ryan's head. "Sir? I know you have a lot of questions for me, but my assistant is out in the auction area. I'm worried about her."

"My people have secured the warehouse."

"I'm sure they have, sir. Cindi was undercover with me. I would appreciate it if she weren't hauled off. I put her in this position. I'm to blame. I'll understand if you need to arrest me, but she needs to be left out of this."

With his hands on his hips, the captain stared down at Dec. And Ryan. Ryan knew the man could do basic math. Dixon blew out a breath. "Neither of you is getting arrested. You have my permission to go and see to her." He narrowed his eyes at Ryan, shot a look at the EMTs racing up, and waved them back. "I assume you want to go with him, Jakes, even though you should be on a stretcher."

"Yes, sir." Ryan pushed against Dec's chest and staggered to his feet. Okay, he tried to get vertical under his own power. It was Dec's strength that really hauled him up. Ryan was pathetically grateful when Dec kept his arms wrapped around Ryan's waist.

The three of them—Ryan, Dec and the ever loyal Pax, who, let's face it, had saved Ryan's life—limped away, curtesy of Ryan's rubbery legs.

They winded their way through the vast warehouse, the sounds of shouts ringing in Ryan's ears even before Dec pushed aside a black curtain and ushered him into the familiar chaos of a round-up. At a glance, Ryan took in a lot of well-heeled and unhappy people. Many of them were uttering threats about lawyers. He wasn't sure exactly what was going on. Irish had mentioned an auction. He'd been so focused on imminent death, though, he hadn't considered what that meant or what kind of undercover work Dec and his admin had been doing.

"What's going on?" he asked Dec as a uniform came marching up.

Ryan recognized the woman the moment she stopped and scrutinized him. "Sergeant Jakes?"

"Yeah, that's me." He managed to say with a modicum of strength in his voice. He really wanted to sit down. Make that lie down. With Dec's arms still wrapped around him. "We're looking for a young woman."

"Dec!"

All three of them turned at the sound. Cindi Keyes, looking like every straight man's fantasy woman, was being led away in cuffs by another uniform.

"She's not a perp," he announced. When the uniform shot him a skeptical look, he added, "She's undercover." The uniform's expression didn't change. "It's complicated. Trust me on this, though. You can clear it with Captain Dixon if need be."

The uniform shook her head and waved the other one over. Cindi shot Ryan a melting smile as the cuffs came off. She didn't even bother to rub her wrists the way people always did when released. Instead, she leaned into him and frowned. "You poor baby. Who hurt you?"

Ryan had to laugh, which turned into a minor coughing fit. Man, did his body ache. Dec only held him closer. "Don't worry. Dec and Pax took care of them."

Cindi beamed. "I should hope so." She patted first Dec's cheek, then Pax's head. "Come with me. I have something to show you."

"Not now, Cindi," Dec said gently. "Ryan needs the EMTs and a trip to the hospital. We only came to make sure you were okay."

Cindi's expression changed back to worry. "Oh, of course." She looked around. "Where the fuck are they, then?"

The change in tone, so gruff and masculine made Ryan smile. Which made him wince. "No," he said emphatically. "I'm fine." At Dec's grunt of disbelief, Ryan amended his statement. "Enough for now. What do you want to show us?"

After a moment's hesitation and some kind of silent discussion with Dec using only her eyes, she turned. "This way."

Ryan staggered after her, Dec's strength the only thing holding him up. He tried to ignore the stares of the remaining cops pulling out the stragglers. Hard to have much dignity while walking around in one's underwear and a suit coat hanging onto someone. But he kept putting one foot in front of the other, determined to see the case to the end as much as possible.

Cindi led them to the other side of the make-shift room and through a slit in the curtain. She tottered along in her mile-high heels with enviable grace compared to his lumbering gait. Another uniform started to stop her as she approached what looked like draped paintings. Fortunately, Ryan knew this cop as well and waved him away. Cindi lifted the sheet off one particularly large piece and exposed the painting with a flourish. Ryan halted, an odd feeling of excitement replacing for a moment his pain and fatigue.

"When Dec didn't return, I decided to do a little exploring on my own," Cindi said with a grin. "I found this right off the bat."

Dec shifted his hold on Ryan. "That looks familiar."

Ryan stared at the magnificent picture of three men in a storm-tossed boat. "*The Storm on the Sea of Galilee*. One of Rembrandt's paintings and a piece stolen from the Gardner Museum."

Dec gasped. "You're shitting me."

Cindi all but bounced on her heels. "Is this like the biggest find ever?"

"Yes, ma'am." Ryan could barely breathe at the enormity of it all. Even though he'd come to believe that famous heist had been at the center of the whole murder, the proof of it still left him breathless.

Dec caught his eye. "I'm not sure I understand. Was this what Place was murdered for?"

"In a way, yes. Near as I can tell from what the guy you knocked out said to Johnson right before planting a bullet in him was that Place showed his treasure room to at least one boy."

"The dead one." It wasn't a question because, of course, Ryan's guy was a smart one.

"Right. And Kenny couldn't keep his mouth shut, so whoever is behind this theft ring and auction house killed the kid to stop him from talking. Eventually, someone might have put some pieces together enough to get a warrant. They never cared about the other art. But this one was too hot. The FBI has never recovered any of the Gardner pieces or arrested anyone for the heist."

"Until now," Dec said.

"Until now," Ryan agreed. "They must have decided Place had turned into a liability and killed him to take back the painting and resell it to someone more trustworthy." A thought occurred to him, finally. Pulling back a bit, he looked up at Dec. "How the hell did you end up being here, anyway?"

Dec winced. "I'll explain later." When Ryan opened his mouth to argue the point, he added, "You really need to see a doctor, baby."

Fatigue washed over him with the unrelenting pain. The "baby" didn't hurt, either. Seemed like he and Dec were on the same page. Ryan could wait to get answers. He figured he and Dec would have a lot of time in the future to talk things through.

"All right. I guess I could use some down time. I'm not going to forget to ask the question again," he added with a frown.

Dec smiled indulgently and kissed the top of Ryan's head. "Of course not, sweetheart."

"If you think you're going to start out our

relationship by placating me…"

Dec stopped Ryan mid-admonishment with a gentle kiss on his busted lips. "I wouldn't dream of it." He treated Ryan to a devastating smile. "I'll have other things to fill my mind at night."

Epilogue

"John Boy, talk to me."

The nightmare started as it always did. This time, however, when Dec couldn't shake free of it and his body thrashed in his sleep, something strong wrapped around his chest and hugged him tight.

"Wake up, baby. You're safe."

Ryan's words pulled Dec up from the depths of his horrible memories and brought him into the safety of his own bed. Ryan's arms held him securely. His warm breath bathed Dec's neck. Dec felt secure, safe, anchored.

"Ryan," he breathed out the last of his lingering panic.

"I'm right here, baby. I've got you."

Dec rolled into his boyfriend's embrace. "I know you do."

They lay together, entwined, Dec's breathing slowing down to sync with Ryan's. He'd had his nightmare three times in the week since the night of the auction. Ryan had been with him every time. They'd stayed together every night, switching from one home to the other. Neither of them had questioned the decision or even specifically made one. They'd simply fallen into the habit of spending every night together.

It had been easy given that Ryan was on administrative leave. Forget his injuries. Internal affairs was looking into how and why Andy had been shot and Ryan taken prisoner by a ring of art thieves. The lead investigator, a woman named Parker Li, seemed fair enough when she'd interviewed Dec. He still worried that Ryan's career was on the line.

Ryan didn't appear to be very worried about it. He'd said Andy being alive was as much as he'd hope for. Dec didn't really believe him. He knew how much Ryan loved his job. The discovery of the Gardner painting was being kept under wraps for the moment as the FBI tried to work their way through the morass of the illegal art auction. The guy Dec had clobbered had lawyered and clammed up. None of the underlings were proving to be useful, either. Still, it would all come out eventually, and Dec had to believe that the cop that was instrumental in cracking the case open wouldn't be canned. Bad publicity, surely, for the city.

His own skin had survived intact, the price for his silence. More importantly, so had Cindi and Mal. And the case was over for Dec. Knowing that Johnson had been the inside man, confirmed that Dec hadn't fucked up his job. Putting in a new security system had undoubtedly been a ruse as had the threats against Place. It was all speculation still about how it all played out, yet the logical assumption was that Johnson had laid a false trail and set Dec up as maybe the fall guy to deflect from the true intent of recovering the painting.

The bottom line was, everyone was safe and Dec had answers. He also had a hot guy in his bed, helping him with his emotional problems instead of running screaming from them. Pax didn't seem to mind Ryan being incorporated into their small family, although being canned as Dec's panic partner at night was harder for her to accept. While she loved the new doggie bed Ryan had bought for her, she still rushed into the bedroom whenever she heard Dec having a nightmare. Ryan swore she glared at him when he signaled her to back off from helping her master. Dec tried to make up for it by lavishing more attention on her during the day. No matter what the future held for him with his PTSD and Ryan, Dec would always want Pax in his life.

"You okay?" Ryan whispered in his ear before licking it. "Shall I use the usual remedy to get you to sleep?"

Before Dec could answer, Ryan was already sliding down Dec's body, pushing him onto his back, and straddling his legs. Dec blew out a harsh breath when Ryan sucked Dec's hardening dick into his mouth. The wet suction had him fully erect in seconds as it always did. This had become part of the new routine. A blowjob by Ryan sent Dec blissfully back to sleep as nothing else ever did.

But it bothered Dec that Ryan never got a return favor until the morning. He decided in a blink of an eye that this night would be different. He trusted Ryan like no other, and to Dec's mind, there was only one way to truly prove it.

"Fuck me," he ordered quietly into the dark.

Ryan instantly stilled. He held Dec's cock in place for a few seconds before pulling off it with a small pop. "What?"

Dec moved his legs, trying to pull them out and up. "I said, fuck me."

Ryan held Dec with his hands, not letting him expose himself just yet. "You don't bottom."

That was true, even more so since he'd lost so

much. The idea of someone covering him made him nervous. None of that mattered compared to this man, though. "Everything is different with you, Ryan. Please. I trust you."

He heard the hard swallow. Ryan hesitated a moment before sliding off Dec and reaching for the nightstand drawer where Dec kept his condoms and lube. Dec took the opportunity to open his legs and pull them up. It was a vulnerable position, yet Ryan took it on a daily basis, completely at ease. Dec could do no less. He squinted at the sudden light when Ryan turned on the lamp.

"I want to see you." Ryan gave Dec an intense stare while covering himself. Like Dec, the guy was hard and needy.

Cupping his knees, Dec spread as wide as he could. "Don't you dare go easy on me. I want to feel this."

Ryan smiled smugly. "You will."

Still, he prepped Dec, using lubed fingers to slowly open and stretch his hole. Dec had forgotten the burn, the pain making his cock harder, not softer. He kept his gaze on Ryan's head of tousled hair to make it easier to relax and open for his lover. His lover. His boyfriend. The man he trusted above all others now, even though they'd barely known each other a few weeks.

It didn't matter. It felt right. So did giving himself to Ryan when he hadn't wanted or been able to with other men over the years. It took no time at all before tossing the lube aside, Ryan wedged his body between Dec's straining thighs.

True to his word, Ryan made sure Dec felt the hard length of him. He pushed in with one, long stroke that sent him balls deep inside Dec's practically virgin ass.

Dec hissed at the way his entire channel fought to accommodate Ryan's thick rod.

"Christ," Dec panted. "You are one big motherfucker." He clenched his bedding with both hands.

Ryan's eyelashes dipped on a low groan. "You are so fucking tight." He placed his palms over Dec's hands and pushed Dec's legs even wider and higher. "That's it, baby. Take me in as far as you can."

Throwing his head back, Dec closed his eyes and tried to give Ryan what he wanted. He tried to give him everything. He squeezed his hole tentatively, and Ryan's pleased moan encouraged him to do it again. He rocked his hips, too, to sink Ryan in that last millimeter. Dec's cock bobbed against his belly, but he didn't try to touch it. This was for Ryan.

Ryan, however, thought differently. He released his hold on one of Dec's hands to reach between them and clasp Dec's dick. He jerked it a few times, wringing moans and groans and gasps from Dec.

"That's it. We're going to come together. I swear we are." So saying, Ryan pinched the base of Dec's shaft to hold back the climax.

Then Ryan started rocking. Shallow thrusts that turned into full throttle drilling after a few seconds of gentleness. Dec bit back the cry struggling to escape. He focused his concentration on the feel of Ryan's cock pumping in and out. The strokes became faster and shorter, more erratic, telling Dec Ryan was close to coming.

With a brief, hard squeeze, Ryan began beating Dec's dick with a punishing speed. He slammed against Dec's ass, grunted, and fell over. He trapped both his hand and Dec's cock between their bodies, still pumping, and sunk his teeth into side of Dec's neck.

As promised, they came together. Dec writhed within Ryan's embrace, trying to escape him and get closer at the same time. Ryan rode out the storm, never letting go from any of the places he claimed. When they were spent, Ryan pulled his hand free to collapse fully on top of Dec. They remained cock to hole, and Dec wrapped his legs around Ryan's wide hips to keep him there.

"Are you all right?" Ryan breathed into Dec's ear.

Dec shivered with the aftershocks of his orgasm and the sheer pleasure of Ryan's breath and weight on him. "I can honestly say I've never been better."

Ryan chuckled. "No pressure there."

Dec pried his fingers from the sheet and rubbed his palms up Ryan's arms. He loved the feel of Ryan shuddering with the touch. "Sometimes the intensity of how I feel for you scares me." He paused. "I guess a lot of things still scare me."

Ryan rose as much as Dec's hold would allow. "It's okay. I'm here with you. We'll face those fears together."

Dec smiled up at him. Ryan was right. He wasn't alone. He might not be in the Teams anymore, but he had a new one—Red Cell Security, Felix, Cindi, Mal, and Pax. Ryan, too, on a different kind of team. He'd make them both work. He had no doubts now.

About the Author

I'm a corporate lawyer, happily married for over twenty years with three kids and three dogs. No white picket fence, but we do live in the burbs west of Boston. While my husband and I still do occasionally lick chocolate off each other, our more typical evening involves lying in bed once the kids are in theirs and reading separate books. Mine of course are romance. I started reading them as a defense against all those boring legal documents. Once I started, I couldn't stop.

I love all types of romance, although my favorite stories are the ones with two heroes. There's nothing sexier to me than an Alpha male, except two Alpha males!

I've also loved erotica since I was old enough to appreciate what sex is. I've been publishing erotic romance since 2009.

Besides my family, writing and reading, my loves include the sight, smell, and sounds of the ocean (I'm a New England girl through and through), chocolate (naturally), prime rib (bloody), and good bourbon on the rocks.

~*~

Visit Samantha at

www.samanthacayto.com

~*~

To chat with Samantha Cayto and other Wild Rose Press authors of erotic romance, join us at

www.groups.yahoo.com/group/thewilderroses.

Also Available

Blue Heat

by

Samantha Cayto

Boston's Brave Book One

https://amzn.com/B00N2AH972

Finn Callaghan's quest to prove his father wasn't dirty and to follow family tradition leads him to become one of Boston's brave. Like his father and brothers, he proudly wears the blue but as an openly gay man. His first assignment—going undercover as a teenage runaway. The sexy detective in charge is a bonus and a distraction he just can't pass up.

Only half out of the closet, Michael Caruso heads a task force to end an underage prostitution ring that preys on homeless gay teens. He has mixed emotions about using the hot young rookie as bait. Finn is perfect for the part, but Michael's attraction to the pretty cop might botch months of work.

Attraction turns to alarm as Finn goes deeper undercover. Can Michael keep him safe? And even if he can, how can he protect himself from the danger of falling in love?

Also Read

Keeping Secrets From Sir

by

Nese Lane

https://amzn.com/B00IT4QLOI

While "hatchet man" Drew Chandler is both feared and revered in the boardroom, he is completely ruled by his need for submission in the bedroom. Dominance and pain give him that edge vital to his corporate success, but Sir has been unavailable and Drew's hold is slipping...

The D/s bond that Kane Devlin shares with Drew is the icing on the cake of their relationship. When problems at work force Kane to sacrifice time usually spent with his sexy sub, the loss of that connection becomes a source of frustration. His patience is tested further as Drew begins to keep secrets, but Kane plans to get to the bottom of things, from the top.

www.ingramcontent.com/pod-product-compliance
Lightning Source LLC
Chambersburg PA
CBHW051521260626
47170CB00003B/730